FOR ALL
the
OBVIOUS
REASONS

Undertow—novel—1993

Fata Morgana—novel—1995

Pipers at the Gates of Dawn—novella triptych—2000

Because a Fire Was in My Head—novel—2007

FOR ALL
the
OBVIOUS
REASONS

And Other Stories

LYNN STEGNER

Arcade Publishing • New York

Arcade Publishing books may be purchased in bulk at special discounts for sales promotion, corporate gifts, fund-raising, or educational purposes. Special editions can also be created to specifications. For details, contact the Special Sales Department, Arcade Publishing, 307 West 36th Street, 11th Floor, New York, NY 10018 or arcade@skyhorsepublishing.com.

Arcade Publishing® is a registered trademark of Skyhorse Publishing, Inc.®, a Delaware corporation.

Visit our website at www.arcadepub.com.

10 9 8 7 6 5 4 3 2 1

Library of Congress Cataloging-in-Publication Data is available on file.

Print ISBN: 978-1-62872-641-1
Ebook ISBN: 978-1-62872-642-8

Printed in the United States of America

To Sam Chase, for all the obvious reasons.

— *acknowledgments* —

The following stories first appeared in:

"Catch and Release," *The Best of Carve Magazine*, Volume Five, 2005; "The New Sister," *New West*, May 2011; "The Boat on the Lake," *Five Points*, Vol. 14, No. 2, January 2012; "Mona's Coming," *Stoneslide*, Autumn 2012; "Rogue," *The Tusculum Review*, Vol. 9, 2013; "For All the Obvious Reasons," *Gival Press*, 2014; "Twins," *december*, Volume 25.2, Fall/Winter 2014.

— *contents* —

FOR ALL THE OBVIOUS REASONS

*W*hat you heard were the hooves of the three horses with the mule at the end, clattering through the rounded stone along the river, the first and the third horse steady, carefully picking their ways, but the one in the middle, a small dark Arabian, skittering and taking too many steps to cover the same distance, some of the steps sideways and even back, *one jump ahead of a fit,* as the man downriver who had saddled her remarked.

"You can handle her." He nodded toward Harry. "Your man says you can handle a horse."

"Sure I can," Charlotte had said.

Harry believed everything she told him. He could afford to believe things and he was generous with that endowment, extending it to everyone. He had had the kind of upbringing that fostered commendable attributes like trust and courage and Honor, capital H. It was what she liked best about him, how clean-swept his life had been. Harry Fairbanks. How could she lose?

Of course it was easier to be honorable with nothing much to challenge those limits.

"I've ridden my share of horses," she had added.

But the other one, the Indian, probably knew better. The Indian hadn't looked at her as she mounted, as she snugged up the reins, slipping her ring finger between the two strands of leather, her right hand clenched and holding the slack off to the right, her posture perfectly trained and the mare already jittering beneath her. The

Indian, a thoroughly plausible individual who did not watch but who could assuredly hear the animal snorting and huffing—she knew that he knew the horse was too much for her. Already dark bands of sweat were spreading like ink along the Arabian's shoulders and inside her flanks, her skin twitching, and not from the flies. Abra was her name.

It was just another one of the things Charlotte had probably lied about. All those years of riding lessons, keeping her heels down and her eyes up, and she had never sat a horse well. Mr. Purdy had said that she wouldn't let herself become *one* with the animal—it was the sixties, and people had begun to say things like that, even riding instructors at fancy clubs—but now, seven years later, she knew it to be true. She had kept herself above and separate from the horses she had ridden, which had not been that many, all told. Horses had been one of her youthful infatuations, and to her thinking infatuations demanded mastery, not union. Mastery, she thought, was a trick of the mind. Something you might try to sell yourself at the end of a long day when it was harder to believe that you knew what you were doing and were in charge.

They made a strange procession, the Indian, the girl, and then the tall man leading the mule, as they set off up the Fraser River, keeping close to the water where there were fewer mosquitoes and deer flies. For a while there had been sandy bars and shores and plenty of open sunlight, with the wet belt of alder, birch, black cottonwood, and willow standing back and letting them proceed without trouble or interference. It was early June, the peak of spring runoff, so the broad banks were often wet from a recent surge, and the wildrye or mugwort or reeds flattened and muddy from the flood water's scouring rush. In the wide swaths of river rock, silt girded the larger stones, and there might be pockets of water warming in the sun from which the bugs lofted as they passed. On the drive up from Vancouver the smells had been of pulp mills and new asphalt where the Ministry of Transportation had been paving over one of the roads the map still indicated was dirt, and of course the smell of the peanuts Harry ate with compulsive intent—"Protein?" he asked, offering her some. Foodstuffs had been stripped of their individuality and trained into conforming ranks of dietary requirements. It was all very scientific. Protein was the thing in 1970, the superstar. VIP-for-protein, Harry once told her. Protein and the wonders of frozen vegetables, though they had conceded to cans for part of the trip.

Now in the midday heat along the river the smell was of rotting vegetation, and at random intervals, when the new obscure tension in her chest became too much, she clicked the mare into the shallows where Charlotte felt she could breathe again. Somehow it reminded her of what had happened, that smell. She could not yet bring herself to say "happened *to* her." She was not ready for that claim that would invite something for which she was not ready, some form of psychic catastrophe, a free-falling departure from the high mastery. She was not ready for much of anything yet, in fact, maybe only this trip, one week long, with Harry and the Indian guiding them up through the system of waterways and lakes that veined interior British Columbia.

It did not take more than an hour or so for Charlotte to give up trying to post, which anyway had been mostly to demonstrate that she knew how. The Arabian's trot was so fast, so frenetic, everything about her distracted and ready to bolt, that Charlotte could not settle into anything rhythmic. It would not have done to let Abra take the bit, but neither did Abra give Charlotte any indication of reliable consent. They were in some kind of standoff without having the least provocation. She was a beautiful little horse, spirited and athletic, big anxious eyes; and Charlotte, at 110 pounds, could not have been more than the lightest of burdens, insubstantial as a toy up there, or dismissible erratum. The standoff felt uncalled-for. They ought to have liked each other, made a pair—that seemed to be the idea back at the outfitter's. So Charlotte simply endured it, her bum, her spine jarred and twisted, Abra's hindquarters suddenly bounding out from under her, her head thrown down, her graceful neck swinging sideways. What a week it would be, battling this four-legged tempest. And yet Charlotte could not help admiring her defiance, her anger, so free and absent of cause. Abra was all heart.

On the first night they camped along the Mighty Fraser; Harry liked to call it that, liked to indulge in small flourishes of speech. The rest of the week would be spent east of the Fraser, in the area between Kamloops and north to 100 Mile House. The Indian was one of the Shuswap, an interior Salish tribe, and he knew the area well enough that even the man with the horses had called him by his Salish name, One-See, because he was the only one left who had seen each of the rivers and creeks, the lakes without names, the trails that vanished into the high timber. Harry's father had used him when Harry was a boy, and later, the boy grown, had tracked him down and hired him for fishing trips with his buddies. This trip was different, because of the girl and what had happened.

At twenty, Charlotte was not technically a girl any longer. But she was so petite and so well proportioned, so big-eyed and doll-like, that everyone treated her like a naïf. Or like something not quite real yet. On campus some of the guys referred to her as Harry's trinket, and there had been two occasions on which strangers had mistaken her for his child. He was ten years older, about to finish his degree in medicine at UBC. His mother had taken ill and he had had to leave school for three years to help care for her. It had devolved into one of those eerily satisfying romantic stories—she had died of cancer, and thirty-two hours later, Harry's father had up and died of a disease no one even knew he had, but which everyone decided was grief, pure and simple. They were a poor couple from the mountain town of Revelstoke, and Harry was the family star.

Charlotte was convinced that it would be the same for her and Harry—they would go more or less together. She did not think that she could bear it otherwise. People left: they broke down and were carted off, or they moved away, or they up and died. But not Harry, not this time.

The Indian unsaddled and staked the horses, then he offloaded the grub boxes and staked the mule too, graining them with hands cupped while Harry and Charlotte leveled out a tent site and gathered armfuls of wood for a fire. There was plenty lying about from the runoff and it did not take long.

"Reuben," Harry said to the Indian, for he would never know him well enough to call him by his Salish name, "shall we try our luck?"

Reuben was studying the surface of the river. He turned and nodded toward the rods, jointed and ready, propped in the crook of a cedar. After he had watched the water and the bugs skimming or dancing off the sheen, he came back and fingered up some flies from the box, then the two of them worked their way downstream while Charlotte put up the tent she and Harry would share. They were four months married but it still felt funny to her, spending all of the night hours with him. Even now, it was exciting to wake up and find him beside her, like a holiday morning surprise with its sudden extravagance of joy that sent a hum through her breast, anticipatory and guilty, as if she were getting away with something. *Still here*, she thought, *still right here*. She had developed a secret habit of happiness, trilling the sheets with her toes, before conceding that the day must end or begin. As a child there had been too many mornings when, awakening, there was no one there.

Charlotte's father was a G.P. in Ottawa. After her mother had been institutionalized, and then the years of him trying to conceal the women he saw (because he was still a handsome man, after all, a vital man with needs, was how the maturing Charlotte came to understand the situation, his beard nicely trimmed, his shirts professionally pressed, no one could blame him, really), he moved to Ottawa so that he could see the women openly. In the tidy little city of Penticton where they had lived, people would have talked. Divorce was out of the question; one did not divorce someone who had had a mental breakdown. One did not abandon the elaborate beauty and comforts of social form for content, no matter how authentic. This was not America, after all, where messy realities throve.

That same fall when her father joined a practice in Ottawa and Charlotte began her freshman year at UBC, her mother was relocated to a Home in Vancouver. In the two years since, nothing had changed for Mary, and Charlotte's visits had dwindled to once a month. But a week ago, just after what happened, Charlotte had gone off-schedule to see her. Ignoring the rest of it, Mary was her mother, and this was the sort of thing you brought to a mother, something only a mother might be able to fix, or at least soften.

"Where are the bruises?" her mother had asked her.

It was a reasonable question. Where were they? Why hadn't she fought?

Mary was having a bad day, they told her, and so the visit had taken place in the special room that was divided by a half wall, with heavy wire mesh rising from the low counter, their two chairs positioned on opposite sides. Her mother pressed her face against the wire, squinting at Charlotte's visible body parts, her face and neck, her forearms, searching for the bruises Charlotte had not thought to earn.

She had been hitchhiking. She hadn't ought to have been hitchhiking.

In a little while Harry and the Indian returned. She watched them coming toward her, their heads bowed in conversation, their boots sinking slightly in the wet sand and gravel. How she liked seeing him come toward her, like a marvelous and improbable piece of news. He brought the whole billowing world with him. And he walked like a man who knew he owned a place in that world. Harry, tall and lithe as poplar, wearing the bright eager expression of a boy convinced he's about to figure out something grand, or very likely already has. His thinning hair was something she liked, confirming his seriousness of purpose. He took her seriously, too, her compact body, her moods, the things she said that often surprised him. Harry did not think that he was easy to surprise, but as it turned out, he was.

Beside him, shoulder-height and still black-haired despite his age, the Indian paced along with a great and serious fortitude, every step somehow both difficult and destined. The sun was down behind the broad canyon walls and with it, the wind had dropped too, so that all she could hear was the water coursing over the river stone, and the hollow knocking of an oil drum that had washed downriver and eddied between a gravel bar and the place where they had made camp; and then once, she heard Harry's laugh, cool, clipped and easy, as if he were trying to draw out a reluctant child. Harry was going to be a pediatrician and it seemed to her that he had chosen the perfect field, one that suited his encouraging nature.

"You didn't catch anything," she remarked.

He shrugged. "Wasn't the point."

Without quite looking at her, the Indian gave a languid side-wary acknowledgment and paced over to where the grub boxes sat beneath a stand of cottonwood and began rummaging through one of them. He was unknowable, moving with a slight stoop that did not appear to come from any weariness but from contemplation to which, so far, he had given neither of them access.

She turned to Harry. "Aren't we here to fish?"

He squatted beside her, offering her a swig from his flask. "This is a salmon river. Sockeye, coho, chinook . . . mostly sockeye. Steelhead if you're lucky. But steelhead run at night. Reuben noticed a pool downriver, a pool with watercress where steelhead like to hide."

It irritated her, his mini lecture. Sometimes Harry knew too much. "So what was the point?" Lately it was important to her that things have a point, a specific and well-defined objective, and it helped, too, to know just how long things would take, each task, each job, so that every bit of every day would be used up doing something good and productive, something worthy that an imaginary presence who was always watching you might tick off a list. She had become a furious housekeeper; she balanced the checkbooks to the penny; she completed and then went back over her homework. Charlotte did this, Charlotte did that. . . . Industry stitched the day together, and so far nothing vital had bled through the open wound that morning seemed to expose.

He placed the back of his fingers against her cheek and gave it a feathery possessive stroke. "Oh, just to try it out, set the mood. We're after trout. That's inland, where we go tomorrow."

"I like it here," she said, tossing a pebble into the river, not wanting to belong to anyone at that moment, not even Harry.

In the flat light of dusk the river stretched away from her to the slanting and distant canyon wall, gray-brown, the water too, gray-brown like tea with milk, but cold, the surface a moving slick of indifference as it slid downward to the sea. The way the water moved, not flowing but huge and muscled from underneath as if it were pushing something impossible out of its way, and that one couldn't see but knew was there just around the next bend—that was what she liked, that pushing, that deep, heavy determination to shove the unseen thing down the canyon and out of the way. Lakes were motionless; lakes did nothing but lie there looking pretty and inviting and stupidly susceptible.

"You'll like it at the lakes too," Harry was saying just then. "You can swim."

"I might not want to swim."

"You love to swim."

"I don't want to swim. Not anymore."

"Sure you'll swim, Char. You'll do everything you were going to do. Nothing's changed."

She tossed another pebble in the water. "Everything's changed."

"No."

"I'm not going to swim."

"Don't be this way, Charlotte. Give it some time. Your feelings will change."

"I'm never ever swimming again."

He sighed, considered the flask in his hand, and then took another swallow. "The lakes are beautiful. You'll see."

"I don't care about lakes or how beautiful they are or how much you think I'll like it or won't like it, or hate it. I'm tired of swimming."

He seemed about to take her hand but thought better of it. "You're in a mood."

"That's right, Harry. It's just a mood. Nothing you have to think too long or too hard about. Call the next patient, order up another tray of animals to dissect, make notes in your notebooks, schedule a follow-up." A mosquito bite on her forearm had made itself known and she was scratching it down to a dot of pulp to put a quick end to the itching. "Consult with Alex," she thought to add.

Behind them the woods crowded down a narrow wet draw ending in a hedge of young cedar so dense that she could only worry about what was behind it. She took another sip of Harry's whisky and glanced over at the Indian to see if he'd been listening. Harry unfolded his long self to help with dinner, leaving her alone. She had wanted to drive him away but was equally disappointed in having succeeded.

She had missed the bus. And she'd seen others, friends of hers with their thumbs out, catching rides with other students into the city, or across the Lions Gate Bridge to North Van where it was cheaper to live. Where she and Harry lived now. Plenty of them did it.

They heated two cans of beef stew over the fire and sopped it up with bread. Afterward, the Indian rinsed the cans in the river, burying them and marking the place so that they would not have to carry them but could pick them up on the way back a week later. He did not drink and he did not eat the candy bars that were Harry's weakness, his only one, so far as she could tell. Reuben and Harry were familiar with the routine and with each other. They did not need to tell stories, the way men did, establishing who they are and what measure of deference or disregard each warranted. Even among men like her father, men who cared for a living, Charlotte had heard late-night versions of Great White Hunter tales, about patients with problems the books never told them about and that were usually the result of some strange thing they had managed to do to themselves, and these were the stories that had bothered her the most—the unavoidable exposure, the hoped-for and foolish trust, then the hunting tales that betrayed them. Once, even, she had overheard her father talking about her mother—'*will you just stop doing this, Mary,*' Bellows said to her. Bellows was a colleague of theirs in the practice. Charlotte had seen the cuts, too, but until that night, she had not known how they got there.

Around the fire the three of them sat. Reuben had found the desiccated root of a cottonwood five to six centimetres in diameter, and had begun carving it. His nose was striking, the kind suburban women with stereotypical views about Indians might want to paint, with a strong straight center bone, the flesh planing down evenly like the sides of a tent, one in shadow and the other a coppery gleam against the firelight. Harry was reading aloud from the fisherman's guidebook about Dolly Varden, the trout they were after, *"maximum weight, six to seven pounds, 18" long, hearty and colorful, stunningly spotted in scarlet with halos of pale silvery blue."* A log had settled out of the fire and he poked it back in among the embers, releasing an outburst of sparks. *"Dollies are anadromous—seagoing."*

Over in the river shallows they could hear the hollow *booming* of the oil drum against stone. It was so deep and muffled by the current that the sound seemed to come to them subliminally, like some kind of animal, a moaning beast out there calling to them, *needing, needing, needing* and not about to give up.

"Expect strikes to be savage," Harry read.

Charlotte had recently begun biting her nails again, a habit leftover from childhood and the time after her mother's breakdown, a habit now revived with a vengeance. The sound of the drum banging restlessly in the eddy was getting to her. Abruptly, she tore her hand from her mouth and leapt up, plunging into the water. The drum sent up a great rumbling commotion when she reached it; under the trees the Arabian began to dance nervously.

The Indian didn't rise to help. Harry scrambled his boots off, but Reuben extended one hand, palm down, and Harry stopped, and then the two of them stared into the fire, listening to her struggle to shove the oil drum out of the shallow eddy and into the main current.

Harry put away the guidebook. Reuben's knife hesitated, then a thin curl of cottonwood grew from it, and then another and another.

"Dr. Schleifer said to talk about it," Harry whispered to her later in the tent.

It was pitchy inside the tent walls, but somehow she could see the negative white of his eyes. "I don't really want to talk about it."

"He said it would help."

"I told them everything."

"Char."

"The hard parts too. I told everyone everything." She was thinking at that moment of the younger of the two RCMP officers doing his level best not to expose a twitch of emotion about what she was being asked to tell them, what she heard herself having to say to strangers, to herself who had now become a stranger. "I'm through with my talking."

The officer had not been much older than she. It was worth hating him for, that and his fumbling inexperience, his dropped clipboard, his fat tender face and the tiniest glint of excitement she was sure she had detected in his eyes. It was like having to talk to a brother, if she had had one to talk to.

Harry propped himself up on one elbow, trying to see her through the darkness. She hadn't cried yet and they all seemed to be waiting for that—signs of release and metamorphosis. A proper lamentation. But what was it that she had lost? What had slipped from her hands? What had died and what could she grow into, now that she had been ruined?

"Charlotte," he whispered, "I'm *almost* a doctor." She could hear in his tone an attempt at some misguided order of distracting levity, a detour onto the sunny well-tended boulevard that was Harry's life and career where it was always safe to talk or cry, or to be yourself, because everybody would still love you. Harry was not afraid to be at anyone's mercy. "Why won't you talk about it, even with me?"

She rolled over. "For all the obvious reasons."

Adoration was a dangerous proposition, potholed with hazards, obstructed by roadblocks, strangers asking intrusive questions that challenged your assumed identity. One day, one look across a room at *him*, and there were things you knew you didn't dare reveal about yourself. Parts of you were quarantined as abruptly and dismissively as if officials had nailed a sign to your forehead—*until further notice*—or until you had somehow determined his receptivity—or his immunity—to the bad habits, the nasty thoughts, the lies that lacked any real point, the silly female rituals of love, the regrettable but not forgettable deeds of youth that you were convinced said more about who you were than all the make-up days that followed or coincided with that downfallen, down-at-the-heels version of you yourself.

She hadn't told them everything. She hadn't told them, for example, that she had been hitchhiking. They might have thought that she had been asking for it, or at the very least, that she had been reckless. Or that she was some sort of girl that she was not, a girl who hitchhiked.

On the second day they rode east along a creek that cut through the mountains, traveling in and out of shadow and then, leaving the creek, they found themselves beneath the tall fir and cedar and hemlock, resolutely in shadow. A disturbing quietude enveloped the Arabian. Charlotte began to worry that something important had gone out of her; began to wish for the fire and fight of the day before. From the trail a damp fecundity issued, and clouds of mosquitoes materialized, with single or double deer flies orbiting her dark curls and buzzing protest whenever one or the other became entangled. The thumping echo of slow hooves marched them along steadily, the Indian, the girl, and the tall young man leading the pack mule, and for a while no one broke whatever spell had been cast once they had left the sound of moving water and entered the silent forest.

Not long after, the Indian turned his horse, a stocky old stallion unexceptional but for a striking compliancy, and came back alongside Abra. "They like hair," he said to Charlotte. "Hair like ours." It was true: the deer flies did not bother Harry with his thin colorless wisps. Abra lifted her nose against the old bay and snuffed as Reuben handed Charlotte a tin of some kind of homemade salve, sharp and bitter smelling, that she was to rub around her neck and tousle into her thick curls. Reuben did the same to his own neck and hair. He had small blunt hands, but they moved—as he did—with a fine deliberation. Everything about the way he moved, in fact, suggested someone conserving himself in the face of an impending battle, an illness that he knew he could not beat, or an unbearable feeling that he knew he would simply and finally have to feel. For the first time since she had met Reuben, she offered a smile and he returned it with a slow solemn nod before resuming the lead.

What possible motive, she had to wonder, could this stranger have for treating her with such unearned and mannerly respect?

Behind her she could hear Harry humming something; he had such a reassuring voice, not especially strong but clear and valorous as rushing water. When the humming stopped she glanced back and saw that he was reading from another of his guidebooks, the one on native trees and plants. It was knowledge that bore no interest for her except insofar as having it might help her acquire some of his power. Harry was a great conqueror of things. When he took on a subject, he took it over entire, not obsessively but with a sanguine thoroughness that sometimes made her nervous, as if, once he had delved *her* through and through, he would leave her behind just as thoroughly. Charlotte did not want to be another topic on which one day he had finally sated himself. Even if there were not other reasons to hold some of herself back, this was reason enough.

And could he ever forgive her for this new knowledge she had not wanted, for what she had learned about men? A sudden raw shame came into her stomach. She was no longer innocent. She knew things, had done things. All of the shine of being Harry's girl, Harry's *trinket*, had been rubbed off. A dirty, needing, wanting world had simultaneously converted and convicted her: she was an adult. Adults did not need protection. And the very last thing she could stand to lose was Harry's protection.

A polite distance had opened between Abra and Reuben's old stallion. She watched the muscles of his rump flex, alternating with each step, left, right, left, right, unhurried and obedient, and felt herself settling into a dozy comfort. Between the Indian and Harry she felt safe; they were keeping her safe, these two men each with his own fields of knowledge, each a conquering hero. For now, she was safe.

And in that safety something terrible stole to the surface: They would not be looking for someone who stopped for hitchhikers; they would be looking for a man with a different approach, more aggressive, more obvious. And there might be another girl out there like Charlotte, just trying it out, hitchhiking for the first time, who maybe was mad about something, in that sort of mood, *the Devil take it all*. There was something real and tangible at stake here—another life, another satchel of innocence someone had managed to carry away from the kingdom of childhood with its unsleeping monsters and its daily traumas disguised as lessons, all of them coming thick and fast as locusts in a private and inescapable parable of biblical proportions. Family bibles, she thought, each one personalized with barren dreams and born crosses, suppers trailing betrayals, doubtful redemptions.

Parables . . . people either broke down or went off, leaving you alone . . . that was what her life had taught her. That was the moral of her story. Relentless contingency.

But there was another life, anonymous but real.

She had missed the bus because she and Harry had had a bit of a row. About a woman who was going to be a doctor too—one of his class- mates. Alex was her name. Charlotte didn't even have a major yet, and was in fact considering dropping out, now that she'd met and married Harry. What more could she want, after all? After Harry.

Alex, she thought, staring into the melancholy depth of the forest whose tree trunks and branches scratched out the distance and held her to the narrow, viewless path. Alex was probably Harry's equal in ways that Charlotte could never dream of being or achieving. Even her name suggested equality, male but not male. Charlotte had not understood that Harry's friend was a woman. Alex this, Alex that. She pictured them side by side, peering into the half-dissected vitals of a bird or a rat, poking about with cold steel tools and making cold steely notations in journals, cracking jokes only an insider could get. Making eye contact.

The bus was gone and there she stood on the curb. Harry was back in the Faculty of Medicine building, and Alex somewhere in there too, and Charlotte was needing to file some kind of cosmic complaint, not exactly for his having Alex, or an Alex, but for occupying a world to which Charlotte would have only peripheral access, wifely access . . . social events or professional functions or perhaps dur- ing staff vacations, she might fill in as the receptionist. She might even help with accounting. She'd always been handy with numbers. Having children would increase the stakes, but just about the time they went off to live their lives, her female charms would begin their inevitable slump and slide. She might take up volunteer work, join a book club, take a last-ditch lover, have a small-scale breakdown. But it would all be part and parcel of the inequality for which she had gladly signed on. She hadn't driven much of a bargain, had she? And here it was, the seventies. From the very beginning she had been dazzled by Harry. She hadn't given herself much of a chance or even tried to be a person yet, she'd been so busy setting herself up as Harry's protectorate.

They camped late along Hat Creek. Using grasshoppers, Reuben and Harry caught a string of rainbows, no more than what they could eat that night, and Charlotte boiled rice, and then there were two cans of Le Sieur peas upon which she had stubbornly insisted. No matter the healthy attributes of frozen vegetables, Charlotte would never give up canned Le Sieur peas. Reuben had gone away and come back fifteen minutes later with a bright orange mushroom, chicken-of-the-woods, which they fried up with the fish. After dinner, after scrubbing the tin plates with gravel and creek water and spacing them out on a downed tree to dry, Charlotte took her towel and wandered downstream until she found a deep enough pool to bathe in. Washing had become especially important, all parts of her body but some more than others. The men had been reminiscing about Harry's father, and Harry's voice had gone wobbly. It had been a long day. Everyone was tired. She did not want to hear Harry's voice with so much feeling in it, not now, not this week. It had the effect of unstitching some of the day's seams enough to send her back to the tent and into her sleeping bag before any more came loose.

Within minutes, a car pulled to the curb, a turquoise VW Beetle, maybe ten years old, judging by the thin chrome bumper and the seat configuration. A cheap car, repainted, balding tires. A student car. Clean—she had noticed that. It had made some kind of skewy difference as she leaned down to look through the passenger door glass. She can't now remember what he said. What she said. What she remembers: nice-enough looking guy, brown hair cut short but not so short that it said something else, something you wouldn't want to know. A man who was too fastidious could not be trusted with the accidents of being human. Small brown eyes, round as beads, olive skin, like her own; a checked shirt on a slim torso; flashing smile, bored, or hurried—one or the other—that tells her he might be doing her a favor, that he probably is doing her a favor. So she gets in. Because that's all she wants right now, a favor from a stranger. Maybe he looks a little like Ricky Nelson, or some other teenage star. She's not sure. She's not sure now and doesn't really want to know, because then she won't breathe so well.

He has his left hand on the steering wheel and it looks like it's trying to be casual, that hand with the fingers draped over the top, tapping, though the radio isn't on so there's no beat to follow. It's the other hand that isn't quite right but she can't say how. Not when it's shifting. When it's shifting it looks fine, but in the space between shifting it seems to scurry back toward his body, or the seat . . . she's not sure. There is a smell . . . vegetables . . . broccoli, it's in the top of a paper bag, backseat—he's been to market. Heading home. His window is half down. Hers is all the way up. The smell of the broccoli is making the car feel smaller than it already is. When she tries to find the window lever, he says it's broken, but it's actually simply gone. Maybe that's the first sign. They're on the Lions Gate Bridge and it's not so far from Lynn Valley, from the neat middle-class neighborhood she lives in with Harry Fairbanks in their rented bungalow, and so she just wants to get over the bridge and figure out the rest of the way some other way. Walk. That'd be fine with her now. There's a lot of traffic that is helping her feel all right about this in a roundabout way. Commuters. Commuters seem to make everything feel normal, crankiness and petty aggressions, tailgating. She's never before hitchhiked, and she decides she's just nervous. Her mother used to say dramatic. That Charlotte should grow up to be an actress. Her backpack is propped in the gap between the driver and passenger sides, and she rests her hand on it, as if it's her dog watching out for her. Some of her friends hitchhike regularly. She ought to be able to do it too, though Harry's always telling her she looks too innocent for ice cream practically. It is something he seems to like about her, so she doesn't tell him otherwise. It is part of the part of her that isn't quarantined, her presumed innocence.

He's telling her that he goes to college too, not university but one of the city colleges. Money, he says, apologizing. It feels like a line he's used to advantage. Struggling, hard-working fellow cheerfully accepting his lot, making the best of things, philosophical about it, not jealous—that line. Some part of her decides to buy this line. And why not? Half of who anybody was was who he pretended to be, or wanted to be, or had to be just to get along. Then he's talking about girls he's dated and how difficult they are, making him quit smoking before they'll kiss him. University girls, not the ones at the city college—most of them smoke, he says. Now she remembers that he's chewing gum. He keeps his mouth closed. Someone has taught him manners along the way, but he has a slight underbite and it doesn't look all that easy. She would rather not hear about girls and how difficult they are. She's wondering why he was driving around UBC when he attends one of the city colleges. "I quit smoking 2.6 weeks ago," he's telling her, and she makes herself mentally deliberate the .6, whether it means 6 out of 7 days or six-tenths of a week, because he's still saying things—about mood swings and lack of sleep and periods of random aggression. He says the word "gum," as if he's saying "uncle" and surrendering, then gestures at his mouth and smiles without parting his lips. It's not really a smile, it's a flinch. She wants to get out of the VW now. A dumb word enters her mind—shenanigans—one of her mother's words. "What sort of shenanigans have you been up to?" Charlotte needs to laugh . . . shenanigans, shenanigans, shenanigans, she repeats to herself, trying to shrink what's happening down to a prank.

At the end of the bridge they drop into West Van and she suggests that he let her off at the next corner. "Right here is fine," she says lightly, trying to sound unfussy, trying not to officially recognize what might be happening, giving him a chance, an out, a merciful lie, and stifling the panic that takes up her chest like a ballooning explosion.

He doesn't even slow down.

By late morning on the third day they made it well into the lake region. Crossing the Bonaparte River at Scottie Creek, following it east, then turning north before reaching the Deadman River, they simply began to wander. Each lake they passed sat quietly hopeless below them, passive and bound up in woods. It was a cloudless day, the sun bleak and ubiquitous. Most of the bodies of water—lakes, ponds, reservoirs, big and small—were named, but the one the Indian finally led them to had no name, or no name that he knew of, and he knew that country better than any, the outfitter had assured her.

"It is called No-name," he told them, which made it worse. Saddened her. It seemed to render the lake vulnerable, unqualified for protection, the formalized namelessness of it. And it was embarrassing too, that it had not even merited a name or inspired a friendly idea, a moment of vanity or possession among early visitors—

Bonnie's Lake, Heartwell Pond, Loon Lake. Here they would find Dolly Varden, fish with a proper name, and yet they too would be violated. The named and the un-named. Sooner or later, everything was violated, driven down to the knees of anonymity. Who were we, she wondered, if we were just like everyone else, dirty and wanting and needing, anonymous as we wheeled toward death in our passing cars?

They had arrived late. Reuben grained the horses and the mule, then she helped him stake the animals in a sunny glen near the campsite where there was a variety of wild grasses growing—wheatgrass, wildrye, bluegrass, needlegrass. The needlegrass sewed itself into her socks as she led Abra and Harry's big chestnut into the glen, the chestnut steadying Abra down to a tentative walk. The trust between Charlotte and the Arabian was still cautious. For a while she sat in the shade, picking out the needles, trying not to think. Harry strolled down to the water to make a few casts at the place where a stream left the lake. Every now and then the light touched his fair hair, marking where he stood and acquitting her of thought. So long as Harry Fairbanks was there, believing she was still who she was, she did not have to think too much.

Soon, two Dolly Varden, not like the sleek silvery rainbows of the night before but fat with a blue blush of color banding their sides and brilliant red spots, swung from a length of cedar that bowed from their weight. Reuben ran switches through them, mouth to tail fin, and they were cooked whole over a fire until their flat glassy eyes hardened, and went as white and opaque as dried beans. Kypejawed, she had to notice, because it reminded her of the man in the VW with his underslung mouth.

The no-name lake and the cloudless sky and the primeval emptiness were conjuring a desolation all their own, as if bad things had once happened in the place. Even the blue smoke from their fire, whorling and quixotic through the trees, seemed baffled. It was too quiet. A breeze that they could not feel up on the slope under the trees was chaffing the surface of the lake, portending trouble they were too ignorant to detect.

After supper, the Indian threw his bag on a tarp down by the water and in the late light, stretched out with a book—poems. She'd seen him with it the night before, and it tended to complicate him in ways she didn't know how to resolve.

Harry was already in their tent, which from the outset had been a concession to his notion that women needed privacy. Harry could be counted on to give up things for her, and though she did seem to need a great deal of privacy right now, his thoughtfulness was galling. Needing it, she felt ashamed. "I would like to hold you, Charlotte, if you will have that," he said in a voice so gravely formal that she felt sorry for him, as if what had happened had forced him back to an era when courtships were endless and women chaste as fresh cream.

Out of the question, she heard herself think. What she said while she sorted through some gentler surrogate words was his name, "Harry," and he took that for assent. Maybe it was—just a little. She kept her back to him though, where the muscles were bigger and blunter and there were fewer nerve endings. Why, you could practically run a needle through them and expect nothing worse than a distant *ping* of alert, the brain hardly bothering to acknowledge pain so inconsequential, so far away. It seemed a good way to be, distant and removed from injury. You could get on with things that way, keep running, keep keeping on. That was what was expected. But why did people expect such grand things of someone they didn't know? To keep living, to keep caring? There was a certain brand of universal importunity obtaining, a kind of species-wide peer pressure to buy the line, all the clever lines, and stay alive no matter what. Life is grand, isn't it? Yes, of course it is. Life is so grand.

Lying there with Harry's breath on her neck, the bunched sleeping bags generous and soft fortification between them, she thought about the eyes of the Dolly Varden, white and impassive in their deaths. It was how she felt now, if it could be called feeling—sightless and impassive.

"Tell me something good," he whispered.

"I can't think of anything good."

"Then tell me a good lie."

She said, "I love you."

Harry gave a laugh that was really just his breath leaving him. "Is that the lie?"

"Water," she said. "I like water."

Glad, it seemed, to have found something that might distract her, he asked her what about water.

"The way it feels around my skin, the way it holds everything in place, the pressure of it, like borrowed skin, except I can still move. I can still get away."

She was no longer sure that she loved Harry Fairbanks, because she was no longer sure who she was, or who the *she* was who had once upon a time loved him. But one thing she was sure of was that it didn't matter either way. Nothing mattered. If she could have she would have erased her name to end once and for all, all mattering.

How would it be when they made love again? When she lost herself in touch entirely, which was what happened more often than not? Harry said that she was a sensualist. No more than the next girl, she thought to herself, though she couldn't help feeling a little ashamed. It was only that she knew how to shut off her mind and for a while live through touch. How would it be if she found herself doing something new? Would he look at her as if he didn't know her? Would he say something awful . . . *do I owe this to him?* "Don't be insulting, Harry," she might say. More likely, shame would exile her to the land of silence. And in any case, Harry would never say anything so awful.

They met on a university-sponsored ski trip to Whistler, Harry one of two leaders commissioned to teach a group of sophomores Nordic skiing. Late one afternoon she had taken off her skis to climb up a tumble of boulders for the view, and one foot had gone out from under her, disappeared down a crevice and wedged. For a slip of girl lacking muscle in her arms, it was all she could do to hang there on winged elbows and bent knee, jackknifed for dear life. Several of her girlfriends skied by but either didn't hear her or didn't take her calls for help seriously, as if they might have been fraudulent. And it may be that they were, that if she had tried harder she might have been able to extract herself. Out there in the meadow with the others, teaching them telemark turns, was Harry, a marvelous skier, and she knew that sooner or later he would come. His irritation with the others for ignoring her seemed to codify the incident and purify her motivations. The sun perched high behind him, the snow was blinding, the air aglitter with icy crystalline flecks, and she could not see his face as he hooked his arms beneath hers and pulled her from the crevice, suspending her for the longest time so that she might work her boot free from the crack. She'd been up there more than an hour, and her hands had gone white. What he did was to lift his parka, his turtleneck, and press her hands in the warm hollows of his underarms. "No," she said, "they're too cold." They *were* too cold. But he only gazed at her, into her eyes, with the intensity of someone sure of himself, of all the right things that there were to do in the world if only you'd had a good solid life, one that let you believe in things. Harry was happiest when he was helping someone.

On her warmed hands his scent, with its salty tang of authority and exertion, suggested all she needed to know about him as a man. His upper lip quirked into an unexpected and unabashed show of passion. Instantly, as if some ancient cog had ground round at last to catch up another cog long ago meant to have been caught, the machinery moving now and something back there in the crowded cluttered clanking works beginning to sing, their meeting animated a classical dynamic: distress and rescue, innocence and protection.

Now Charlotte wondered how much she had not seen gazing up at Harry in that dazzling white light. How much she had tricked him into imagining about her.

Sleep was a valuable enterprise. She was not sleeping so well. Night terrors; gory images; weird sex. How was it that these terrible things were inside her? Where did they come from?

Human beings were horrible, one way or another. *God curse us, everyone.*

She reaches for the door handle, ready to jump out as soon as he has to brake at a light or a stop sign, to jump out no matter the stopping, the going, but the door doesn't open because the door's locked and at the base of the window, the up-down button is missing. He says something, something that goes with another flinching smile. Charlotte can't remember that part, what it is that he says at the very moment she understands with every cell in her body that she's no longer a part of the world out there, the one washing by her window; she belongs to this world inside the VW, and the other world, her world, is past and gone now, zooming out and away like the expanding shock waves of an explosion.

He takes her into the neighborhood where she lives with Harry. The man doesn't know it and she decides not to tell him. Maybe she is protecting it, her home. Or maybe it is as if she has already said good-

bye. Has already entered this new order. They roll by the house; she can see the lawnmower where Harry left it by the side gate, and the three pots of herbs on the front stoop. She is supposed to water them when she gets home. It is the only moment that opens a thin crack, a welling of tears. Time is stopped, or ripping past, or launching her into fright—it has so completely lost its measured and faithful validity.

He is holding himself. He may have been holding himself for a while, maybe six or eight turns, one quotidian block devolving into another, all the houses with trimmed lawns and topiaried hedges gazing sightlessly on her and her captor as they pass by in the slowed motion of nightmares and car accidents and suicide jumps from window ledges. She never learns his name. No-name. He takes her just four streets away, to a cul-de-sac formed by the western edge of Lynn Canyon, and turns off the engine.

"You don't need to do this," she says.

"Now, why is that?" he asks.

She can't really hear him; she seems to see the words in her mind, minus whatever personality inhabits his voice.

"You're a perfectly nice-looking fellow." Having just seen her home with all its now bygone promise and possibility has imparted some strange state of calmness, as if just seeing it must mean she will see it again. At the same time it is as if she was viewing old photographs in the album of a lost life. "You can ask girls out. You could ask me out," she adds, trading in a concept that belongs entirely to this new order. The one that is telling her that she must survive.

The knife has been there all along—she realizes that. It must have lain alongside her backpack, slightly hidden, occupying his right hand whenever he wasn't shifting. A long steel blade like the kind her father uses to carve meat. When he isn't touching the knife, he's holding himself. There is a lot of flesh rising between them, flesh and steel.

"I would go out with you. If you asked me out properly, I would accept. You're a nice-looking fellow. You don't need to do this."

"Describe it," he tells her.

It takes her a little too long to understand what he wants, and he has to say it again.

She does what she is told to do. That and the other things. He wants her underwear; she removes them, he puts them in the bag with the broccoli while she pulls her pants back up. So far he has not touched her, and she takes this as a good sign. She has been instructed to touch him, but he has not actually touched her. Maybe, after all, he's just a pissant, a coward. She begins to feel sorry for him, to need this badly, to take these actions; she is, in fact, embarrassed for him. Her own base instincts, like that one at the very bottom, the one that is telling her to stay alive, she is still reticent to expose. Exposing her own needs would put her at his mercy. Right now she still owns some of the action, some of what will end up being deeds.

She talks about school, about her life, peppering the surface of this new world with casual chatter, as if they are indeed on a date. She never mentions Harry. She says again, "Why don't we go out for a regular date? We could do that, we could just go out on a date. I would like that."

It may be that he did touch her. But she just can't remember that part.

They have entered a place that is a time without name. It is all action, with deed as the outcome of that action, the past tense of action. Or maybe the past tense of action was regret. Time and space are one in such scenes. And she is trapped in such a scene before it must be condemned to deed.

That night, Reuben told her, she went down to the lake, walking into the black water with great quietude and courage, as if there was someone out there she was scheduled to save. She was wearing one of Harry's white undershirts, and so was visible even in the snuffed light of the new moon and the hard little stars pinned into the night sky. Thirty or forty yards out, she stopped and floated on her back. Then she began to swim toward shore. He could see the white of the undershirt and hear the movement of the water, and he knew—he told her—that she was at home in water, and so he was not yet concerned. It wasn't until she reached the shallows and the sloping bank touched her feet that she awakened. And then immediately he entered the water to catch her, her breath coming sharp and fast.

"You were asleep," he said.

She stared at him. He still had his short, strong arms around her rib cage. He was not an attractive human being, his face too broad and his skin damaged, but he had the sweetest eyes she'd ever seen. She started to cry then, crumpling against him.

"To see in this darkness what you don't know . . ." he settled her on her feet before him and opened his palms to the hard little stars, and nodded, "that is something. But to see what you don't want to see . . ."

Once, when her father had gone off to a conference in Toronto for four days, her mother had all the stone in the house painted white. One coat for every day that he was absent, so that by the time he returned, the glossy paint was so thick, and still not quite cured, that you could press tiny frowns into it with your thumbnail. Her father had loved that stone wall surrounding the hearth; had laid it himself; had run his hands across its rough surface in thought, in boredom, in appreciation of its tactile proximity to earth.

She had every tree on the place cut down, too, even the mountain ash he had nursed from a seedling.

She slashed a giant X into the mattress and packed the wound with rotted apples from the neighbor's orchard. Then she used the knife to carve words into her arm, not so deep to kill, but still legible: *a pity about the nights in bed.*

So. So . . . her father had seen what he had not wanted to see.

They have been parked on an ordinary neighborhood street, houses facing other houses and at the end, a guardrail that keeps cars from plunging over the bank and down into Lynn Canyon. They are stopped parallel to the guardrail. It is not yet the time when families have all arrived home from work or school, and the street is quiet, though she is hopeful that inside one or more of the houses there are people beginning to wonder about the turquoise VW parked on their street. He tells her—and once again, she can't really hear his voice, can only see the words scurrying across her mind like terrible rats in the Devil's own penny arcade—that they, meaning he and she (they are a couple, it seems, in this new order), they are going to go down into the canyon together. He doesn't pretend to anything ordinary, like a nature hike or even a fete of groping and drinking that young people enjoy under trees and beside bodies of water. He says: "We are going to go down there now."

"Why?" she asks. The fear that she has held back suddenly dissolves into some kind of icy liquid metal veining through her body.

"I'm taking you down there now."

"Why can't we just have a date, a real date? You don't have to do this."

He says things . . . about how she looks and that he's sorry she had to be so pretty.

Had.

"I'll come around to the door and let you out," he says finally.

"You don't need to do that. I can let myself out. It will look funny, if you come round to let me out. People might notice. And anyway, you can trust me now, can't you, to let myself out? Here we've been sitting and talking about everything under the sun, and a date, a real date, and surely you can trust me now to let myself out of the car." In truth, it is only she who has been talking.

"A date," he says, flinching up his smile, emitting a huff. "Sure."

He studies his reflection in the knife blade. "I don't believe you."

"Look, I'll give you my number . . ." she fumbles in her backpack for a pencil, a piece of paper, adding cheerfully, "Friday's best for me. Only one class, early. You can pick me up in the same place."

Somehow, it is this flurry of routine date-making details that causes him to hesitate. Looking not quite confused and not exactly off-balance, maybe wobbled, maybe even the slightest bit pleased, he accepts the piece of paper she extends, her number and address—both false—scrawled on it. For a half a second he seems to belong to, or to recognize, the old world, the real world, not the one he has been busy creating inside the VW. Then he reaches in his breast pocket and extracts the up-down button for the door lock and simply hands it to her. He zips himself up. If they go down there she figures that he will have to kill her. In every terrible chaos of action and details, there is usually one point of exit best recognized by someone down there in the cellar where good and bad, black and white, freely consort. This is her point of exit. At the same time, she has accepted this new world so wholly, and acted so well across its stage, that she is actually worrying about hurting his feelings even as she casually, casually, screws the button back in place, opens the door, and runs.

He starts the engine and as he spins the car away he throws her backpack out the still-open passenger door.

No backpack, no identification, no name, no blame.

So, after all, he is a pissant, a coward.

The door is open at the first house she comes to, the screen door in place. A man is sitting on a couch in a dimly lit family room, watching the television. She cries through the screen door, "Help me, please, he tried to rape me, I need help! I need a phone . . . police . . ."

The man says, "I don't want to get involved," and rises to shut the door.

Next door, a woman in a kitchen, her husband approaching behind her. Charlotte says the words again. The woman picks up the phone. Her husband leads Charlotte into a living room, a cozy quiet sanctuary where good lives have gone on, and offers her a place on the couch. When the RCMP arrive, the couple hover in the doorway, looking worried about Charlotte, looking beautifully wonderfully human.

The kindness of strangers.

The owl woke her up. Harry was already gone. It was sitting in the Doug fir that towered over the tent, looking for the world like a small amputated human being, all torso. Heart's home. Somewhere not so far away that she couldn't tell its northerly direction, was another great horned owl responding to hers, questioning her identity. *Who, who, who.* She did not feel so bad, or not as bad as she thought she would after the sleepwalking.

They were probably fishing. It was early, only five, and they had to have gone down to the lake to cast when the fish would be feeding.

Comfortably abandoned, she squizzled back into her sleeping bag, glad for the time alone and sad for it, as well. All the mornings of her world with Harry would be spent like this, with him gone off to work and the silence of the house and a day, already fractured, that she must learn to piece together. But how? She hadn't given herself much of a chance, had she? She'd stuck out her foot and tripped herself at every turn, hoping for someone to pick her up, someone who might restore what had been taken a very long time ago.

Overhead, the owl *who–who-ed* again.

And if she didn't know who she was, how could Harry? If she had to conceal so much of herself, lie about the unsavory bits, or maybe it was mostly the unlucky bits, to hold him, then she could not finally keep him. To have and hold him, she had to consent to letting him go. The idea of leaving him felt brave and cleansing. Even noble.

Anyway, she couldn't have told him everything, how people survived one blow or another, that sort of thing. Mothers who had gone round the twist, pissants who would as soon kill you as date you. It was no one's business how one survived; survival was a private matter, and the capacity to inhabit other worlds, however temporary, to understand a murderer's heart, for instance, or the strange everywhereness of knives and fear, was no one else's concern. Harry Fairbanks had never *had* anything, really, to survive. It was Harry who was the innocent.

Finding in this realization a hard satisfaction, something she might feel, like a flat stone in her pocket, as she walked away, Charlotte tried to smile, tightening the sleeping bag around her shoulders. A fine mist of condensation had formed on the ceiling of the tent, evidence of breath and warm-bloodedness, and she reached up to run a finger through it. . . . *Charlotte*, she wrote, the name disappearing even as it took shape.

In memory what was a life anyway but a series of *tableaux vivants* that you visited now and then, like any tourist? Harry, her fellow tourist, appreciative, eager to believe, had thought that she was actually living when what she'd been up to was arranging things for his, and perhaps everyone else's, approval. What was left now to believe in? What was real?

Briefly, she thought of the Indian's solemn expectant face, the way little girls' faces were . . .

But people do survive, she thought again. Somehow people survive, though the means are not always salubrious. Of course, it may have been better not to have survived. At the very least, there would have been some clarity in that. Things would have made better sense, responsibilities assigned, punishments meted out, rewards awarded. Her mother had not survived, not intact. Her father was in Ottawa, making an ad hoc go of things. Their little family had been cut down back in Penticton, right along with all those trees. But Harry's parents . . . even dying, they had survived together. What a marvelous legacy.

The owl overhead had been silent for a while.

She would have to tell Harry that she had been hitchhiking, or tell the authorities—someone who might keep it from happening again to someone else.

She felt strong and somehow better—briefly—than the human that she suspected she might be.

Harry. Thinking his name, she wanted to cry. *Beautiful man.*

Harry was the sort of person you became if you'd had a normal life.

Harry was also the nicest thing that had ever happened to her, making him wholly unbelievable.

It was best, really, to remove herself from his life. She simply didn't deserve him. He would argue with her, but it was not an argument he could win. He had never been much good at the mazy logic of emotions.

An exciting and headlong uncertainty rushed over her. She could do anything she wanted, wreck anything she felt like wrecking. No one would care. She might even secretly survive, which would make for a different sort of wreckage. Live a solid, solitary life, independent of anyone, needing no one. She could be a gardener, a landscape architect, as they called them now, helping things to grow and thrive. People might even admire her solitariness, her way with plants; might wonder among themselves about Charlotte as she aged away from the possibilities that radiated like rolling green fields around youth.

A sound suddenly, then in the next moment a shadow spreading over the tent, followed by the laborious *whoop-whoop* of the owl's wings lifting him heavily away. Everything fell before it could rise. Even great owls.

With the owl's departure, Charlotte decided to pay a visit to Abra, say hello. The long grass was soft and dewy up to her knees, and she was glad to be barefoot in the cool morning, glad that Harry was gone and that she had had the owl to herself, glad to have Abra to visit. Dropping over the rise and down toward the glen, she saw that all three horses were gone; Reuben too she discovered gone. Only the mule remained to eye her dolefully and waggle its halter, asking for grain and attention. What every creature needed and sometimes deserved.

Rushing back to the camp, she found everything eerily in place—grub boxes, tackle, the fishing rods secured against a tree, last night's plates stacked on a log. The lid to the coffeepot was off and the pot itself filled with water and sitting on the grate, but no one had started the breakfast fire. A loaf of bread sat on a board, one piece sliced, the knife half embedded in the loaf for another piece. Off to the side Reuben's tarp lay neatly folded with a stone on top to hold it down. His book of poems too, and the cottonwood root he'd been carving. She picked it up. It was Abra, her angular face and in-pointing ears. Had he carved it for her? Harry's can of peanuts was just over there in the pine duff, exactly where he had left it when they'd been drinking whisky the night before, waiting for supper.

Why had they left her? Where? Why hadn't they waked her? How could they have left without her? Something terrible had happened and they had simply left her. Or something wonderful, and they had ridden off to see it and had forgotten her. Or she was too small, too weak, too much trouble, not worth it . . . She glanced over at the tent, the Doug fir towering over it, the owl gone. The air, the trees, the water, all was perfectly still, the absence of sound frightening, as if the world had sucked back into itself and left her utterly alone to fend for herself.

Abruptly it seemed important to be dressed, to have some protective coating, to be ready. In the tent she pulled on her boots and a wool sweater. Still cold, she dragged the sleeping bag with her to the stump she had occupied the afternoon before, and sat to wait. Her legs felt leaden, her hands were shaking. They had taken her horse, too. They had taken her way to get away. The mule was no good. You couldn't escape on a mule inured to pack. And anyway, where to go? How to go? And what if it wasn't Harry who came back, or Reuben? What if it was someone else who found her there alone, who might take advantage, who might hurt her? Nothing was as it once was; everything felt empty and alien and hollowed out with menace. The world was no place to be.

If she hadn't reason enough to leave Harry Fairbanks before, she did now. He would pay for this. If he came back, he would pay.

She had never been that important to Harry, *never*—she realized that now. Perhaps she had known all along. It was his work, his colleagues, like Alex, who really mattered. Who held his interest. He had a whole life, rich and rewarding, and she was just . . . just a girl. Or another one of the subjects he had swiftly dispatched.

For the first time in her life, she hadn't the faintest idea what she would do. As if to sort it out somehow, to stumble upon the thing she must do, she got up and walked down to the lake, looked at the water, flat and impervious, knelt to feel the temperature—a swimmer's habit—without really noticing it once she had. She went and looked at the mule again, who this time ignored her. She stared at the impressions left in the long grass where the other three animals had stood and stamped for oats. No good at making fires or at cooking over one, and not even remotely hungry, she nevertheless picked up Harry's tin of peanuts and rattled it gently, carefully replacing it within its perfect circle in the duff. As afterthought, she kicked it away, finally surrendering to tears and the increasingly familiar chaos of fear.

If Harry returned she would not submit to him, to his reliable kindness, his love, his male assuredness, his categorized food. Whoever she was or might become, it was equal to Harry Fairbanks—different, but equal.

God, she hoped he would come back to her! Then she might properly leave him—on her watch. But just to see him again, coming toward her . . .

It was two hours before they returned, trailing Abra, lathered and wild-eyed.

She threw her head back and released a sound that might have been a word, or a hundred words.

"We almost lost her," Harry called to her with a big smile. His face was red, his eyes brightly popped with that incurable enthusiasm of his, and he looked for the first time not so perfect.

Charlotte was already up from the stump, taking Abra's halter, touching her neck. "You okay, girl?"

"She made it all the way to the other side of the lake, she was tearing up to the plateau like the world was on fire."

"Well, it was," Charlotte said, "in her mind." She pressed her face into the crease behind the Arabian's soft ears. "Abracadabra," she whispered. Then she turned to Reuben, not yet ready to look at Harry. "There was an owl right over the tent."

"An honor."

"Yes, I know," she said without really knowing why or how she knew, without caring about her tears.

Harry was beside her, one hand squeezing her shoulder and the other on the chestnut's bridle.

"I don't ride well," she said to him coolly.

"Who *could* ride this screwy mare?"

"Don't be so tolerant, Harry. It's rather mean, when you think about it. And no, I don't ride *any* horse very well. Never have."

She looked up at him then, feeling ready finally for something unnamable but essential. "And don't do that again. Go off without waking me, without telling me something."

He tipped his head and removed the hand that had rested so comfortably on her shoulder, and shoved it into his pocket. "All right, Charlotte."

Charlotte, not Char, she noticed. He was looking at her differently, as if she had changed her hair or something, but not without a curious bit of appreciation. "I guess I'm still getting used to being two."

"Yes," she said, "well, I suppose we all are."

CATCH AND RELEASE

*T*he kid has that look, deer in the headlights. He stands on the dock as I flip in the fenders and untie the bowline, and it isn't until I toss him a life jacket that he sets the tea tin down. It hurts to watch the way he first brushes the boards off with his bare fingertips, and we both have to look at the tin before getting busy with something else. I tell him he can handle the stern line and that seems to shake loose the stare he has going. The ladies are already onboard—two aunts, a cousin, and the stepsister. What a piece of work she is.

Early in the morning, Tahoe is like it used to be—empty, quiet, blue like blue is supposed to be. The summer tourists are still in bed recovering; man, all they do is come up from the Bay Area and cut loose in our backyard. I wonder how they'd feel if we herded down to their hometowns and partied every weekend. Not to mention that around here locals can't afford to eat in our own restaurants anymore, the way Bay Area bucks have driven up the prices. So it's nice having the lake to myself. Yeah, I have to admit, it's sweet heading out of Agate Bay with the Merc chugging along like a big black dog going about his morning business, and the ladies back there on the padded benches chatting each other up like they're birds getting together after a storm and so much pecking to be had that they can afford to put it off. The sun is still riding below Marlette Peak, but sending pink and orange flares up and out across the lake. The water is flat enough that I can stand with one hand on the wheel, my other arm along the top of the windshield, and my knees not even flexed. It's my lake again, or our lake, the people who really live here. Like I'm that king we all started out being before we grew up and got the bad news.

The kid looks out of place, but he isn't. Maybe the only one of us who isn't. That orange life jacket bunched up under his chin—well, jeez, I guess he is only eight—and the tea tin sitting empty in his lap, waiting. There is some kind of picture pressed into the tin, little house on the prairie type thing, but no color. Gray and serious, you know. The tea tin was his dad's idea. Dad is out of town, as usual. The guy's a Suit, a first class Suit, always gone—Hong Kong, Japan, Bangkok, Korea. Techielands. Who knows what he does? I mean, do these guys really do anything?

I come home from the job and my back tells me what I do, my back or my hands, banging nails all day, and now even my ears. The MD says I've got hearing loss, being around power tools so long. That's the way he puts it too: you have some loss. Now how do you *have* something you lost?

Well, it feels like I'm about to find out, along with the kid.

He has both hands wrapped around the tea box. A death grip.

I ask him if he wants to sit up front with me, in the port seat, but no, he shakes his head and stays put in the second row by himself. Behind him on the padded benches the ladies face each other with the box mixed in between them. They don't seem to remember that he's around or that it's his mother who just died.

About two hundred yards off shore I goose up *Angel*, and she noses straight down the center of the lake. Maybe the kid'll dig it, I think, but all he does is check out the bigger wake, then twist back around, like he's in church and doesn't want to get caught not paying attention. Over the engine noise the ladies are shouting now, but they all look real happy about it the way people are at a party that gets loud after the first round or two. The sun pops off the eastern ridgeline and sails up fast, like a gas balloon, yanking all the pink streamers out of the west. It's going to be a day, hot even.

After about ten minutes one of the aunts wobbles forward. Debbie. Does the X-ray shots for a foot doctor in Reno. She's okay. A plain talker. Has a family herself. But even she went along with the kid's mother—the spiritual mumbo-jumbo, the nutzoid cleansing diets, the hot tub ceremonies. God, you would not believe it, you would just not fucking believe it.

"What do you think, John?" she says.

I'm about to answer but here comes the cousin from nowhere, short tubby Trish in her flowing getup. "This isn't the center, it has to be the soul-center of Lake Tahoe."

"Amber said the middle of the lake."

I throttle down. We are in the middle, east to west.

Trish does this thing with her hand, like I'm supposed to keep going and never mind Debbie. Which I ignore. Hey, she's not my wife, I'm just the next door neighbor who owns a boat. I get enough of that shit on the job and at home, the hand signals, like words don't compute. "Oh, John," she says, sweetening right up, "can't we go just a little more that way?" She jabs a long red fingernail toward South Shore. You can tell those nails are fake.

I smile at Debbie and give the kid a nod. "Is that what all of you want?"

The kid looks at me like he doesn't even want to be asked, he wants me to decide for him, decide everything. Poor guy.

"Fine," says Debbie. No expression. She has a way of never letting on what she thinks. And after that day I have to wonder if she ever thinks past the sign hanging on the front door of anything, if maybe that's why it's all fine with her.

Debbie pinballs back to the stern seats and the three back there go on shouting at each other over the Mercury while Trish hangs up front with me, perching like a fat pigeon on the edge of the port seat.

She thinks I can't see her, she thinks I'm actually driving the boat, or Jesus, I realize finally, she doesn't care that I can see her dig up inside her nose and basically do a nasal D & C, scraping it clean. Then she gives me a look, like oh, are you there, like I'm just something stuck to the steering wheel, and rejoins the flock in the back.

We motor along, eight, nine miles, and I have to admit I'm enjoying the scene. Which I try to hide from the kid. He's a cute bugger, blue eyes, freckles, the works. I notice his buzz cut has grown shaggy. Mom was pretty out of it at the end, and no one yet has figured out his hair needs cutting or combing, but hey, he's still a cute kid. Has a proud little way of walking, but not like the punks around the neighborhood. Naw, he's just a new little guy, and hasn't had it ripped off him yet. I'm thinking maybe I'll see if he wants to go fishing.

Most of my water time is spent over at Boca, not Tahoe. Boca's a dirt reservoir north of the Lake, just off I-80. Guys from Reno come up in the summers to cruise and drink beer; they don't even bother with the fishing excuse, these guys. In winter it's weekend snow-mobilers. Basically you're out of the High Sierra there, on your way down to the Nevada desert, so there's nothing showy about the peaks, they're low and rounded and like dirt mound mountains, and it's drier stuff that grows, you know, ponderosa, manzanita, even sage, but not a lot of variety because of the low rainfall. Nothing classy about Boca; it's what it is. The yahoos from the Bay Area don't bother with it, I can tell you. Sometimes in a dry year Boca's so low you can count a dozen bathtub rings in the banks, and don't expect anything fancy like white sand, it's dirt with plenty of sharp volcanic chips in it. But I like it. No one's ever going to throw up a condo village at Boca. It's a rough place, not pretty enough to rape and wreck. And still wild. I've seen plenty of bald eagles, even a golden once, lots of coyote, maybe bear in the summer when there're people with picnics around. And the wind howls and the snow freezes up hard as a sheet of plywood, and I don't know, you kind of know who the hell you are out there and what's what.

Naw, most of the time it's just me and maybe three or four other die-hard fly fishers, and then we're spaced along the Little Truckee River with bends and brambles in between, and I can go all day and never see anyone. I don't catch much, throw back what I do. Liz, my wife, and Ashley, my daughter, they don't like trout—too many bones. Liz, she could care less about all the fishing I do. She's got her bunko girls Tuesday nights, her investment group another night, and this gym thing she does after work three days a week. Liz has got a figure that keeps going and going, ever-ready, you know. She's been with the same title insurance company for ten years; they can't wipe their asses without her. And I don't mind saying that she makes more than I do, it's a true fact. Naw, the fishing doesn't bother her. I am a free man. She even chains up her own car now. Hey, one day last winter we were waiting for a load of lumber, and I ran over to the 7-Eleven to pick up a grinder for lunch, and there she was in her miniskirt, if you can believe it, chaining up for the grade into Tahoe Donner. Said she had to meet a real estate agent up there. And no, she did not want my help. I had to admire her. Thirty-five years old in a mini-skirt, and it's dumping a fresh load of Sierra cement, and she says she can handle it. Doesn't want me to catch shit from the foreman. Now how many women would think of that?

Yeah, I've seen plenty of the dependent types and I got a wife who is definitely not that. Have to admire it, I guess, but it's funny, I didn't feel too good, eating that grinder back at the job site with her out there in that skirt 'n all in a snowstorm, and some real estate jack-off waiting for her up in Total Downer, tapping his foot. They're supposed to bring it to her office, all that paperwork. She shouldn't've had to drive it up there, no, she shouldn't've done that. Damn, I wish she had not done that.

The kid's got his arm out now. The tea tin is squeezed between his knees and he's got his arm out, his hand flat, starting at the bow where it peels back the water, and following the white cut water all the way back until it's just the wake curling out. I've seen him do this thing before with his lab, start at the dog's nose and pet him all the way back to the tip of his tail. It's so slow that the dog has a hard time standing still for it, but you can tell that the kid doesn't want to miss anything, he wants to love the whole damn dog. Yeah, he's a funny little guy. I've watched him since the beginning. My shop's off the back of the house, and the property runs out into Forest Service land, so no one on our street's got fences. Their hot tub sits right out there, big as you please, and Amber was always in that thing, her and her cronies, every one of them bare-ass naked. Even the stepsister. What a piece of work she is. Right out of Cinderella. But who could blame her, I guess. Simone. One of those phony French names. She got stuck with the kid a lot of the time, just plopped him down in front of cartoons, and his diaper full and his nose running green. The kid always has some sinus crap going. Simone and Ashley, my girl, they don't have anything to do with each other, even though they're both sixteen. Ashley's on all the teams, volleyball, basketball, soccer, and I don't see her the way I used to. Boyfriends, it's a regular parade. And they're all on teams too, humping for scholarships. Truckee, that's what you hope for, athletic scholarships. It's not like down in the Bay Area where there're private schools and universities and the kids don't have to hope, they're so busy *aspiring*.

Simone, she's a druggie. Basically. Out there with her low-life friends in the driveway, smoking. What does she want to be? A tattoo artist. Perfect. Amber wouldn't let her smoke in the house, but fine, do it in the driveway so all the littler kids in the neighborhood can see, right? A fine example. There they'd be, lined up on the bumper of Dad's brand new Explorer, dragging away. And Dad's gone, as usual, off making the big bucks, doing what, I can't figure.

So there was Amber with her girlfriends in the hot tub, middle of the day, and the kid was wandering around naked too. I had my belt sander going so they knew I was there, but they never cared or maybe they liked it, I don't know. Amber used to be a looker and she thought she still was. Red hair, a real fine face, the kind that's like an old-fashioned doll's face, wide with the kid's big blues, but she didn't seem to realize that the weight sort of changed things from the neck down. This was summer, maybe five years ago. The kid had a red plastic shovel and he was minding his own business, just going about his world, heading for the sandbox, which they never cleaned out for him, you'd've thought they'd've kicked out the pine cones at least, those things are sharp. And Amber breached up out of the hot tub like a whale and pointed at the kid's pecker and said real loud, "Little Penis," like she just made a sighting on *Wild Kingdom*. And all of them, the stepsister especially, dug up a real gut buster laugh. The kid stopped. He was still holding the red plastic shovel, and he kinda lifted his arms up and out, like he was hanging on a cross, and he dropped his head to stare down at himself. "Little Penis," he said, and tried to laugh. But he didn't get it and I didn't get it either, it was a funny thing for a mom to do. And I don't know, I don't know but she called him that more than once, maybe a lot more, could be that's just what she called him. It was a weird thing for a lady to do.

The breast cancer happened the next year. And get this, she decided she could beat it with organic food, you know, seeds and nuts and liver flushes. Liz said she spent five grand on a retreat in LA with Dee Chalk Poker, or whatever his name is, eating nothing but rice to clean herself out. Wouldn't let them come near her with the chemo. Finally her doctor got her to agree to radiation. Did that for a while.

Even had all her fillings replaced, though I never could understand that one, something about bad metals. But a year later back it came, this time in her lungs too. She ditched the natural food cure and went gangbusters—chemo, surgery, radiation, the full monty. Her red hair fell out and grew back looking like a terrier, but she was going to be fine, she told my wife, and she told me, and she'd tell anyone who had a couple of hours to spare that she had beat the big C, maybe, basically, by talking it to death. In her mind she had it whupped. The kid's dad was home more, but not that much more. Signed up for some kind of emotional therapy to deal with the scene. And the kid, he talked about his mom's cancer like it was her cooking. These people, they didn't know the first thing about how to hide anything, even from a little kid. One of these "open" families, everything right out loud, you know? *Did you take a good crap today, dear?*

Six months ago she began dropping the weight, I swear it looked like five pounds a day, but she was still out there in the hot tub with the candles and incense going and the Hare Krishna music and her girlfriends jawing it up, and she was going to make it, she said, it was Not Happening. Two months ago Simone put the cover on the hot tub and pretty soon I saw that there were pine needles and crap collecting on it. And the kid was in the backyard by himself, bouncing up and down, up and down, on a trampoline day after day. She couldn't drive. The pain pills, you know, they kept her pretty looped. I saw the kid wandering around the neighborhood with his dog, dinnertime would come and go, no one paying attention. Even the hospice people didn't seem to get that there was a little kid living there. And without Mom to rein it in, Simone was running rough-shod. One day I was driving in from work and I saw her flick her cigarette at him, and I hammered the brake, opened my window, and told her, "No," like she was just the bad-ass dog she is, and she gave me this look like yeah, right, I'm gonna listen to *you?*

Dad managed to be home for the death. That was last week. The sisters arrived, Debbie and Fern, the cousin from out of the woodwork, Idaho, I think, the girlfriends, Simone, plus Amber's creepy brother. They cleaned up the house, which was a total mess, and threw together one of these homegrown funerals where people get up to say things, sing a song, whatever. Maybe thirty people, mostly just neighbors thinking they should. The kid goofed around with some of the other kids, then I saw him sitting in the middle of the trampoline, picking his nose. The stepsister, she had on this dress, it was right out of Club Med, some red flowery thing, no straps. Go figure. Dad looked like he couldn't wait to get back to the office and count paper clips. There was a lot of food, but no one stayed long enough to seriously get into it, and the women, they acted like that was the way it was supposed to be, you know, like the spread was for show. They were shoveling it into Ziplocs before I was even out the door. And man, that was it. End of a life.

Except for the ashes. She wanted them scattered in Lake Tahoe. And the guy next door's got a boat. Do they even know my name, these ladies?

They're back there, they've got cans of Coke, some cardboard tray of Costco muffins, and it's the party barge, right? The wind is making sails out of Trish's flowing getup, and I can see—my luck—her belly rolls stacked up like bike tires. Simone's smearing on lipstick, Debbie's sitting there like she does this kind of thing every day, scatter ashes, and the other one, Fern, who looks most like Amber, is listening to Trish explain something real important, I bet, like why Kenmore washers are better.

The kid and I don't exist.

I cut the engine.

Right away they put on their *concerned* faces. They look around. I'm staring at them. They decide not to complain. Amazing.

Debbie starts tearing the white paper from the container. It's about the size of a cake box, maybe slightly bigger but a helluva lot heavier. When she gets to the metal she's stumped. The thing is sealed, I mean, really sealed, like a can of sardines. I have to use a screwdriver to pry up one corner, and then pliers to peel it back. The kid is watching it all, like it's a horror show. Debbie takes his little tea tin, scoops out some of the ashes, and hands it back to him. There is stuff on the outside of the tin which he gets on his hands and you should'a seen him trying to figure out what to do with that, his mom's ashes on his hands. So I help him lean over and do a scrub off in the water. "It's what she wanted," I say quietly, "to be in the lake."

He nods with zombie blues.

Meanwhile Debbie's hanging off the stern with the box. There is not the whiff of a breeze, and the ashes are dropping straight down, and the thing is you can hear the *plop* of bone shards. Trish is reciting something, Simone is trying to squeeze out a few tears, Fern is kneeling on the padded bench with her eyes shut. And the kid and I are standing there like we crashed the wrong party, big time.

He opens the tea tin and looks in at his cupful of Mom, gives it a little shake, and yup, you bet you can hear there are bone shards in there too. That's when he pinches up his face and starts to cry. I'm standing right behind him and I can see the life jacket shake. He's got his mom's white skin and it's as red as raspberries. I give his arms a slow kind of rub, the way he does with his lab, then leave a hand on the back of his neck, and he stops crying about as fast as he started. Kid like that, it doesn't take much to comfort 'em, he's so hungry for it.

Then the real weirdness begins.

"Let's swim with her," Trish says, "let's swim with our water sister." And she does this twirl around with her hands up in the air, like she's God's girlfriend or something. And I'll be dipped, the others are going for it.

Basically I tell them I'll hang up front, give them some privacy. I hear three splashes, then a fourth, then Simone says, "Not you, Little Penis." And one of the others kinda laughs, probably Trish. "Water *sisters*," Simone says. "What, are you a girl now?"

"Come here," I tell the kid, and sit him down on the driver's seat between my knees, put his little hand on the throttle, and together we shove it forward. We can't hear what they're saying, they're just birds cheeping, but we can see their pink faces bobbing above the blue water, and the cloud of ashes around them, and the wake opening like wings.

It's pretty warm out, I'm not too worried. And the kid, he's smiling. He doesn't smile much, this kid, he's serious, like he's always trying to figure out what's going on, and he's getting it finally, but he wishes he wasn't.

We buzz a few coves and run a big doughnut out in the open before we start back real slow for the water sisters. I tell him that sometimes all you have is what you lost, and that's better than nothing. It's like throwing a fish back; it's almost the same as losing it, right? That's how you have something you lost, I tell him, and that tea tin he's keeping of his mom's ashes, that'll remind him.

And I'm thinking okay, so the wife cheats on me, I know, I know, and my kid, Ashley, she thinks her dad is yesterday's lunch. And this kid next door, his dad's basically absent and his mom wasn't much even when she was around, and now she's been thrown back. But hey, I'm here and the kid is here.

"Brian," I say, "you wanna go fishing with me tomorrow?"

"Cool," he says in his emptied-out voice.

"Catch and release," I tell him, "that's what it's all about, catch and release."

THE NEW SISTER

*I*t was almost noon as the children walked up Orchard Lane, the shadows cowering into small gray blots that seeped out from under the backs of their tennies, like sweat stains. They passed Mrs. Myer's house, the third grade teacher who they had found cooked the strangest sorts of foods, including artichokes, huge and barbaric things, and if you swallowed any of the soft prickles at their base, why, you could die. That was what she had told them and from such knowledge they had made a stupid song: "Arty choked on his artichoke and couldn't get up in the morning." Then came the yellow house where Ronald and Donald lived, identical twins who went to a private *academy* up the peninsula during the week, not the new public school three blocks over with its tetherball courts and walls checkered in brightly colored construction paper. The Decker twins were nice boys, clean and round-eyed as marionettes; their mother used something in their hair that transformed the tufts and cowlicks into a surface that resembled grooved plastic. Ronald was just then returning home, having gone somewhere on his bike, and when he saw them, he coasted down his driveway to join up, making lazy loops in the street to slow his wheeling pace to their Saturday drifting and dawdling.

In front of the adjacent house stood Mr. Kesselman, hosing off the sidewalk. Louisa squinted down at the nearly white cement, scoured under the noonday sun, and remembered not to step on the cracks, but really, it was too hot to be that good about anything. And Louisa was a good girl, everyone agreed on that. But not so many thought so after what happened that day.

"Off to the pool, kids?" Mr. Kesselman held the hose to the side, letting the water plash with heavy flaccid clarity into the lawn as they shuffled by. The smell of grassy mud sagged down toward them, warm and vaguely sickening.

"Yeah," one of them mechanically intoned.

They had not yet decided where they were all headed, or even if, wherever that was, they would go together, since it was only Jimmy and Dan who had planned to hook up, but then Louisa had begged to go along, and when they passed Julie's, she had trotted down from her front porch where she was practicing posting on her imaginary horse, the black one with the star on his forehead, and if Julie went then Robert too, who had a crush on her and who lived across the street and could see any activity, and when they had passed the schoolyard and there was Todd Wolfe, bereft of his usual band of lesser bullies, he had ambled after them, sniffing for trouble. No one ever said no to Todd, and even if they had wrestled up the courage to tell him to bug off, it was practically impossible to get a word in edgewise. He hardly ever shut up. A short, thin, wedge-faced kid who seemed a man in a boy's body, and with a muddled birthmark like chocolate splashed against his neck, nevertheless, Todd commanded respect as the worst of the neighborhood torments, an avowed thief and an apprentice pyromaniac. It was not that uncommon to see parked in front of the Wolfes' house the fire chief's car with its official Santa Clara County crest decaled onto the driver's side door, and Mrs. Wolfe following the chief down the walk, her hands wringing promises that her son would not keep.

Maybe they would go to the Club, maybe not. There were always a lot of adults on the weekends; a lot of other-parents' eyes noting who snuck out of the kid's pool over into the big pool, maybe even into the dangerous, and for the youngest children, forbidden deep end.

Things happened in the deep end, aching ears and secret touches; once Louisa had seen a human turd floating by the ladder. Even though it wasn't hers, she had felt somehow responsible for having seen it, and so she hadn't told anyone.

As for Mr. Kesselman, it was usually best to simply agree with him. He was what Louisa's father called a "free thinker." Mr. Parker's admiration of people who were "free thinkers" conferred upon him a certain high-minded insubordination of which he was manifestly proud. Louisa and Dan assumed that their father had been a "free thinker" at one time in his own life but wasn't anymore because now he had a family. He had lived in France, briefly, during his college years, studying painting at one of the *écoles*—a word he pronounced with unsettling pleasure—and to that experience he returned again and again in conversation or reverie, in vacation dreams the Parkers could not afford, and Louisa had come to think of her daddy's time in France as a pretty little raft that for a while had taken him away from the island of his life. "The pursuit of joy," he liked to tell her, "is a radical act."

Mr. Kesselman was the manager of the local department store next door to the Ben Franklin, and as a free thinker he was always debating the "pros and cons" as he liked to put it, of everything and anything, from ladies' pumps to Reagan for governor. He would have kept them there in the heat, undoing the suggestions he had just made, only to instantly revive them.

"Yes, sir, the pool," Todd threw out, probably figuring it was better to support this collection of losers than to endure Mr. Kesselman's studied double-mindedness.

As soon as the children had passed the boundary of his property, he thrust his thumb back over the hose end and aimed the now-hard white rush into the cracks of the sidewalk, washing the bits of gravel and dirt over the curb into the gutter. "Stay out of trouble," he called after them. "And the deep end."

Louisa had stopped listening. There was a blinding, dazed quality to the light and somehow the hose water made it seem worse, beyond relief, cleaning out one or two cracks but not cooling the unending black and white surfaces of street asphalt and sidewalk cement. The squares of sidewalk marching one after another, the little lawns, so brightly plaintive, like hungry puppies; the flat bleak glare of midday, the sun not an object, not a thing up there, but a no-thing, a small searing hole in the top of the sky directly over the top of her head; the dry heat that carried—not entirely incongruously—the scent of Mrs. Parker's seasoning cupboard, which itself brought to mind something just about to burst spontaneously into flames; and then Todd Wolfe skulking along at the back of their group, waiting to angle in and snag down one of them, maybe Jimmy this time for finking on Todd about the magnifying glass stolen from the science room . . . well, it was all making Louisa feel funny in a bad way; everything was fizzling out from her into a hot, washed-out emptiness. No matter how hard she tried to keep it back—whatever *it* was—things weren't mattering the way they were supposed to. Louisa Parker was not feeling like Louisa Parker that morning. *I'm me, I'm me, I'm me*, she insisted furiously to herself.

"Hey," Todd said, addressing himself to Dan, "where's the new sister?"

"How should I know?" Dan shot back. Louisa watched her brother quicken his pace, keeping his eyes fixed on the sidewalk. The Cabaña Club was only a block away. They could already hear the weekend squeals of little kids in the baby pool and occasionally the lifeguard's piercing whistle followed by the bullhorn telling someone to *walk, don't run* around the big pool deck.

"So. How'd that happen, Danny-boy? A ready-made sister. Let me pull a sister out of my hat. *Poof!* No doubt about it, I gotta get a new hat." It was a near-perfect imitation of Bullwinkle the Moose and in spite of the gravity of Todd's feared though still unformed intentions and their possible dire consequences, some of the more oblivious kids smiled.

Jimmy leaned in to whisper something to Dan, caution or comfort, maybe both—Louisa couldn't tell. They never stopped scuffling along and the others in the group kept up, with Todd nipping at their heels like the school janitor's nasty terrier. Louisa had lately been practicing a risky authenticity to which she felt she had earned the right to treat herself, just by having been a nice girl for so long. First grade, second grade, third grade—nice, nice, nice. She had done all the extra credit work, she had stayed to help out Mrs. Myers when they had made a mess of the classroom with a papier-mâché project, and she had refused to join some of the others teasing the retards who had their own classes, but who shared recess and lunch with the normal kids. Before first grade she couldn't remember whether or not she had been nice, it was all just a whirl of unformed memories, like the dust and debris that finally balls itself up into a real planet. Nothing official, nothing that counted.

Now she turned, set her hands on her hips, and stopped Todd Wolfe. He had a hurried, shambling way of moving that was never quite straight ahead, so that after she had swung about, she still needed to readjust herself in order to properly square off. Todd actually waited while she found her final stance, his head cocked with a merciless amused curiosity. Louisa said, "She's our *half* sister," exaggerating and slowing her mouth workings as if to assist the deaf, and at the same time to try to memorize the lesson herself. *Half sister, half sister....*

The boy seemed momentarily flummoxed, probably by both her age—two years younger—and her blond, blue-eyed, doll-like and yet soldierly manifestation asserting itself in his way.

Finally he said, "Yeah?" and released a smirk; the way it started on one side and slid to the other reminded Louisa of a pet garter snake her brother used to keep in a shoe box under his bed. "Half what?"

Then Dan was beside her, gently shoving her away. Dan with his crazy mop of hair, his freckles, his nice and easy way. "Half us," he said. "Half Parker. What'd'ja think?" Normally, Dan would have added *stupid*, but after all, this was Todd Wolfe.

Maybe it was just too hot, maybe Todd didn't think it was worth it, especially without his usual cohorts backing him up, but instead of tackling Dan Parker, he just gave out with a single chopping laugh and resumed the Saturday migration toward the Cabaña Club.

It had already been a whole *month* since their new "half" sister had arrived, right out of the blue. One whole long lousy month, Louisa told the sidewalk.

***

"You have a sister," Mrs. Parker told them that Sunday night four weeks ago in the TV room. When she entered, she had turned down the sound, but the children could still see Ed Sullivan, his head slunk in and bobbing as he clapped for the last act. It was clear that by some private compact just executed, Mrs. Parker had been designated the spokesman, because Mr. Parker stood slightly behind her, his hands on her shoulders not lightly draped in that proud proprietary husbandly way, but nervously fidgeting, his eyes darting from the faces of his children to the olive-green shag carpet. It looked as if he had been crying—the end of his nose was red. The least bit of excitement showed up in the end of his nose.

Louisa stared at her mother's flat stomach where a baby couldn't possibly be living. "Her name is Miriam, but apparently your father is calling her Mimi."

At the word *apparently* Mr. Parker made a sound with his breath as if something had lodged in his "Sunday pipe," the one you weren't meant to employ for food.

From behind her back Mrs. Parker produced a small canvas, framed in gold, the vivid pastels smeared approximations of the girl's features; there had been no attempt at realism; the artist had wanted to capture the subject's character and spirit. There were very dark brown eyes, almost black, with dabs of white that made them bright and hopeful-seeming, the cheeks were pink patches below high sharp dashes of bone shadow, and the mouth was ripe and hurt-looking, like bruised fruit. Her hair was long and black and perfectly straight, and at first Louisa mistook it for a veil of some sort. Their new sister was not smiling in the picture. She was just looking out at them.

"What's her last name?" Dan said. And everyone was relieved, even Louisa, though she couldn't have said why exactly.

"She has the same last name as we all do. Parker." Her mother was using the singsonging voice that she reserved for situations in which she wanted her children to do something without any fuss *whatsoever*, if there was no time, for example, to explain, or they were *in public*. Being *in public*, Louisa had learned, was far more serious than any state of affairs, more than being *in church* and even more than being *in trouble*. In fact, you could get into big trouble just by saying or doing something *in public* that you had been doing regularly at home for a long time and without anyone once protesting.

"Why?" It was Dan again—*big brave Dan*.

Mr. Parker reached and clasped his wife's hand, and when he tried to say something, she gave his hand a quick resolute squeeze before releasing it, almost angrily. "A long time ago, before we left Chicago and even before you were born, Louisa, Daddy, well. . . ." She smiled weakly, grimly, then glanced at the TV as if there was help to be found there. Ed Sullivan was flinging his arm out and stepping aside as the next act emerged from behind the curtain. ". . . stubbed his toe," Mrs. Parker announced, and in the weird bluing of the TV, her smile flashed like scrap tin in a vacant lot, sharp and dangerous just for being there half-hidden in the thriving weeds. "We are going to love this girl. All of us. Daddy stubbed his toe, but we love her anyway. She has our name now, and she is your sister, and that's all there is to it."

Of course Louisa knew this was not all there was to it. Gamely she prepared for their sister's arrival, taking certain covert measures as well, including emptying the spare change from all the coat pockets in the hall closet. This had been a steady source of income, funding not only candy bars and Fanta sodas from the Club machine, but also the eighteen-cent McDonald's hamburgers that the school offered every Wednesday. She also thought it smart to hide particular personal treasures—a new box of BBs, a golf ball that had been painstakingly skinned down to the tight fist of rubber band at its core, the nicest of the Barbie-doll clothes, not the torn or homemade ones; broken bits of costume jewelry from her grandmother, Nana Parker, who lived back in Chicago; a miniature troll Louisa had forgotten to pay for at the Ben Franklin.

Over the next few days they managed to discover several more details orbiting "the situation" as Mrs. Parker was referring to it. Mimi's age, for starters. She was nine, a year older than Louisa and a year younger than Dan. "You know what that means, Lou," Dan had said under his breath. Louisa wasn't sure but didn't want to expose a lack of worldly knowledge.

Second, Mr. Parker had just recently found out about Mimi, and only because suddenly the girl needed a responsible parent.

Also—and this was the best bit of information they had gleaned—
Mimi was part Navajo Indian, Mr. Parker told them when Mrs.
Parker was off doing errands. In spite of "the situation," Mr. Parker
seemed pleased by this fact, the same way he was about having been
a free thinker. He was wearing an expression like the one he wore
whenever he drove his old Citroën around the neighborhood. He
had an everyday car, a Plymouth he took to work, but he kept an
antique Citroën in the garage, which he enjoyed waxing and polishing and taking for a spin on Sunday mornings when no one was
up yet and the light was still gray and the round, bugged-out eyes
of the Citroën's headlights shone hardly at all, a dim dying amber,
like history fading or the end of a story. Before Mimi arrived Louisa
often went with him. A thermos of coffee squeezed between the
seats, they tooled around one corner and then another, often ending
up near the entrance to Laurelwood where there was a big field with
a falling-down old house at its center. It was not a haunted house, he
assured her, just abandoned. A family had lived there once, long before the grid work of the neighborhood was laid out; a fruit-growing
family. Eleven kids, Mr. Parker told his daughter, every one of them
with extra long arms for picking. Then he might wink and gravely
say, "Now and then they would misplace one of the children. Under
a chair, or behind a dresser, or accidentally left up in the top of a
cherry tree, living on cherries, poor thing. They found the youngest
child in the cellar, nestled in with a nice family of coons. Quite happy, the girl was. Didn't have so many siblings to share with."

"I don't blame her," Louisa said, thinking that occasionally even
Dan was annoying, or in the way, or getting a bigger half of something.

Sometimes Louisa would climb into the Citroën and pretend to
drive it, fast, along a foggy sea cliff, the lights really quite pointless,
yellow stains in an endlessly vaporous world, nothing seeable, and
anyway, what did it matter? She was having free thoughts, there in

her daddy's Citroën, and it seemed to her that being a free thinker would offer both protection and good reason. "I hope you have good reason," her mother was always saying. "I just hope for that much." But Mrs. Parker really wanted more than good reason; she had Visions for Louisa—of learning to type or of becoming a nurse, acquiring the sort of get-along skills that were valued when she herself was a girl. Typists met executives, nurses married doctors. Dan was exempted from her visions; boys had careers while girls either got married or knew how to get along.

***

Mimi had arrived on a Monday before the children got home from school. Mr. Parker had taken several days off in order to make the drive to Arizona and bring her back, and when Dan and Louisa slammed through the front door, heading for the cookie jar, there was Mimi, already in their house. She was standing before the sliding glass doors, her hands behind her, staring at the plane tree in the backyard where, Louisa observed, absolutely nothing was going on. Her hair was so long in back that she could fiddle with its ends from behind, but she stopped long enough to accept Dan's hand. "I'm Dan," he said. "Wanna cookie?"

Most of the time Louisa appreciated the way her big brother could be a gentleman whenever it might prove useful, but at that moment she didn't see any reason why he had to be that way, there was nothing in it for him, no adults around to impress.

Mimi shook her head once. You couldn't say that she looked at all like Mr. Parker, but there *was* a quality around the edges of her, a shining sort of imprudent hopefulness, that brought him to mind, even at that earliest meeting when she stood there in silent contemplation of Louisa. There was such a purity to the silence that

Louisa wanted to yell, or break something. Instead, she said, "Come on, I'll show you my room." *We are all going to love this girl*, her mother had unanimously vowed.

Mr. and Mrs. Parker were already in there, rearranging things to accommodate the addition of Mimi. "It's just lucky we thought to get a double bed for this room. Isn't it lucky, Louisa, that you have a double bed . . . now that you have a new sister?" Louisa noticed that her mother did not refer to Mimi as a new daughter.

"I guess," Louisa replied even though her mother didn't seem to be talking to her really; she was just mindlessly peppering the air with words.

Mimi went over and stood along the edge of the bed, looking first at the two pillows, then immediately at the small window on the far side of the bed. She pointed to the pillow beneath it and then Mr. Parker said, "I guess you're used to a lot of the great out-of-doors, aren't you, Mimi? I'm sure Louisa will be happy to give you that side of the bed."

"Sure," Louisa agreed amiably. That was the side where, if there were bad things, they hid, between the bed and the wall, and under the window through which they came and went.

"Well," Mrs. Parker began, "well, now that's settled, we'll let you two get acquainted." She gathered up several empty shopping bags—Mimi's things had come in paper bags and at first Louisa wondered if they were all new from the store—then Mrs. Parker fled. They could hear her out in the hallway, "Isn't it lucky, it's just amazingly lucky, isn't it, Thomas?"

"What?" he asked. And for the first time Louisa heard a strange festering sort of irritation, the way Dan sounded when he had no choice, when he was positively *stuck* doing his chores, usually watering the backyard plants, and his mother called out to him from the house, cheerful and triumphant, *Don't forget the azaleas* or *you're doing a wonderful job, dear!* "What?" Mr. Parker repeated. "What could possibly be lucky?"

Mrs. Parker lowered her voice. "The double bed."

"For Christ's sake, Mary. Her mother's just died."

A burbling sob ruptured the surface of their civility. "Oh, Thomas, how could you?"

***

Laurelwood was one of the hundreds of new, planned neighborhoods in the Bay Area, most of them with an elementary school and a recreation club of some sort. The development had the standard-issue pseudo-grand entrance flanked by two cinder block walls painted white and about thirty feet in length, one side bearing the name of the tract in scripted metal letters, Bella Vista or Hillhaven or The Oaks, something fancy and picturesque-sounding. Situated between the entrance and exit lanes there might be a turquoise fountain pool or a ring of flowers, the kind they plant along freeways because it takes a lot to kill them off, or sometimes even topiary, hasty and when you got right down to it, basically just a hedge of something green and equally indestructible. All the houses looked pretty much the same, except that the garages might be reversed one house to the next, or there might be a curving driveway instead of a short tongue of cement that lapped straight down to the street. There was always a postage stamp front lawn, a low, flat border of juniper maybe, and against the house, standing bottle brush or bulging oleander, sometimes red or white ornamental rock to set things off in the garden, and stepping stones of exposed aggregate that circled round to a side gate that let into the backyard. Outside, shake shingles curling in the California sun, stucco, board-and-bat redwood fencing; inside, three bedrooms, two baths, shag carpet, and skip texture. Everyone knew where the powder room was in everyone else's house, and if there was a problem at a neighbor's, where the water and power shut-offs were located.

It was terribly handy, the neat functional repetition. Depending on where you had come from—what part of the country, where in the pecking order, how much money you had had before and how much now—the uniformity, the *equality* was either reassuring or insulting. A local ordeal that effectively disclosed which reaction a new family might be having was the block party. This was a potluck affair held in the nearest cul-de-sac and featuring bags of barbecued potato chips, roasting dogs, macaroni or carrot-and-raisin salad, with Fudgesicles for dessert. The Parkers had not missed any of them and were generally considered a nice addition to the neighborhood.

Mr. Parker worked for a business machine company. When they were living in Chicago he used to have to travel a lot, but he was made "management" and put in charge of the latest expansion office in San Jose that still smelled of synthetic carpet and roof tar. The family had moved into Laurelwood a year and a half earlier and hadn't quite got over the sunshine, the mild wet winters that promoted Louisa and Dan to weather authorities, since most of the other kids had never even seen snow. Of course *they* had in their possession all the local mysteries: how to build forts from the newly cut mustard weed in the orchards; where the drainage pipe was that dropped four feet down, then fifty feet west and out into Howard's Creek; when the Dempster Dumpster used for collecting old newspapers was at its fullest and best for burrowing through; why the dirt clod fights were ideal after a little rain but not a lot.

"You've been into the newspapers again," Mrs. Parker said to her children three weeks after the move West.

"We have not. Promise." Dan could gaze into his mother's nice clean blue eyes and lie angelically, the two of them plainly aware of their dueling counterfeit innocence and taking some kind of genetic pleasure in it.

"Yes, you have. You are fibbing, young man," she would say, raising her eyebrows and smiling with a satisfaction that was—to Louisa—baffling.

It was some time before the mystery—of how she always *knew*—was solved: their clothes were smeared with newspaper ink. Louisa had felt strangely betrayed by her mother; it seemed cruel of her, to let them tell the same lie over and over, and never once reveal her method of detection. The other thing was that Dan's share of the lie, though not exactly excused, was somehow accepted, like grass stains on his jeans, but Louisa's role resulted in lengthy installments of "trust-building." These periods just about broke Louisa's heart, she wanted so to be considered a good girl, a perfect girl. And they seemed to have no end point; Mrs. Parker never said, "I trust you now, Louisa. I believe you."

The young children of Laurelwood were never allowed past the main entrance. This had lately developed into an awful problem because of the 7-Eleven that had gone in just across from the entrance, and which was selling something called a Slurpee, an icy slippery drink flavored with cola. Some of the older kids were bringing them into the neighborhood, giving the littler kids tastes and daring them to cross Station Road. Until recently, until Mimi arrived, Louisa would never have done that sort of thing, no matter how tempting it was; maybe her big brother Dan might, provided someone kept guard. But there was something about the new sister, the sudden inescapable and still not plausible fact of her, that was pushing Louisa beyond her own familiar boundaries. The whole thing did not seem real.

There was in fact a way you could get to the Ben Franklin and down Station Road to the 7-Eleven without actually crossing the road—by dropping into the drainage pipe near the edge of the or-chard and then through it to Howard's Creek, and then up its other side through the walnut grove and onto the street of another neigh-borhood called appropriately Walnut Grove. You could tell that the houses were older by the colors of the stucco, brighter and less taste-ful than the pastels of Laurelwood, plus the bushes and trees were bigger, even while, overall, things just looked less tidy, less respecta-ble. In Laurelwood, if someone hadn't mowed his lawn for a while, a neighbor might offer to mow it for him. There was a *divorcée* (a word that practically jangled jewelry and gave off whiffs of perfume and cigarettes and other nighttime artifacts) living around the corner from the Parkers, a Mrs. Springer, who didn't keep up with things, and so the fathers took turns trimming her hedges and mowing her front lawn, and Coach Brace, it was said, even spent a lot of time fix-ing up her backyard, which no one else cared much about since you couldn't see it from the street. One night soon after Mimi arrived Mr. Parker was told by Mrs. Parker that Mrs. Springer probably had enough help. She gave a shrug of somber regret and then mentioned *building trust*, whereupon Mr. Parker turned and walked right out of the kitchen and into the garage. Presently they heard the automatic garage door opener followed by the growling fits of the Citroën, and then passing the window Louisa saw the yellow lights crawling away through the night, dim and forlorn.

***

The apron of lawn around the entrance to the Club was a shiny tan-gle of bikes hastily cast onto their sides. With a healthy fling, Ronald added his Sting-Ray. Jimmy said, "Wow, it's sure crowded." Jimmy Snyder was slightly older than Dan, a responsible boy who had land-ed the local paper route and who usually kept an impressive and worrisome roll of bills in his pocket. What if someone tried to steal it? As both a target and a leader, Jimmy was someone to pay attention to. When the children pushed through the tall swinging gate they saw the usual bunch of kids in the shallow end of the big pool but the rest of the pool was likewise dotted with bobbing heads. A patchwork of towels covered the lawns and every single deck chair was supporting the baby-oiled body of Laurelwood's finest. Tucked around the corner next to the fence the little pool seethed. There they spotted Mimi, a brown girl standing in turquoise water, playing solemnly with toddlers. Because Mimi had lived on a reservation where there weren't any "bodies of water," Mrs. Parker would not allow her in the big pool, not even the shallow end of it, which, even to Louisa, seemed overly cautious and maybe just plain mean. Mimi was supposed to learn to swim first, only there hadn't been any lessons scheduled.

The parents lounging on towels and chaise longues didn't seem to know how to talk to Mimi Parker, so they simply kept an eye on the girl. Mrs. Parker had felt insulted when they first introduced Mimi around the Club. "They keep a weather eye," she told Mr. Parker. "Imagine!" In spite of Mimi's silence, she seemed harmless enough. Sturdy—not fat—there was an unnerving quietude to her broad handsome face, her eyes the color of molasses, her lips that never seemed to move even when she had made a decision to produce human speech.

The minute she saw them, Mimi climbed out of the pool and came over. She was wearing one of Louisa's old suits, noticeably too small, a fact that both embarrassed Louisa and prompted familial protectiveness. Not for Mimi but for the real Parkers. Julie said hi; so did Ronald. They were both nice without having to think about it, which meant it didn't really count. Dan nodded even as Todd said, "Hey, it's the new sis," loud enough for anyone on that side of the pool deck to hear. Louisa had been digging in her pocket for a quarter and when Mimi had just about reached them, she spun off toward the Fanta machine where she studied the flavors with conspicuously fake interest. She always bought grape. Whenever she was in Mimi's company she felt a strange urgency, like needing to pee, or noticing that there is something unidentifiable there in the shadows just behind what you're doing that you'd rather be doing. Plus, she was still feeling sore about missing out on the trip to Willow Lake with Jimmy's family last Saturday. She hadn't felt like having to play with their new sister again, so she'd made the long trek through Walnut Grove and across to the Ben Franklin to buy a Nestlé's Crunch Bar; but it hadn't been quite enough to satisfy that new unnamable need in her, so she made her way down Station Road with the cars roaring past, scary and threatening emissaries from the world *out there*. In the 7-Eleven she purchased her first Slurpee. It wasn't as good as she thought it would be, and she ended up pouring the last of it in the gutter. When she'd got home an hour or so later, the Willow Lake party had already left.

"We looked for you, dear," her mother said. "Everywhere. Really sorry . . . oh, poor dear."

Sick with grief, Louisa curled up on her bed, the tears instant, unstoppable, and so complete that it felt as though her entire body were twisting up tight, wringing out the anguish of her loss; as if there were nothing that could fit inside the world but her pain, it was so overwhelmingly enormous. All she wanted was for the day to *please end* so that she might at least know that they weren't still at the lake, her brother, her friends, Mimi, having fun without her at that very instant. The simultaneity of her misery and their pleasure was maddening.

***

By some vaguely democratic process led by Jimmy who couldn't find his trunks in the cubby assigned to him, the children exited the Club, having now added Mimi to their ranks who filed along behind Todd Wolfe. She walked like a person trying to make things last as long as possible, steadily and evenly and with all of her deep-eyed attention. There was no hurry in her, nothing she ever mentioned looking forward to in the future and no one she seemed to miss, not even her mother. She liked to look out—out windows, doors, a seeker of horizons; anyone could tell that much.

"What's it like on a reservation?" Todd asked over his shoulder. They were shuffling along in the general direction of the entrance to Laurelwood, and now with the daily default of the Club behind them, there really was no destination, it was all just the meaningless-ness of the heat and a dangerous itinerancy.

Mimi answered, "Quiet," which for some reason did not make Todd laugh. He just appeared thoughtful and preoccupied.

"You live in a teepee?" This was not provocative; he seemed genuinely curious. That was the thing about Todd Wolfe—he was smart. There was nothing to get him on, except maybe the birthmark and the fact that he didn't have a dad, no one knew why, though it was rumored that Mr. Wolfe had "taken his own life" and that "the kid" had been the one to find him.

"Hogan." Twice Mimi pronounced the word with momentous formality: "Hogan."

Todd bunched up his chin and nodded. "Hogan," he repeated correctly.

"We had a house too."

"Yeah?"

"All the same, like these," she said, making a sweeping gesture with her hand. "But smaller. The government builds them cheap."

Todd started to ask another question but Louisa broke in. "Quit bugging her," she said, wildly overconfident and aware, too, that it was she the questions were bothering.

Again, Todd considered Louisa Parker with calculating amusement, letting her know—in so many unsaid words—that he was willing to put up with her bizarre and risky behavior so long as it struck his fancy, but that she was beginning to definitely push it.

Now they were angling across Orchard Lane and turning left onto Thrush. To their right lay the empty field, the house sitting in soundless vacancy at its center, as if it had only just that morning been abandoned by its people. The ground was a ragtag of mustard weed, oxalis, and matted tufts of native grass, gray and tall as a man's thigh, leftover from the summer before. Once every year someone came with a tractor and plowed the field to reduce the threat of fire, and every year some group of concerned neighbors with aspirations of a soccer or Little League field tried to buy it from the orchard family descendants, as the developers no doubt had tried not that many years ago when Laurelwood was built. But the descendants wouldn't sell, wouldn't even tear down the old family house. And there it was yet, a California ranch house, spreading out one way and another, with sagbacked porches and two chimneys, and behind the house a redwood tank splitting its sides up on a rickety platform. There was not a living tree in sight, not one, they'd all been ripped out or left collapsed in a desperate snaggle of bare branches clawing up toward the sky, the old limb crutches hopelessly splayed. Which was why Louisa didn't want to go out there. It was already so hot, so bright under the pressing weight of the noon hour sun, she felt she wasn't seeing clearly. That her eyes were like the yellowy balls of the Citroën whose light never went out anywhere, never penetrated the early fog or even merely the leaden veil of dawn that only the earth's turning could lift or alter.

They made their way across the field, the eight children. Because of the recent plowing the ground was uneven, the dirt clods dry and crunchy, some of them as big as a softball so that when they broke up under Louisa's modest weight, sharp crusty bits cut into her ankles or scratched her calves. It was not long before she noticed Dan rubbing his fists into his eyes; he was terribly allergic to mustard weed. Maybe he would make them turn back; maybe what was already happening could be stopped.

Julie was trotting about and rearing, pretending to be Blackie, and Robert, always trying to please, cantered in close affectionate circles. Every so often Todd picked up a dirt clod and lobbed it against one of the broken trees, most of his shots finding trunk wood and exploding satisfactorily. He was trying to get Mimi to join him but she just kept plying her way across the uneven ground, like a herd animal of some sort, a water buffalo or a cow or the last elephant in one of those trunk-to-tail processions. Finally he pressed a clod into her hand, as if to teach her, and obligingly, shockingly, she made a quick sideways flick of arm, wrist, hand, and found the same tree trunk. Along with the dirt clod, something inside Louisa shattered. "Hey, nice shot," said Todd.

Once inside the children discovered that the center of the house, roof and all, had imploded; there was a bright sunny space carpeted with ceiling boards, scattered shingles, and precarious sections of old wallpapered walls seesawing underfoot—it was like a fun house gone crazy, everything topsy-turvy and not funny, eerily serious in fact, as though something terrible had happened and the house itself was trying to cover it up. Weeds grew wherever raw dirt had been exposed. A toilet sat in what must have been a parlor and in the same room atop a miraculously intact brick mantle there was an armless doll whose black button eyes surveyed the scene. In this place a girl had once loved the doll.

To no one in particular Louisa shrugged and said, "It's just been abandoned." But it was generally understood, maybe even by the lately arrived Mimi, that there really wasn't any appreciable distinction between an abandoned house and a haunted house.

"My dad says . . ." Louisa began.

"Mine too," Dan reminded her, not even glancing her direction as he scrambled about the small side rooms whose walls still stood, peering into closets and aimlessly flipping defunct light switches.

Louisa stared at him savagely. "Fine. *Our* dad says that there were eleven kids in the family that used to live here."

"And we're the kids!" Julie shouted. "We're the kids and our parents are gone, they left us and just never came back . . ."

Heat dazed and oddly frightened, Louisa murmured, "There's not enough food . . ."

Dan, passing behind on his way into another of the little peripheral rooms, stopped, and looked at her. "What are you talking about?"

"The food is running out," she told him, angry frustration in her voice, in the word *out*, as if it was all incredibly obvious, everything that had happened to her, to their family, and that was still happening, the catastrophe of things not mattering, and the heat . . . how could he not realize?

Robert climbed over a heap of rotten studs to get into the kitchen and began slamming the old cupboard doors and clanging a dented sauce pot against the enameled sink. "The cupboard is bare!"

Between the kitchen and living room stood an old wood box on which Todd perched, one leg bent so that he was resting his chin on his kneecap as he fiddled with a small rusty device. It had a cogged wheel and a handle, and might have been an egg beater or an apple corer. "There's only eight of us," he observed matter-of-factly.

"Two are twins," Ronald said. "They ran away. They joined a rock band that's friends of the Beatles. The Beatles love them."

"Okay," Todd said drily, "still one unaccounted for."

Unaccounted for . . . yeah, Todd Wolfe was smart, and for a while Louisa supposed that that was what had sent a flush of raw heat up her chest and face. "She's lost," she informed no one in particular, staring down into the hole where the cellar used to be. "They forgot her, everyone forgot her, there were just too many . . ." Her voice trailed off. The dark opening at her feet and the hot sun overhead were creating a terrible tug-of-war inside her. There was no place she wanted to end up, no comfort she could imagine or hope to find. She was quite simply and completely miserable and the misery blew over her like a vast hot wind that came from no direction and went nowhere that was *away* and that would never stop.

That was when the game started.

The abandoned children in the abandoned house have to fight for the remaining food. Broken plaster bread, brick meat loaf; Julie gathers mustard weed and fox tail to toss a salad: it is arranged prettily on a section of wall lying in the sun-blasted space, flowered wallpaper transformed into a tablecloth, sticks of kindling for silverware, shingles for plates. The children contest each other for the food, at first any way that comes to mind, but then someone—Robert? —mentions Mrs. Myers's artichokes, *Arty choked, couldn't get up in the morning*, and the terms of engagement become choking. In fact, the only way you can win is by choking the food out of your opponent's mouth. Dan climbs atop Jimmy's chest, trapping his victim's arms beneath his knees; Jimmy pretends to cough up the fare he has just eaten. For verisimilitude he hocks a loogie, then claims his turn choking the food from Dan's mouth, Dan making a great show, rolling his eyes, lolling his tongue, which reduces both of them to hysterical laughter. Julie and Robert are at each other, except that Robert spits out the cherished and imaginary food before Julie can properly choke him. "You can't just give it to me," she complains.

"It wrecks it." Ronald and Louisa take turns strangling each other, Louisa hanging on to the stem of Ronald's thin white neck until he yields up the life-giving rations.

And then with her customary silence Mimi walks over and lies down beside them. Ronald must feel funny about it, maybe because no one really knows the Parkers' new sister. Leaping up, he vanishes into some other part of the house. In fact, everyone seems to vanish, faces and voices retreating at breakneck speed as if the camera is zooming out to a far-flung setting in which Louisa Parker's life used to take place. Then it is just the two of them, Louisa and her half sister, in the hot, bright, laid-open space where the orchard family home has fallen in on the heart of itself.

"You first," Louisa says out of the habit of being nice.

And so Mimi sits on Louisa and squeezes her neck. The pressure is intermittent and bearable but there is a part of a moment—just the smallest inside pocket of one—when it seems maybe scary, when Louisa might be detecting a twitch of wildness, of lost control, like something slipping naturally into what it used to be, or is used to being, the way Louisa is used to being nice. It could be that she is hoping for that; it could be that Louisa has been longing for a peek at the malice she is sure this girl has brought with her into the very center of the Parkers' house and home. Like an infection. In her own mind Louisa is positive that she has seen it.

(She told Dr. Pearlstein that, but that was much later and by then the idea had gained strength.)

The sun is up there behind the black veil of Mimi's hair, up there like a bad halo, and at the same time the edge of one of the boards beneath Louisa is digging hurtfully inside the crevice of her shoulder blade, and vaguely she is wondering where exactly the hole is that opens into the bottomless pit of the cellar, is it nearby? Will she break through and fall forever into it? And wondering too where

Todd Wolfe is only because it is what you have to do with that kind of simmering human hazard, keep track of what state it is in, how near it is. The air begins to prickle. Then the bad halo and the human shape that is the void of Mimi in the noon light slide off to the side. The hard white light takes over. Her throat feels . . . *exercised*, not sore.

"Now I eat," Mimi says without triumph, without expression, and she cups her hands over her mouth, dutifully acting her part.

So it becomes Louisa's turn.

From the broad plain of her face, Mimi's eyes gaze up at her as if she is an animal forced to monitor a distant bird of prey winging back and forth across the sun. Her eyes are dug into her face like a couple of silent caves. Louisa wishes the caves are not there, or that whatever is in them will stop peering out at her, watching. Louisa looks at her own hands at the ends of her own two arms and remembers the extra long arms of the orchard family children, and the armless doll, and the girl who lived in the cellar with the coons; she thinks of the deep end of the pool where things happen; and Mr. Kesselman's free thinking that never settles down anywhere, everything is always in doubt, nobody seems able to solve anything once and for all. She wants—suddenly, desperately—to have *good reason*. But what things come flocking to mind, like riotous black wings, wings without birds, birds without bodies, are Dan saying *he's my dad too* and Todd Wolfe pressing a dirt clod into Mimi's capable hand and how hot the sun is in the hole above her head and the way Mimi cupped the imaginary food and brought it gently and weightlessly to her lips. Then Louisa watches her fingers wrap around her new sister's neck, the thumbs lining up in a way that makes it seem right. And she simply squeezes as hard as she can. She is aware of wanting to squeeze away everything that is between her fingers; of wanting to end up with air and her two hands meeting in a state of happy old reassurance, like twins who have been cruelly kept apart.

She might hold on to herself again and not feel a stranger huddled under the noonday glare. It is easy, really quite easy, shocking, nothing, really, at all, and it takes almost no time to make Mimi cover the caves of her eyes and lock away what is hiding inside them.

***

"There was a sound," Todd Wolfe told the fireman. "Like a dog who's got something whole down its throat."

Almost everyone, except people like Mr. Kesselman, was surprised that it was Todd who yanked Louisa off the girl and he who ran the two blocks back to the Cabaña Club. It happened that there was already a fire engine there, because one of the poolside adults had suffered minor sunstroke. Of course the fireman knew Todd Wolfe, owing to the episodes of pyromania, and was disinclined to believe the boy until the arrival of a second youngster, one of the Decker twins, persuaded him that there was in fact a problem over in the old orchard house.

"Just *throttled* her," one of the other parents said.

***

Mimi Parker was in the hospital for three days. The Parkers were quiet during that time, not exactly tiptoeing around the house but moving about as if through some thick resisting medium and murmuring behind their bedroom door late into the night. They were awfully polite with Louisa, less so with Dan. Louisa might have been a guest who had come from another continent practically. Africa maybe. Dan went to school and still had his chores to do, but he wasn't complaining, at least not during those days. Louisa got to stay home and watch TV—a lot of it—*Captain Kangaroo*,

Have Gun Will Travel, Lassie, The Rifleman, Flipper. She felt peaceable now, played out and peaceable. Then one morning Mr. Parker put his hand on her shoulder and walked her out to the Plymouth, and drove her to the airport. She stayed with Nana Parker in Chicago for a while. Chicago was where she went to Dr. Pearlstein. They had talks. When Louisa came home to Laurelwood she found that her daddy's Citroën was gone and that the garage where it had lived had been made into a room for Mimi with tall windows that opened to the east through the foliage of the young plane tree in the backyard. Now their house was the only one that didn't look like all the others in Laurelwood.

***

"Remember the block parties?" Louisa asks her sister.

"No," Miriam replies.

"That's right," she says, glancing off, "we stopped going to them after you came."

The waitress appears and Louisa orders a Diet Coke. Miriam asks for a glass of Chardonnay and when it arrives she sees that her hand is shaking and reaches quickly for the steadying stem. She is in town for only two days. This lunch is her idea. Like many of her visits over the years, the last one three months ago was bad—surreptitiously; only the two of them, the sisters, can say exactly where and when the tiny assaults occurred, so remarkably accurate, the standard defenses triggered, enacted, the snipes and blows, the unheard underground melee. It was a birthday dinner party for Louisa's husband, Conner. Miriam and four couples, all *dinks*—dual income, no kids. They have decided against children, Louisa and her husband.

Mr. and Mrs. Parker are long gone; Dan was killed in a boating incident, aged twenty-two. That was fifteen years ago. So they are it—the last repositories of those years, those people, those memories.

"Do you ever drive through Laurelwood?"

Louisa lifts an eyebrow. "In my business ..." Her manner is casual, almost blasé.

"That's right, of course." Nodding, smiling, Miriam is hopeful that this might actually work.

"The Club is gone. And the trees—huge. The whole neighborhood is shady now."

"What about the orchards?"

Louisa sucks on her straw but stops long enough to say, "Condos." Like her husband, she is a real estate agent, fit and petite, who handles mostly million-plus properties and who likes to attribute her success to attention to details. Miriam has one of her magnetized business cards, the kind made for refrigerator fronts, with that phrase, *attention to details*, beneath her name. But she does not think that this is the secret to Louisa's success. It is the kind of success that Miriam has not been able to care much about—financial success—though she has never let on because it gives Louisa something on her. Tangible and widely agreed-upon, a recognizable American virtue. Louisa has always seemed to need that. Miriam teaches in one of the reservation schools and her husband is a blacksmith artist. Already they have three children. Real money is probably not in their future.

The sisters have never talked about what happened; maybe they couldn't afford to, or maybe it's because they are women. Miriam believes that women often make bargains with themselves to not remember, or to rearrange memories and impressions in order to be able to stay comfortably related. Certainly she has. What if I ever need a kidney, she has said, half-joking, to her husband.

The waitress comes by for their order, and Miriam tells her that they are taking their time today, smiles apologetically, then sips at her wine only once to convey a leisurely pace. The restaurant is filling briskly with young business types laddering their way up; there is an eager, toothsome quality to their conversations, as if they are feeding on that as well, on anything that wanders within range. For some reason the restaurant has chosen an elephant theme, which Miriam has trouble fitting with food or dining pleasures. Across the table, behind Louisa there is a massive elephant head emerging from one of several merely decorative columns, its trunk uncoiling down behind her back.

"Lou," she begins, "how can we make our relationship better?"

"Are we here to talk about that letter? Is that why we're here?" With each word her head nods encouragement and agreement. "Because I might lose my appetite if that's why we're here."

It's a funny little threat. Nevertheless, Miriam does think—momentarily—about Louisa's appetite. Losing it.

"Well, not necessarily. I just want to know how we can make our relationship better. I want to try."

"Don't send letters like that. If you want to improve our relationship, don't send me letters like that. Ever." An instantaneous hardness invades her tone and actually takes Miriam by surprise. (In recollection, she is ashamed of herself for that surprise.)

"I was being honest," Miriam says quietly. She is also surprised by how fast, how sharply, things have taken a bad turn. The lunch is beginning to feel irretrievable. They haven't even ordered yet.

"It was bizarre. Now all I need to do is show people that letter and they know how bizarre my sister is." Louisa says this as if she has been patiently waiting to stumble upon some form of proof, supportive evidence of a long-standing hypothesis. She has pushed her glass of Coke away from her and is pressing backward against the booth, both hands rapping the tabletop, daring Miriam to utter a response.

"The view is different from my side of the street. I showed the letter to Scott, to the kids, to a friend who's a counselor. Before

I sent it. They all thought it was a good letter, hard to write, but . . . necessary. Because, Louisa, if you don't want to see me, if that would make things easier for you, it would be better if you just told me."

"I was the hostess!" Louisa says, almost shouting. But by now the restaurant is loud and the business types, so edgy and animated, are in the throes of their time-limited feeding, and no one has heard, or if they have, the words are instantly disregarded spikes on the radar screen.

Miriam gazes openly at her sister, trying to recover her footing on the path. She has always been okay with silence, with just looking.

After several minutes, in a voice as flat as pavement, Louisa says, "The inscrutable Redskin."

"Oh Louisa . . . please."

"The Parkers' . . . inscrutable . . . Redskin."

There is a fist of grief augering its way up Miriam's throat now. "I'm speaking to you as my sister, not my hostess. Yes, you invited me to your home, but you let me know in every other way, in the stiffness of your embrace, in the way you asked about Scott's cancer, so offhandedly, *now tell me about Scott's cancer and pass the salt* . . . in your little public sniping at me . . . so many ways . . . you let me know that I was not really welcome."

"I invited you to our home. I was the hostess!" This time two young men, both wearing white button-downs, glance over. One of them scowls briefly, then lets out an appreciative snort, as if the two women are part of some luncheon entertainment provided by the establishment.

Though her heart is pounding sharply, Miriam is determined not to show how upsetting this is, not to cry, not to raise her voice. "Yes, you invited me and that was the end of it. You could check it off your list of details. After that it just did not seem to me that you really wanted me there. Why did you want me there? Just to punish me?"

Louisa leans forward. Something has happened at the center of her face, it has collapsed or cratered subtly in a vague sort of square that runs from her eyebrows down along the maceration hollows and then straight across her mouth. Her eyes have always been on the small side, a perfectly nice hazel, but now Miriam notices that the whites have gone pink, almost as if someone has droppered a touch of red dye into them. "I was the hostess. You were in my home. You were eating my food." Her voice is graveled back and down, like a tractor in low gear pulling up something enormously heavy that has been long and deeply buried, and now Louisa is standing, heading away from Miriam, making a gesture with both hands along her sides, a final flicking-away motion. *No more* or *that's it* or *I can't stomach you one second longer.*

Miriam is afraid to lift her eyes and see who has witnessed this violent domestic exodus, this final abandonment and dismissal. Instead, she runs her fingers gently up and down the stem of the wineglass and sips occasionally, supposing that the wine might help. The elephant head with its uncoiling trunk is peering blankly across the table. The elephant in the room, she thinks without even a grim inward acknowledgment. *I am left with that.* It is a shame to waste the wine, to waste anything, there is sometimes so little to go around. After it is gone and a respectable enough time has passed, she tells the waitress that they have had a change of plans and must go now. She thinks about simply leaving a twenty on the table—far more than necessary—and just exiting, but decides against it, not wanting to expose even the slightest trace of desperation. The bill paid, she leaves an appropriate tip.

Out in the rental car it is a while before Miriam can stop crying, and it takes the rest of the day and night, plus dinner with an old friend, for her to accept this end and the huge sadness filling in the blanks around her. Not that long, considering what was at stake.

On the flight back to Arizona she realizes that it is a relief not to have to try any longer. The plane, shuddering skyward with its fragile cargo, reminds her of the jocular remark she made to Scott, about some day needing a kidney. No chance of that now, not from Louisa anyway. The stranger strapped in beside her was a more likely donor, and after all, hadn't this always been so? Now she would have to take good care of her own two good kidneys. She would have to take very good care of herself.

MONA'S COMING

*I*t was after 1:00 p.m. when I telephoned my old college roommate, Kaplan, assuming that he would at least be up, maybe already in the kitchen, preparing his usual toasted bagel with bacon, mayo, and cherry tomatoes—and he *was* up but only just. A conspicuous hesitation followed by his voice, cold and irritated, acknowledged that it was in fact he, "Sidney Kaplan." Needlessly I identified myself and he replied, "Oh." The singularity of the word together with the sound it made between us, like a dull book slammed shut, set the usual tone. And so I was well into the routine of the opening gauntlet predicated upon the crime, so far nameless, that I had committed and for which it seemed I was calling to offer a rather tardy apology.

"This a bad time?" I asked. I think I always trumped up something along these lines.

"It's all right," he said slowly, without inflection. His voice is deep enough to be forbidding.

"I can call back, if there's a better time." I knew of course that he wanted to talk; I knew I was probably the only call he had received all week, except for the daily flurry of handymen, tailors, mechanics, gardeners, carpenters, and the like. By my count he had only one other friend left, fellow from Chicago, some jazz authority I used to see quoted in liner notes. And the women—they called, they came. Otherwise, what friends he had acquired over the early years he had managed to offend into the wounded stupor of the past.

"Well, I am having my breakfast."

Typically by this point, I found myself growing weary of the old game, but I really did want to talk with him, so I said playfully, "Let me guess," and I could hear something release, some held tension dissipate on the other end of the line, and he softened into the commerce of a thirty-year friendship, if that was what it should be called. That I kept track of his habits, what he ate for breakfast, that sort of thing, never failed to please him.

I told him that I was not only coming to New York but that I would be in town for six months; that I had arranged a midtown flat near Gramercy Park, and would be working at the Humanities Institute, but that there was a last-minute foul-up with the lease and I found myself homeless for the first two nights. Could I shack up at his place?

"Mona's coming," he said.

"Ah, a new one."

He chuckled. He's always been proud of the parade of women in his life, ever since Judy left him. "Mona's my cleaning lady."

"She doesn't clean at night."

He cleared his throat. "I have to prepare for her."

"Yes?"

"Move some things out to the deck."

"Not to be pushy, Kaplan, but how long can that take? I'll give you a hand." Of course I was being pushy, because I did want to see him—he's one of the smartest men I've ever known, too smart for his own good, and he is always thoroughly entertaining, especially the bits about the women he meets through the personals. Romantic tales replete with minutiae, intimate to the pores. Added to that was the practical aspect: with the Kennel Club show in town, every hotel in Manhattan and beyond was booked solid.

After a good deal of needling and wheedling, he finally consented and even seemed to warm to the idea. "I've got a new hand truck.

Bigger wheels." He was awfully excited about the hand truck. In truth, I was surprised he knew its name, or what one was and how it might be employed. Kaplan is what has become known as a metrosexual, finical about everything, expensive taste, cups of coffee that come with a provenance and a preface, personal trainers who work with him at increasingly ungodly hours, a bimonthly stylist. He has his initials sewn into the pockets of his shirts, keeps several pairs of Italian driving shoes, and he's a tan-orexic. To the opening night of the opera, he might wear silk Mondrian-print slacks and a jacket of woven mink and cashmere. At certain hours of the late afternoon, when the light hits his floors just so, he is known to run his industrial buffer, the one with three heads and a cord as long as a city block, to bring up the grain and gloss of the oak. Naturally, my sartorial indifference provides no end of comment and mock disbelief. He gloats over the contrast, particularly if he has one of his babes, as he prefers to call them, on arm, and if he can amuse them not with my rumpled appearance but with what it highlights: his own excruciating standards of perfection. I like egging him on; it's all part of our duologue. Metro meets retro. When I told him that Costco and Sam's Club serve as my haberdashers he rolled his eyes to the ceiling and emitted an operatic bellow of disparagement. It was therefore something approaching incredible that he owned a hand truck.

"Hand truck?" I said. "Jesus, what are you moving? A refrigerator?"

"Well, not exactly."

"Not exactly?"

"Look, Paul, just come. I'll see you in a week," he said, and there was a staccato chord of impatience blending with anxiety, as if he were saying, *let destiny take the stage, come, accuse!*

Despite my awareness and even the amusement I took as a bystander of his subclinical OCD tendencies, I was nevertheless vaguely dissatisfied with his explanation, *Mona's coming.* What sort of impact could the arrival of a cleaning lady have on anyone's life? As one of the "new historians," more and more of my job consists of finding the questions that were never asked of long-standing material. I am not interested in the available answers. They are all someone else's lies, stale and uninspiring.

It was mid-February, cold, clear, and bracing. I had already shipped most of my things to the apartment, and arrived at La Guardia with only a small carry-on. The cab driver spoke choppy English and dropped me off half a dozen blocks from the address I had given him, but after the long flight from San Francisco, the walk suited me fine. And it gave me time to prepare. Sidney Kaplan had become a kind of living satire of himself, the man having been blotted out by a towering persona. Visiting him was like attending a performance that demanded audience involvement. I would have to be amazed, amused, outraged, disgusted, delighted, and even jealous of the stories he would unravel at a pace so leisurely, so comprehensively, that whole nights might be swallowed up. I would have to supply booster shots of encouragement, ask questions that would leave no stone, no pebble, unturned, no detail not picked at and preened. All must be anatomized until what it was about, what was at issue, had scattered to the winds. Lacking a center or guiding purpose, even, minimally, something he absolutely had to do each day, his life over the years had frayed into trivialities. If Kaplan had ever been moved to curse the bread, he'd have found only crumbs. Crumbs, clippings, and punctilios. For a man that bright it struck me as mortally wasteful.

Kaplan owned a three-story brownstone in Brooklyn Heights, near the Promenade on Remsen Street. He didn't have the view across the East River, but he had lived there for decades and the house was exquisitely appointed and beautifully, obsessively maintained. The corner lot meant that his brick-terraced garden and cedar deck enjoyed plenty of sunlight, and beneath that were no less than three—three, in the Heights!—garage bays, two of which he rented at substantial rates to neighbors. The third one he kept for his Alfa. His was a life of cosmopolitan indolence and ease. Three times a week he played squash at the Heights Casino. Twice a week he attended a world-class live performance of one kind or another, theater, symphony, opera, ballet. On his kitchen counter, next to the phone, he kept half a dozen restaurant guides and his were always the latest reservations on the books. He went to bed at four in the morning, rose at noon, then spent the afternoon dealing with service people. People, in other words, he had to pay. Some time around the customary dinner hour, he worked out, either at the casino or at one of several private gyms. After which he showered lengthily and dressed impeccably for one of his dates. These dates graduated from the personals through a grueling sequence of phone and email interviews that of course included recent photographs. Very recent. He had a penchant for thin, boyish women, women who—I observed cautiously—resembled Judy. An ounce of fat or bona fide bustage and Kaplan fled, on one occasion, literally. Mostly the ads were elaborate self-portraits detailing his education—a law degree from Harvard, never put to use—his preferences, everything from arugula to Erroll Garner, his experience skiing the Alps, driving racecars in Italy, and tasting wines in Napa Valley. The fact of his wealth didn't need mentioning, though I happened to know that most of it was held in Berkshire Hathaway stock, and that he owned enough to warrant attendance at the annual shareholder meetings in Omaha, Nebraska. After all, he didn't have a job that required his presence.

To his ads there were always dozens of responses. If any proved acceptable after the calls and emails, a coffeehouse encounter ensued. If the coffeehouse encounter went off, then a dinner date was scheduled. And the dinner date threw open the curtains to what he was really after—any and all manner of sex.

Sidney Kaplan was a player. Back in the eighties it was called swinging, and ironically, that was how he lost Judy. The group sex parties were too unfocused, too chaotic, and about that time herpes was becoming a deterrent, because once you got it, you had it. At least it wasn't going to kill you, like AIDS, but no one then had had to take sexual pleasure and its risks that far, to the screen door of death. It certainly undercut the advice, *be here now* and *love the one you're with*. Eventually the Kaplans settled into a safer and more regular private threesome with a derivatives man from Goldman Sachs. William was the only name I heard—first names only, of course, in these matters—and after Judy ran off with him, Sidney referred to him as Billy Goat, or just *the fucking goat*. When the reality of what had happened, what he had created, finally flared like klieg lights in the deepening gloom, their delicious sport-and-pastime gone disastrously afield and he the loser, Kaplan devolved into bitter alienation. I had to stop calling him. It was like talking to a man on death row, minus the possibility of religious conversion. All of what had made him uniquely appealing, his sense of humor about himself, his curiosity, his brilliant aperçu—all were lost.

His final act of retribution against Judy was, of course, a virtuoso performance of the blackest nature: He arranged for an acquaintance of his from a local body shop where he had his Alfa detailed to break into Judy's little rented parking space in Carroll Gardens one night, silently roll her white Saab out of the garage, and in four hours flat, paint and return the vehicle to its berth before dawn. What he had them paint on the hood of Judy's Saab, in graceful, three-foot-long Puritan script, was a scarlet A. *Quel sentiment exquise.*

I could appreciate the timing, the elaborate calculations, the literary connotations, the loyalty he had to have paid handsomely for, because, after all, it was a crime, what he did; I could even admire what I imagined was the startling redness of that single letter against the cold vacuity of the hood the next morning when Judy discovered how badly, how meticulously, she had been violated. But actually I could not appreciate the sentiment. Dr. Frankenstein made the Wretch; Ourselves are Fate, as Melville asserts.

The thing of it is, he really loved her. Every woman after Judy—and there were some fine women, lovely, educated creatures seeking companionship, a protector, a bit of fun in lives that were bending in toward the bleakness of solitude—every one was just a babe to Kaplan. It stuck in your throat sometimes, the way he treated them, correcting their grammar or deriding the idealism that was like a toxin to his opinions, fingering in conspicuous silence the shabby, narrow-wale cord of a blazer, or eyeing the inappropriate open-toes of pumps she had dared wear to the symphony. For every date I might have, he threw twenty away. It was hardest on the older ones, the divorcées already sobered by life. The younger ones, some of whom asked too many questions about his money, could take him because they could also leave him. And they had no sense of time yet. Anyway, Sidney Kaplan's bizarre schedule often proved impossible to girls with real jobs. How could she stay up all night, frolicking, and make it to work by nine the next morning?

We saw each other sporadically, once a year, once every two years, whenever one of us swapped coasts. Harvard proved a lasting bond; we were permanent members of the same tribe. I hadn't been to the house on Remsen Street for several years, since we were just as likely to meet up in restaurants, but I knew that it would still be elegant, not ostentatiously, and that the Scotch would be single-malt and old, and that when Sidney Kaplan opened the door, he would be frantic about some matter, a plumber who hadn't showed, or a speeding ticket he was trying to worm his way out of, or a babe who was pressuring to move in. But what happened was this: he unlocked the interior door of the vestibule, then the outer; he said my last name in that clerkish, informing tone of his, as if I was expected to memorize it for a later test; I stepped through the vestibule and into the living room, and then I gasped, audibly.

"Yes, well ..." he said, letting one of his hands fall open toward the room, then close in retreat against his thigh.

"You need more than a hand truck, man."

I watched him wend his way through the piles, each one three or four feet high, quite neat edge to edge. In that one room alone there had to be forty, fifty piles—newspapers, books, magazines, mail, clippings, menus, playbills, receipts banded in boxes, along with (apparently) notes to himself—with a grid of trails crisscrossing among them.

"Seriously."

He turned around. He is a tall man with an arrogant bearing, and he has a way of moving, of conducting his body, that is at once graceful and vaguely stiff, as though he has had to practice and practice choreographed steps. At age thirty-seven, around the time Judy left, his hair simply went white, thoroughly white, obviating any thoughts of modification. The cotton-puff unreality of his white hair, the yoga sweats, and the faded Brooks Brothers shirt, all seemed to infect the mood with a languid, drugged quality as if I were visiting someone who had been living in an institution longer than planned. He said, "I've been meaning to get to them."

Now it was my turn to flatten my voice into what I hoped was a bottom-line, no arguments tone. "Bullshit. You have a very real problem here, Sid."

He shrugged. It struck me that he looked surprised and maybe a little bruised. "All right," he said slowly. "Possibly."

"The last time I was here, what, maybe two years ago, there were a few. Nothing like this."

It was about four in the afternoon, but the piles sent the room into a steeply plunging twilight. Left of the fireplace, occupying the best wall and presiding over Kaplan's interior kingdom, the life-size por-trait of Judy still demanded attention—a lot of it. It was a brightly daubed impression of a jazzed-up woman, mature but still confi-dently sexy, wearing a sequined cocktail dress and canting her head so far sideways that she was like a broken doll. The eyes were starry, unfocused, so that she did not seem to be listening intently to the viewer's thoughts about her, but rather, indulging in a wacky show of girlishness, caught in a private, but not-private, moment, vainly dancing. I was sorry to see it still hanging.

"I'm getting you a Scotch," Kaplan called from the kitchen.

I wandered about the room, picking up one item, then another. There did not seem to be any filing system; everything was stacked with everything else. Time seemed to constitute the only organizing conceit, old with old, the new with the recent. "Is this it? All of it?"

"See for yourself."

And so I climbed up to the next two floors and then down to the basement studio. The only room that had been spared was the mas-ter bedroom. Even the bathrooms held miniature columns of print matter, and every tread on the staircase supported two, one on each side, so that there was left only a narrow parting path. He had saved himself a space on the kitchen counter about the size of a placemat on which apparently he prepared what meals he took at home. Oth-erwise, the whole of his elegant brownstone had been given over to words waiting to be read.

We sat on the stools in the kitchen, he with a cold glass of Chablis and I with a solid Scotch, and he confessed that what used to take several hours—moving the piles out to the deck so that Mona could properly clean every two weeks—was now taking almost fourteen hours. Everything on the second and third floors had to be carried out, which explained why those piles tended to be much small-er, but the hand truck dispatched the living room and basement studio, which had its own small courtyard where the garbage cans were kept. He no longer knew how many subscriptions he received. He also insisted that he had every intention of reading every bit of it, the back issues of the *Times*, the ancient history contained in *Newsweek*, the articles recommended by friends; that he would of course chip his way down through the sedimentary layers of *The American Bar Association Journal* and the *Harvard Law Review*, and meant emphatically to expand his understanding of the human condition through the novels, the lit mags, the obscure volumes of poetry. And once he had, once he had read it all, he would . . .

"What? You'll do what?" I threw up my hands. It was all so obvious. He'd gotten himself stuck. After Judy left, his life ground to halt. The other women were simply diversionary tactics. And the piles, they stopped him in his tracks; they were a maze he would never escape. Until he read his way through all of those piles, he had no hope of a future. Sidney Kaplan, not I, was the real historian, the one who could not abandon the past, who must ask and ask and never know, not for sure. "What will you do?" I repeated, and I could hear the vicarious desperation in my voice.

He looked at me, his mind working. "I don't know, I don't know," he murmured, dropping his head finally and giving it a sad shake. "And Mona's coming."

"Never mind Mona. What about the women, what do they say? Your dates? What can they think about this?"

"Babes," he said, curling his lip in faintly amused derision. "The last one had about a teaspoon of brains." He got up and lit his cigarette, the one he permitted himself each day, and gazed out to the terrace. All but a few of the plants had been trimmed back to winter dormancy, and the tired leaves of the ivy clinging to the wall of the next house were dull and dirty. It was so still in the room among the piles that I could hear the faint clicking of an insect that had gotten trapped behind the calendar hanging on the kitchen wall. In the delicate fan of white lines around Kaplan's eyes there was a distant shattering; his mouth tightened perhaps with regret or guilt—it was hard to peg—but in any case, when he said, "Babes, just babes ..." all of the strength had gone out of his voice.

We went to dinner. By the end of the meal I had him convinced to try some psychotherapy.

And then there were the piles to deal with, because Mona *was* coming, coming like the scythe of Time.

***

It had taken longer than expected for me to settle into the routine of the Institute work, so it was almost three weeks before I called him. My fellow fellows were accomplished and interesting so far as their fields of endeavor took them, to the fence line, in effect, but they were no good to socialize with. I needed one of Kaplan's all-night stories, good food, and gory details. But I never managed to clear the gauntlet. He sounded seriously irritated. Finally I said, "What's eating you?"

"You took liberties with our friendship," he said. The words dropped like stones to clay, singly and heavily. "You had no right. I see you hardly at all. You had no right."

"I'm sorry."

"To say what you did, to treat me like a freak." There was a pause. "You gasped."

"It was inadvertent."

"This is my home."

"Look, Sidney, I was worried, that's all. Shouldn't have said anything. You'll just have to accept my apology. Let me buy you dinner."

"Busy."

"I'm sorry, man. Really."

"You think I don't know, don't have eyes? What kind of presumptuous new-age prick walks into a friend's home and blithely . . ."

"Nothing blithe about it, Kaplan. Anyway, forget I called."

And that was how it was left. Given his sensitivities and proclivities, I did not expect to hear from Sidney Kaplan, not for a long, long while, and I was certainly not going to telephone him. I had wanted to help, truly. After all, the obvious was obvious.

Then one day in July I ran into him in the subway. In spite of his means, he liked taking the subway now and then; it was what he called his "exposure to the real world." *Exposure*, as if he were risking contamination. He looked altogether different, hollow-eyed and nervous, his chin stubbled with several days of growth, the raincoat a mess, his khakis soft and almost boyish without the ironed crease breaking trail. He was wearing a pair of his Italian driving shoes, but they were badly scuffed, and there was an unguinous stain across the toe box of the left. No socks. I might not have recognized him, but he appeared at my elbow, he placed a fluttering hand on my arm, he said my name between shallow breaths, "Paul."

"Kaplan," I exclaimed, turning to face him. "What's happened?"

"Have you seen her?" Back and forth, his eyes scanned the platform; it was as if he were in a waking REM state. "Have you seen her?" he repeated.

"Who?" I thought he might mean Judy—it was that look, the old desolation. The white tile of the subway station, sallow and oily seeming, spread out behind him. There had been thundershowers on and off throughout the afternoon and the station air was a fug of diesel exhaust and crowded impatience. People stood about, minding their own business without visible effort. We were alone.

With a measured urgency in his voice he said, "The woman. The young woman. Red glasses, frames, like feathers. Bright red. Little scarf about her neck, knot at the side, like this," he gathered his fingertips at the base of his neck, "she's distinctive. You would know her."

"Sidney."

"Black hair." He nodded as if to confirm what he had said, held up his palm and quickly flashed his fingers, to make sure I had learned this essential detail. "Black."

"Listen, Kaplan, I've no idea who you're talking about."

A train came and together we stood watching as the doors slid open, travelers spilled out and new ones pushed in, and then it disappeared into the dirty tunnel. It might have been my train, but I had already decided to stay.

He looked at his watch and again searched the crowd around us, and then peered intently across the tracks to the opposing platform, so intently and with so much yearning that I found myself searching for her too, for the red glasses and the black hair, the distinctive young woman who had apparently eluded Sidney Kaplan.

"One of your babes?" I asked, trying to lighten the mood.

He gazed at me with a kind of horror and said nothing.

Five minutes later, another train arrived and departed. Then another. Each time we searched the new tributaries of humanity, flowing out, flowing in. Finally he murmured, "It's too late now," and shook his head, staring into the bottom of the dry murky canal where the rails lay.

"Let's have a drink, Sidney. I'd like very much to have a drink with you. A cold dry martini. Perfect in this kind of weather. We'll go to the Oak Room." And so up I led him to street-level and we took a cab to the Plaza where I secured a booth to give us some privacy. After ten minutes or so, the martinis before us, he sank into a sad sort of calm, as into a pond in a sudden forest clearing. Taking several deep draughts and fixing me with a glittering eye, he began then to tell me what had happened to him, his face and voice entranced. The images, the story they start and cannot end, have never left me—not for a day.

***

"It was May," he said. ". . . very late . . . I had decided to take the subway home. The only other person on my side of the platform was a young woman. On the opposite platform, a young man. He was also solitary, or maybe not. He was alone, in any case. Then as I waited a performance began. The young woman paced across the platform. She was not tall, but she walked in strides. A strong carriage, a dancer's carriage, her hands too, the way she moved them. At first it was not clear to me that she was performing for the young man across the tracks, but then with a small smile she stopped and faced him directly and extended an arm in his direction. Her hand made a pistol. She drew her other hand up along the barrel of the weapon that was her arm and took aim. The young man hardly changed expression. She fired silently.

"I thought that might be the end of it. But that is never the end of anything.

"She put her hands around her mouth and suddenly there was a sound so remarkable I wasn't sure it had come from her. Short, deep, not human, but emphatically human. Again, I thought it might be over, this strange underworld performance, completely intimate, and completely public, but she launched into a series of long, bellowing, wordless calls. They didn't sound as if a human voice had produced them. They didn't sound like an instrument either, not one of our Western ones, in any case. What they reminded me of were those long horns, the Tibetan ones. It was otherworldly, the sounds she made. A young woman, not a big woman but an ordinary young woman with a heart and a life like any other.

"On the facing platform the young man listened to these mating calls with what looked to me an almost perfect placidity. Then the train. I made sure I got in the same car as the young woman. While the train waited for the signal light, she mimed the final moments of her play. She lined her fingers along the rubber edge of the doors and made as if pulling frantically, as if trying to reach him before it was too late; he looked on with that same show of indifference. When at last the train rolled away, she went immediately to a seat and calmly sat down. At Borough Hall I exited. She was still sitting quietly, looking straight ahead, and you would never have guessed what she'd just been through. The anguish."

Kaplan drank down the rest of his martini and we ordered another round. I hardly knew what to say, and found it uncomfortable, making eye contact. I felt like the Wedding Guest in Coleridge's Rime, stayed but not yet stunned. Finally to say something I offered up the apparent conclusion: "And you've never seen her since."

"Seventeen days later. Same station."

"No!"

"And every day after that until . . ."

"Until what?"

"Until I never saw her again." These words he uttered as if I ought to have known, and with a faint, very faint, trace of the old existential irritation. It gave me hope.

"Did you talk to her?"

"I watched her for a week, waiting for her train. I never knew where she came from because I was always just waiting at the station. I did determine that she walked down from the north, because on one of those days I was bold enough to wait on the sidewalk, at the subway entrance. The late-night encounter would be impossible to predict. And it could never be repeated. She'd been with him. That night. And now she was not with him. Not after that performance. I kept hoping that she would complete the story, but of course it was impossible. In every way, impossible.

"Eventually, maybe immediately, who can say, she saw me, or perhaps she knew me from that night. I summoned the courage, I approached her. She said, 'Do I know you?'

"I said, 'No.'

"She studied me. She had immense eyes, like the world opening and closing around you, brown and shining, the whites flawlessly white. Amazing teeth, very white. I think she was Spanish. 'I bet I do,' she said.

"'No,' I replied, 'but I saw you. That night. I was there.'

"'What do you want?'

"'Just to know,' I stammered. After all that time, it wasn't easy, talking to her. 'Just to know what it was about. Why.'

"She looked away toward the waiting crowd.

"'You made as if, well, as if you were killing him.'

"'I had to kill him,' she said matter-of-factly.

"'But you didn't.'

"'It is the same thing.'

"'He's out there, somewhere. He's alive.'

"She inspected me through her red frames. 'He is dead. You are dead. I can tell you are dead too.'

"I drew back from her. Something seemed to tear open in my chest. I heard myself gasp. Gasp, like you, Paul."

***

I don't call Sidney Kaplan anymore. It is not often that a man sees all of who he is, or who he has been in one moment thrown open to the unmitigated light. At last Mona had come, come sweeping the lies away; his life had caught up with him.

No, I can't call him. I don't know who will answer the phone, the one before or the one after; the tall polished man with his babes and warren of words, or the Ancient Mariner collaring innocents. I don't know; I don't think I want to know. It is so much easier, not to care.

THE ANARCHIC HAND

*I*t was not beautiful, the first time. *Toothsome.*

He had left the car at the Civic Center garage and, returning for it, had gone into the restroom, into a stall for some reason. Half a minute later, the door to the next stall opened and closed, and he could see the shoes. Purple high-tops, the kind, though not the color, he had worn as a kid playing basketball. They were big and clean, the laces still white and the bow nearly perfect. A band of thick cotton emerged from the tops—gym socks—then some skin.

His own stall door had been etched with names, numbers, pictographs, random instructions and comments about life. Our species, he thought with disappointment. Scanning the inscriptions, he felt a sudden and desolate fear, as if he were falling slowly into a deep hole that had been there all along, in the backyard on Hadley Street. He was utterly alone in that hole; no one would ever find him. He read the writing on the door again, wondering how long it had taken the authors to carve their messages, how empty or listless their lives must have been, to permit time for writing in public lavatories. Next door the shoes shifted and a kind of wild panic overtook him. As if he did not want them to leave or he needed more time. But for what? His stomach lurched, releasing a sensation that fluttered up to his throat and caught. To hold off the panic or, optimistically, to sort it out, he focused on his own shoes, expensive loafer-like walking shoes made in Maine, three hundred a pair. Molly had insisted. Molly was always insisting. It was one of the early things about her that he had found so compelling, the way her cheerful insistence somehow became cosmic authorization. *Oh, let's take that trail, buy this house, have another slice of cake.* Give it a rest, he had said the other night.

His own shoes, too familiar to hold his interest, did not keep the panic at bay either, and now he could not locate a single thought in his mind. It was as if someone had pulled a plug and everything had abruptly drained from it in a perfect disappearing spiral. He saw the purple high-tops, the bows, how nice they seemed in their near perfection, how sweet in their failure. What was it about those bows? That morning, twice, a small routine gesture had been made toward protection, security, beauty—maybe only that. The effort away from our flawed status.

He cast a wild glance at the hieroglyphics of life, then thrust his hand under the partition. Instantly, another hand grasped his.

After the encounter he thought, *This cannot turn out well.*

That was how it had begun.

Molly wanted details, but with her he declined. With the therapist, because of the money, he tried to tell it all. For 250 an hour he had better maximize the investment. It was Molly who had insisted on a therapist, and after several more encounters, which he did not disclose to her, he had telephoned a shrink who had an office near the Presidio, so that after sessions he could drive immediately to the Philm Works only a mile away to meet his lover. That way he could economize the time investment too, telling Molly that he found he needed to take a long walk after therapy.

And so he entered into the lively commerce of lies, brokering one fib for another as the mood demanded. He felt exhilarated, guiltless, and, inexplicably, owed.

My lover, he said to himself. And at the barber shop one day, in one of those suddenly candid conversations that people fall into with certain categories of service people, he heard himself say, "I have taken a lover," as if to justify the haircut, but really, it was that he felt that it made him sound sophisticated and arrived. Especially the word, *taken*—I have taken a lover. He did not tell his barber that the lover was male. Robert was the sort of man who patronized old-fashioned barbers, who would not consider a "stylist," though a stylist would have been fine about his having taken a male lover.

Robert Treadwell hadn't had a clichéd childhood but he had made a clichéd life somehow. It was so clichéd—his life—that in the end it . . . wasn't. It just couldn't be, finally; a tipping point had been reached, and then Fate gave a bit of a shove.

His mother had died of an aneurysm when he was young, only nine, and his father, who was in the foreign service, sent him to the Christian Brothers school north of the city. Some of his classmates told him he'd been parked there, because he only went home at holidays, never on weekends, but Rob knew that not to be true. The senior Treadwell loved his young son and if he wasn't sure quite what to do with him, how to act whenever he was back in the States, he never arrived without exotic gifts and stories and frequent, brisk embraces, words of endearment spoken mostly in other languages, to make it easier for both of them. It had been a second marriage, but the older half siblings, a brother and a sister living with the first wife, did not complain of less despite having little to do with Robert. The sister was especially attentive when, years later, her own son applied to Brighton, and as Assistant Head, Robert was pleased to ensure his nephew's acceptance, pleased without needing any false familial gratitude. The nephew was certainly of Brighton caliber.

At the Christian Brothers' Robert had been perfectly satisfactory, a B student who excelled at math, and a solid basketball player. He was tall but not so tall that opposing team members worried much until Treadwell laid up half a dozen or so shots, then they did what they could to keep him out of the box. After that he went to

San Francisco State for a Masters in Education. The default field. The one that you uttered behind a cough. Everything had interested him equally, and *not* interested him equally, and in the end, his advisor recommended Education just to break the eddy fence and get him into the current, going somewhere. He'd always loved the atmosphere of schools; they had been, after all, his home. From teaching statistics at Brighton, then later, Religious Studies because he knew the subject and the administration didn't want to hire someone else who might have had a "real agenda"—Brighton was a nondenominational prep school—he'd been promoted to Assistant Head.

At the time of the promotion Robert had thought about his not having any *real agenda* with self-satisfaction, a character trait he hadn't been able to properly appreciate because it hadn't ever been articulated. Other words welled up from that same spring: even-handed, dispassionate, four-squared—all scrubbed American words anyone would be happy enough to have. The position had not been any sort of back door inheritance; the former Assistant Head had been demoted, in point of fact, to make way for the more broadly qualified and more genial Robert Treadwell. Students didn't mind looking up to him because he made it seem somehow optional. Friends referred to him as a "lovely man," and Molly always smiled like someone confident in her own consistently solid choices.

The Treadwells' two sons were in college, one at UC Santa Barbara and the other, the older academic one, had gotten into Dartmouth. They had gone off just about the time the Oedipal turf battles had become vaguely earnest and irritating. Freed of daily parenting, Molly opened a little antique shop on Sacramento Street, volunteered at the shelter, and had a group she walked with four mornings a week, the walking women, they were called. Her prettiness had not yet abandoned her. Even as a young woman with her heavy honey-blond hair dropping straight to the small of her back and hardly concealing the contraption she had had to wear for the better part of her youth to correct severe scoliosis, she had been pretty. A funny girl, too, with dark glistening eyebrows working into mischievous darts and curves and a big smile broadcasting well-being. In a room with such a smile, everything was always all right. Robert had counted on that. She had come from a good family down Peninsula, father a judge, mother whose maiden name came preceded by the article A. Molly and the Fitzharris family had a grand way of straightening out all the wobbles.

Robert and Molly had met in, of all places, a bar in the Haight. The Haight wasn't the Haight, not in the eighties; it was a memorial version of itself, a staged show, and even the hippies on the street, some of them getting, as she put it, a little long in the tooth, seemed to be trying out for roles as extras. Molly's slumming adventure proved entirely safe. Her two friends had left with a couple of guys who advertised Humbolt weed, and Molly, never into pot, was just trying to pay for her Campari and soda and leave before she might have to seriously deal with anyone.

"One dance," Robert said. He'd been standing by the door, actually, *in* the doorway, checking out the scene, trying to decide whether or not to stay.

She looked him up and down, tipped her head in a slow exaggeration of head-tipping, slit her eyes. "Why?"

It was a gay bar and the women were there because the dancing was famously hot. A lot of women went to the Bar-None for the dancing. He had always figured that she assumed he was there for that action, and not the other. That was what he thought, after all. That he was there to dance.

"You have a nice smile," he had said in answer. It ushered him safely into the Bar-None, that insistent, everything's-gotta-be-fine smile of hers.

How was it he had known about the restroom at the Civic Center?

Buckley. Several weeks earlier, after the symphony; the four of them had gone for light fare and drinks, and Buckley had quickly gotten a snoutful and was entertaining them with raunchy tidbits, and he had told them not to use the restrooms at the Civic Center garage where they had left their cars. "That's where they meet, any and all times of day. Hooking up. Been like that for so many years the cops have written it off."

Molly had said only, "There's not much room in a stall," and Robert could see that she was trying to puzzle out how it was done, what kind of sex two men could have in a stall. Molly always had to settle the mechanics of a thing, the underlying nuts and bolts, before she could go on to understand vital points or central themes. If he were reporting an incident at Brighton, she wanted first to know the name of the student, class standing, parents' occupations, even when Robert was trying to get at something entirely unrelated to the specific child or to the incident in question. For instance, she wanted to know what day it had been. That day.

"Wednesday," he had said. It did make it easier, beginning with the innocent details, the ones that could be thrown overboard without regrets. And it got things going, the tale he felt bidden to tell.

Trying, it seemed, to make some sort of profound connection, she said, "Then I was at the shelter."

Wednesday Robert had left Brighton and driven downtown to meet with their attorney. Robert's father had recently died and they were told that it would be prudent to make adjustments to their living trust. He parked his car in the Civic Center garage and walked three blocks over to Hays to sign the new documents. On the Civic Center plaza, squares of pavement flanked by manicured grass and rows of sycamore trees, there were a couple of street entertainers each competing for the attention of a raggedly assembled crowd. Robert paused on his way back to the garage, but by that time the street performers—a contortionist escaping from a web of chains draped and padlocked about his torso, and the other a magician—had fallen into an argument about whose crowd it was. Between appeals to the audience, cloying, amusing, they shot sidewise insults at each other, and some of them were starting to get ugly. People with children began moving away.

It was a gray day, damp without rain, not a remnant of morning fog but the real thing, and the light was so flat that everything stood deprived of shadow. The trees at the Civic Center had had their winter trimming that amounted to drastic amputations of everything but the essential limbs of life, and each of the remaining short, thick, barren branches ended in a clenched fist. Robert looked away, up at the trees, whenever one of the performers abandoned his illusion for an under-the-breath cut at the other. The change in tone from jovial showmanship to guttural invective was so abrupt that it was embarrassing. Tourism was down because it was winter; they were grown men in need of money. When the contortionist shed the last of his chains and began working the crowd with his hat—a beret—collecting donations, the magician leapt in and with a great flourish, extended his own hat—a seemingly bottomless stovepipe. The stocky and muscular contortionist barreled across the plaza, took a swipe, both hats flew, and the crowd scattered like starlings from a shaken tree.

In a world of dazzling deceptions, reality could break in at any moment. Robert wanted to stay, to help somehow. He was the kind of guy who would stop and help people. He had liked the contortionist better, because he had seemed friendlier, but that did not make him more worthy in the end. And the magician had not been the first to verbally complain, though that was likely because he had shifted his act over from his end of the plaza when he'd seen the larger crowd gathering around the contortionist. A man, half-naked and struggling in chains, was probably more immediately gripping than sleight of hand. But they were both just trying to get through the day. Escapism or trickery: what did it matter, how they managed their worlds?

Robert turned and made his way toward the glass vestibule of the Civic Center parking garage. He could hear behind him the scuffle, one of the men grunting in pain, and it was making him feel very bad. It was like the fights at the Christian Brothers', his classmates tumbling about in the dirt. Half the time it was about nothing, the rest of the time, some scrap of forged honor no one could remember the next day. Only humiliation proved finally indelible, though like everything else, after time, it shifted shapes. Some older boys had humiliated him once—*grab your ankles, grab your ankles*, they had shouted, mimicking Brother Ignacious—but it was not the paddle with its well-known penalty of five swats that had humiliated him, but the boy himself, and the others who held Robert in a headlock, and the long awkward walk back to the dorm, awkward not only for the pain but for the secret excitement he had felt. A prank: that was how he remembered it now, its final morphology. One day he might have called the boy a friend because they had known each other so long ago. Because school was home and these boys were his family and you could not betray your family without risking all. And anyway, time could conjure kindness, even love, from the day's refuse. So perhaps it *was* the magician who had found the best means.

The fight was progressing and Robert quickened his steps. Across the plaza on Larkin Street a bus accelerated and a cloud of exhaust hung like a blue ghost in the place where it had been stopped. The trees with their fists clenched at the sky, and the indifference of the tall buildings standing in silence around the plaza, and everything without shadow, without effect, everything seeming just what it was and no more, nothing to hope for, and neither with nor without apology, but just what was . . . it was unbearable. How pointless everything seemed. How literal. If this was all there was, how could anyone go on?

His father was dead. His father had had a life of certain weight and worth, just as Robert now had. Robert's sons were gone to college to make lives of weight and worth. Robert's wife knew how to be. Molly. Molly knew how to make things that meant something to her, to save, to volunteer, to ask small questions that combined to make bigger understandings. She could find the questions and that was probably better than any answer. Answers could not be trusted anyway. She smiled no matter what, and it was that—the smiling, the laughing—that had left the only memorable lines in her face. But then, Molly had always known exactly who she was.

Watching the ground, he gave his head a single shake. Grown men, he thought, fighting over a hatful of coins. But it wasn't that. It was the show that had gotten to him, the waking dream waked; curtain torn, wires and workings exposed, the grubby hands of the puppeteer large and menacing. Grown men acting like scrabbling children. We are, he thought, just that.

In the glass vestibule where the elevators were, the flat light of the day had nevertheless managed to rouse a kind of false and sticky warmth. The glass was smeared and dirty and despite the lack of clarity, he felt too visible and a little nervous, perhaps because of the scuffle, or so he reasoned at the time. Other people entered and stood nearby, a couple with a teenaged girl, waiting for the elevator, but they seemed to regard him oddly, as though he might do something weird or gauche, the father especially. Discreetly, Robert checked the zipper of his fly, then in a show of casualness, removed his blazer and hung it over one shoulder. The elevator. The girl screwed in earbuds and thumbed her iPod as the room jolted down. On the second level,

Robert exited. Passing the restroom, he stopped and gazed like a blind man into the air in front of his face. Then he went back.

If anyone had seen him at that juncture, a passerby with the ability to see not with eyes but with heart, he—or she—would have witnessed a slow and heavy sadness finally rising like oil to the surface, to the light.

He told Molly about the magician and the contortionist, but not about the shadowless day. He told her about the hot exposure of the vestibule, the family in the elevator; he told her that he had not been thinking anything. He did mention the purple high-tops, but not the laces. And she stared at him as if it was all completely mad.

The young man's name was Charlie. Charlie Rawlings. Actually, he was not as young as he seemed—he was thirty-three—but whether because of his occupation drawing for the animation studios at the reconstituted Presidio Philm Works, or because of the intransigence of his wardrobe, he looked about twenty-five. Above the purple high-tops were knee-length, brownish plaid shorts, a Gogol Bordello T-shirt, and in San Francisco in January, a lightweight down jacket with a small X of duct tape on the left shoulder. (He'd been packing for a backcountry ski trek and had accidentally slammed the trunk on the jacket.) The duct tape charmed Robert, it was so ad hoc, so boyish. "Duct tape," Robert said, touching it.

"God on a roll," Charlie had smiled.

Robert was in love with Charlie Rawlings. Never before in all his life had he felt anything so true. Nothing could touch it. By its very existence it justified itself wholly. It was so unexpected and so explosively *everything* to him that he was convinced he had been waiting his life for it. Or that all he had never done, never thought consciously about doing, was suddenly at hand. A dream he had not let himself dream. How could he not share it with Molly?

"So that night, in the Haight . . ."

"No," he said. Then, more thoughtfully, and to show how honest with her he meant to be—they were, first and foremost, friends—he added, "You know, I don't know."

"So is that why you were there?"

"I said, I don't know. I didn't think about much in those days."

"Why not?"

He shrugged. "There were always other people, the Brothers, my friends, doing the thinking for me. That's the way institutions are."

She went into their kitchen and poured herself a glass of Chardonnay, impolitely filling it past the widest part of the glass—something he remembered later, this newfound capacity to act outside the law. It was eleven in the morning, not the morning after though. A month later, when he could bear the secret no longer. He didn't mind the lies; it was the size of the knowledge he carried that had been ripping the seams.

"What does he look like?" It was not much of a Molly sort of question. A truly quintessential one would have concerned what he was wearing, or which stall they had used.

"He's tall. Taller than me." He was trying not to smile, but it was hard. Charlie was beautiful, carrying his height with a kind of apology that won you over instantly, slumping in order to drop in close to Robert, face-to-face. "Brown hair." Robert shrugged, leaving out the blue eyes that searched a little too deeply and cared a little too much. And he did not mention the seductive lips, as if bruised, that Robert would have flatly stared at had it not been so obvious. He did not tell Molly that Charlie had an intelligent way about him, a considering manner, and that when Robert looked at his face, he could see that

Charlie was afraid of close contact, but brave and kind and willing to trust. When he thought these things in these words, Robert felt foolish; they were, after all, simple, iconic words that ought to have long ago lost their meaning, never mind their impact. Robert was fifty-eight. And for the first time, he realized now, gazing at Molly's conventionally pretty face, he was in love. In love!

"Are you sick?"

"What do you mean, sick? In the head?"

"Cancer. Terminal illness."

For a long moment he shut his eyes and felt the lids pressing him back into his own corner. She was serious. "No," he said. Robert was a lot taller than Molly, and as he passed her on his way into the kitchen for a glass of wine, he made a point of passing closely, to intimidate, even while he knew he had no right to be angry.

"Sometimes people try things, when they know. Things they may have been curious about."

"I'm not sick," he repeated.

"All along," she added, as if not hearing him.

"Sorry to disappoint. Healthy as a horse." He drank half the wine he had poured in one long gulp, then topped it off again.

"Would that make it easier?" it occurred to him to ask. "If I were dying?"

"Until you did," she said coolly.

He had laughed, sort of, at that—ever-forthright Molly.

She asked him how many times they had been together, and he asked her what difference it made, and she asked him why he wouldn't tell her that when he had told her the rest, and then they were silent, nobody budging.

Molly stood up and walked to the bow window that hung out over Hadley Street. The light outside was clean and washed from a rainstorm, and she was an uncertain shadow against the Vermeer light of the pastel houses climbing the hill across the street. "I read somewhere that after four times some kind of hormonal bond sets up, and it's harder to break," she murmured absently.

"I didn't count."

She said, "Oh god," and put a palm on the window glass, three fingernails finding the crease of the mullion and digging in, making a claw of her hand.

He *had* counted, but it was still obscene, her reductionism. This was not just a well of hormones on a time-release schedule. Her matter-of-factness was wounding, diminishing. On the other hand, what had he expected, a celebration of his happiness? And anyway, what did it matter? If anything, he had been more attentive to her. Something uniquely true had come into his life, and he had a real sense, perhaps for the first time, of the depth, the richness, the color of human existence. The splendor.

These words, he thought again, giving his head a shake and marveling at the sea of abstractions into which he had plunged and in which he now paddled about willingly and foolishly, like a big yellow dog snapping at wave froth. He could not help wondering if deeply felt emotions always surfaced in clichés.

She came over to him, dropped her delicate chin, and studied him from under her remarkably frank brows, black inverted checkmarks. "Robert, I know that you're caught up in this thing right now. Let's put our heads together and figure this out."

"Figure what out?"

"Let's get a hold of a therapist, a good one. You are using a condom, I trust. Tell me that much." She turned away as she gave this last verbal command in that perfectly reasonable voice of hers, the one she used whenever she felt unsure of her position.

"None of your business."

"Well, yes, in fact it is. It is very much my business, because it's my life."

"Molly."

"I'll get some names. You can pick one. Let's work together. We've always been a team and we're not going to stop now." She smiled but it was a smile that seemed to prematurely fossilize. "In the meantime, I want to meet him."

He felt a hot rush of horror that in an instant iced over. "Not in a thousand years."

"Well, we can sleep on that."

And that would be the next question: how and where to sleep? Now.

He was wishing, wishing profoundly, that he hadn't told her anything. She gulped down the last of her wine, straightened her spine in that habitual way she had been taught as a damaged but nevertheless obedient girl, and as she returned to the kitchen, she let her hand rest on his shoulder a moment. Her hands were small but weighty, like those beanbag creatures the boys had collected, and he could feel the palm of her hand with the attached fingers conform neatly to the curve of his shoulder.

"Condom?" she asked again.

"What do you think?"

"Do you want to lose me?" she asked point-blank. It was a real question, nothing rhetorical about it. That was Molly, as artless and straight-ahead as a freight train. At moments like these he was reminded of the expense of her upbringing, of the strong, well-bred women arrayed like colonnettes around her.

"No."

"Are you sure?"

"Sure."

"Sure," she repeated, cutting her eyes, drumming her hip with one hand. "That's convincing."

If he had lost her at that moment, he could have managed it. Because suddenly he felt that all those years ago she had tricked him, Molly Fitzharris and everything she represented, everything that he had been poised, at least unconsciously, to tumble away from that night at the Bar-None. Molly had always liked a challenge. Now he suspected her of intuiting the direction of things for him that night as he leaned uncertainly in the doorway of the Bar-None, and of derailing his train just to see if she could. Molly took certain pride in being a can-do American girl with loads of potential. When he met her she had had that American-made boxcar of potential but nowhere to drive it except into the business of others. At the time, that business had been Robert Treadwell.

Even if there had been nothing deliberate about that evening, what happened did happen: he had been set on a course away from himself, from the man he ought to have been and the life he might have been living. How could a man make good choices when he was not the man he was meant to be?

They made it through the rest of the school term and the rest of spring and into the late-lifting fog of summer. The world felt muffled over and unseen, those long days of summer after the night fog had moved in and stayed like a mood or a drug you had no interest in or energy for shaking off. You were just willingly *in it*. Being here now. Molly gained weight, mostly in her bottom, and the weight immediately unbalanced her and taxed her distorted spine and she went around with her right hand pressed to her lower back. She had her long heavy hair shingled short and then several weeks later, when that hadn't been enough somehow, she had it permed, but it made her look arrested rather than younger. Or like someone who had come back courageously from a long illness. What he assumed she was after, at age fifty-two, her husband in love with a young man and her sons cut loose into lives of their own, was youthful vulnerability, the kind that inspires a rush of masculine protection. It was a while before he realized that she was hoping to simulate a boy. A hairline crack opened in his heart.

Robert slept downstairs in one of his sons' now-empty rooms. The general plan seemed to be that they would wait it out as Robert went through this *phase*, and then they would pick up where they left off, and maybe even laugh about it privately from the frayed edge of a cocktail party when something reminded them, the handsomely shined-up Treadwells, of that crazy time in their lives. As young parents of two boys, Robert and Molly had regularly consulted the child-rearing books, each time reassured by the universality of the problem they were facing, problems that had ranged from imaginary friends to defiance to porn magazines that lived between the mattress and box springs, problems that now seemed to oddly echo his own. Molly had painstakingly consigned Robert's activities to that hopeful, temporary category of "a phase," and Robert did not try to disabuse her. Now and then he wondered himself at the reality of what he was involved in, because never in his life had he abandoned himself so completely. Never in his life had he had an *agenda*, though to be sure, it was a rudimentary agenda: be with Charlie. Things with Charlie were still moving fast, galloping and gulping, and Robert had no interest in controlling himself or what was happening beyond fixing the next date, the next call, the next kiss.

They were trying things, amazing things, with their bodies—*my god, the trust, the power* . . . it wasn't about anything as banal as *sex*. He was beginning, just beginning, to know where openness led, and what it felt like to be at peace with the human possibility.

Then it was early July. Robert had spent the better part of an afternoon at Charlie's apartment, having luxurious sex. When it was over they fell asleep—or Charlie did. After an hour, lying there thinking, listening to the foghorn om-ing across the bay and then a si-ren rounding a distant corner, his lover's breathing, Robert crept out from under the white sheet and came around to Charlie's side of the bed. Naked and kneeling there, he gazed at his lover, the long length of body mounding under the sheet, and thought of Jesus and shrouds and gods and then of gardens with rows and rills. How present he was, how improbable. There the sexy rush of beard, inadequate to the task but game; the soft lips swollen from their afternoon efforts; the subtle hues of erotica in delayed retreat from beneath his otherwise anemically pale skin. Beloved skin. Robert wanted to protect him from everything, forever. To put a fence around the world and present him with it. This lover, this love. This perfect gesture of life. This gift, this good news, this mortal god. This god of heavenly mortality.

If he was stricken with adoration—and there could be no question—it was a malady he welcomed.

Before Charlie it had seemed to Robert that you simply couldn't get lost anymore. Where was the excitement, the joy in that? In knowing where you were at all times and where you would be tomorrow and the next day?

He was lost in Charlie.

Charlie opened his eyes and reached over, lightly trailing his fingernails across Robert's back. Looking at the hand and not at Robert, he pronounced the name he had adopted for him: "Ro."

They hardly needed speech; they could look at each other and just know.

"What's wrong?" Charlie asked.

Those lips.

Robert closed his eyes. "I can't talk. I don't want to talk."

"Ro."

"I can't."

"I love you," Charlie said softly. "You can say it. Whatever it is."

"She's threatening to kill you."

A spectral bit of charcoal sketched a frown between the young man's quiet blue eyes and just as quickly was smudged out. "Do you believe her?"

"It's hard to say if she has it in her. That sort of thing."

"Not much of a sort of a thing, is it? Murder? It's a definite thing thing." The boy—he became a boy suddenly—smiled winsomely, fatally, and glanced over at the mirror that miraculously threw the two of them back into the room together.

Robert dropped his face into the mattress beside Charlie's arm. "Oh god," he sighed, and then out it spilled. "She doesn't drink much, you know, only when she's really at a loss. She's been drinking a lot lately. I came home and found her on the kitchen floor, passed out in her own vomit. There were broken dishes everywhere, two bottles of wine, empty. She hadn't eaten, she'd just thrown the dishes, one by one. I managed to get her up and into the bathroom, and clean her face, her hair . . ." (he thought then of her sad hair and of the effort she had made, consciously or unconsciously, to be what he wanted) ". . . then I got her into bed. All night long, gibberish, angry invective and gibberish. How she's going to ruin me, my reputation, and dishonor the school, and publicly accuse me of things with students, and then the same with the Philm Works. After that, after she's laid us all to waste, she's going to shoot you, then me, and then herself. I can see the headlines."

Charlie leaned up on one arm and combed his fingers through his hair. "Hmmmm . . ."

"Right."

"Bravado?"

"I just don't know. I've never seen her like this. Molly is, Molly's like a little tug boat. Always able to handle anything, always strong and level-headed. A lot of bottom, as they say." He hadn't meant it that way, that she had gained weight in her bum, he'd meant only that she was steady and good for the long run. But he added, "that

Anglo-Saxon heritage," to cover the insult to his wife that only he could have known about. "Her mother was a Copperthwaite. I've told you that. Her family's as beamy as they come, nothing sinks them. Same holds for the Fitzharrises." There was something that Robert could hear in his own words, something that made him feel ashamed. "She wants me to herself, just for a week she says. So that how I feel about you, my obsession as she puts it, doesn't corrupt, as she puts it, her time with me."

Charlie said thoughtfully, "I can understand that."

"A camping trip. That's what she's proposing."

"Where?"

Robert shrugged slightly; he could feel his forehead tensing. *What difference could that make?* "A week," he said. "I owe her that much."

Tipping his head, Charlie said gently, "It's that I don't want it to be some place I was hoping to go with you, Ro. Someday."

Robert leaned forward and kissed the cool pale drum of his lover's abdomen. They had begun to make plans, to talk about a future, *the* future, about being old together, a cabin in Tahoe, hiking Desolation Wilderness in the spring before the rookies arrived. Robert was still in great shape; he often took a group of Brighton boys up to Desolation. They had talked about cooking dinner together, how extravagant and joyous that alone would be for them. How simple and joyous life could be. In San Francisco, in restaurants and museums, people smiled at them. They made an appealing couple, the tall boyish Charlie with his serious expression and Robert, almost as tall, so genial, so easy-going, so protective of his blue-eyed catch. How could he give up something that even strangers could see was right? They joked about a story Robert knew, "The Earthquake in Chile," in which two lovers, separated by the ways and walls of a society, are fatefully united after an earthquake destroys their city. The lovers discover each other in a refugee camp and now anonymous, are free to have a life together. The earthquake in Chile became code both for a future they dreamed of having, and for the increasing powerlessness Robert felt. It would take an earthquake.

After a while, he said, "How about Yellowstone? I've been there with her and the boys, it wouldn't be new, it would be . . . memorial. You and I will go new places together. I want only new places with you."

"You do what you need to do, Ro. But if it makes any difference, I've never been a geyser kind of guy."

They smiled.

The trip was planned for Columbus Day weekend in October. Robert would take a few extra days and they would make a week of it when the park was not so crowded. The fall semester at Brighton could commence smoothly and the year's momentum firmly established. Charlie had a big contract due in the fall, so he would be busy anyway. But the promised camping trip didn't stop Molly's threats and her tolerance for the ongoing relationship was falling precipitously. Charlie did say gently, carefully, that he hoped Robert would not let her control him with that kind of threat, that it was no way to live, and that he, Charlie, was prepared to deal with whatever came along. One night she called the Head of School, then hung up when Robert passed her room. She had already called Charlie the night before, and had rung off before any real words were exchanged. Each time she told him what she had almost done. Each time she was drunk, this woman who seldom drank. But on that last night he happened to see her computer screen, a page displaying handguns; she had bookmarked it. At the center of the page was a woman's hand holding a small Deringer. The image sent him back on a swift and strangely truthful journey, back to his own hand reaching beneath the stall door . . . two hands acting in opposition to the accepted state of affairs, and contrary to known personae; two separate anarchic hands behaving against the wills of their masters. Robert had completed his anarchic deed. Molly was still thinking about hers.

He knew then just how angry she was, how pushed to the brink of who she had been, or thought she was. Beneath the enameled life that had been Molly's—Copperthwaite, Fitzharris, Treadwell—was something that had not been civilized, that was still savage. It shocked him. He began to reconsider her motives that night years ago at the Bar-None. And he was afraid for Charlie, for his Beloved.

He and Charlie communicated largely via email, fully half a dozen each day, with another two or three phone calls or messages left on cells. *I'm just thinking about you*, or *what are you doing right now*, or *I just discovered the most amazing Burgundy, a gamey Corton Bressands*, or *Charlie, you're probably sketching in the evil on this week's villain*—a lot of messages hamming up suppositions and wild guesses—*you must be bungee jumping with your stylist*, etc. So that night when Robert ceased completely to email, to call, to lovingly speculate, when silence descended like a Biblical plague, Charlie would know—Charlie *did* know—not to email, not to call, not to try. Three days later he sent Robert a long missive, wrenching in its exposure and grace, and set him free. That was it.

The camping trip now seemed moot. She had gotten what she wanted: uncorrupted time with the now corrupted Robert Treadwell, her husband. Still, Molly was dogged in her plan to cast the episode as a phase, and even managed to find a self-help book identifying various examples of "acting out" that accompanied the empty-nest stage of marital evolution, including homosexual experimentation. She insisted on the Yellowstone trip, jollying him along as they cleaned up the camp gear and purchased newer items to replace the ones that storage had compromised. A new, three-man tent with a star-gazing ceiling of dark netting supplanted the large family octagon that still bore not-so-faintly the smell of white gas one of

the boys had spilled and delaminating nylon and insect repellent—
and not faintly but vividly, memories that had been for Robert nice
memories, or certainly good-enough memories. He had known exactly where he was and what he was to be for each of them, and he
had done it all well. But he had not been lost, not felt heart-bursting
exhilaration; he had not blindly *adored* another.

Robert drove and Molly sat beside him, vibrating with happiness,
chirping her approval of the scenery, lining paper plates with crackers and sliced hard-boiled eggs daubed with mustard, a favorite of
Robert's. Tentatively she began to flirt around the perimeter of a ren-
dezvous that they might have soon, back in their own bedroom, or
if he thought he might be ready now, in their new, star-gazing tent.
This had come up several times already, and whenever it did, he could
literally smell her anxiety about it, a nervous small-animal smell, and
it both pained and disgusted him. As sweet as she was, as eager as he
was to do right by Molly Fitzharris whom he knew he had wronged,
whom he knew he had pushed to her Anglo-Saxon limits, he could
not imagine touching her body ever again. And he was already devis-
ing not a means of avoiding it—it could not be avoided—but a way
to touch her from the other side of a wall he had been in the process
of constructing, brick by brick, day by day, inside himself ever since
he had turned away from Charlie. That wall was about complete.

One thing he knew definitively: he could not and would not imagine Charlie while he was with Molly. It would have been the cruel-
est violation of what to him was now sacred and sanctified by the
inaccessibility he himself had chosen.

Just before sunset on the second day somewhere between Salt
Lake and Jackson Hole they stopped to camp. It was nothing like
the Park Service campgrounds or even the BLM waysides that had
at least cement tables; this was a private operation. For fifteen dollars a night it provided a marginally level parking pad, a fire ring,

and a small square barbecue mounted on a pipe and containing an iron grill sway-backed from high heat and overuse. No toilets. No small, tastefully brown or green signs, advising this, warning that. The camp host was not at home in his single-wide, and judging by the leaf and trash-blown premises, had not been around for some time. It was, after all, off-season. But Robert dutifully stuffed the envelope with a ten and a five, dropped it in the indicated slot, and he and Molly made camp. The featured attraction of the campground appeared to be a ledge—Nichol's Ledge—from which a stone cliff face sheered straight down about a thousand feet into a small muddy reservoir. The view east over the reservoir toward the Salt River Range was pretty nice, he had to admit.

"Pretty nice?" Molly said, jumping up from her folding chair and dancing over to the edge, her arms thrown out. "It's God's own backyard," she exclaimed. "And we've got this place all to ourselves. It's like the dawn of time and we're the only two people alive on the planet."

Robert leaned over to assess how much she'd had to drink. The metal go-cup sat beside her chair, the gin and tonic still mostly there. Then he tossed a piece of juniper on the kindling fire he had started in the ring, and sat watching the flickering shadows deepen with the dusk as the circle of light spread outward.

Molly turned and faced him, the ledge behind her. The stone was not a single block but a series of flat broad segments stepping a little up here, a little down there—toe stubbers. It would be easy to fall. Now he turned his attention to the coals, poking at them with a metal spatula. They had purchased a couple of thick pork chops, something he rarely ate except on camping trips; meat was straightforward, easy to deal with outside. It was what you did when you camped, you cooked meat over a fire. Robert was determined to do what you did.

"I'm so glad we're doing this," she was saying. "I'm so happy we made it through . . . you know, everything."

He glanced over at her. Her cheeks were rosy from the brisk October air and he'd finally gotten used to the new haircut. She was pacing at a walking rate along the rim of Nichol's Ledge, maybe a foot or so from the drop, when abruptly she did a kind of skipping step-ball-change. As a girl Molly had tap-danced in part to learn a dancer's balance (her mother's insistence), and in part to get the exercise her back brace kept her from, the competitive sports that had been prohibited. "I'm so very happy, Robert," she said again and though he couldn't see the tears—she was about forty feet away—he could hear them pinching her voice down.

Molly *was* happy. How could you begrudge anyone that? She was happy with him. He had restored her. The murderess was gone, the dancer was back.

Watching her near the edge, skipping along like a girl, was doing something funny to his head, what he couldn't say; it just felt as if it was getting tighter and tighter in there, as if there was a great to-do going on inside, a ruckus that needed clearing out. His teeth began to itch. He stared at the two chops side by side on the plate, ready to cook. "Hey," he hollered over to her, "not so close to the edge there." To him it sounded like an order he might have given one of the Brighton boys he cared least about, a rote but still genuine caution, one that you were required to make and of course, *would* make.

"What? You don't trust me?"

"Seriously," he said, "the stone's uneven. Get away from the edge, Molly." It was pissing him off, her showing off like that.

"Okay," she said. Just like that, not insisting.

Carefully he lay the two chops on the grill, not daring to look at her as she came back. As a youth on idle weekends when he and his buddies could not choose what to do among several equivalent options, they would flip a coin, not to determine what they would do, but how they really felt about each option. This meant that they would flip until they got the option that did not feel somehow like a disappointment.

Two days later Molly did insist, as she was wont to do, cheerfully, optimistically, and in perfect character. Instead of cooking another fireside meal at their Yellowstone campsite, they had dinner at one of the park hotel dining rooms. A treat after four days of "roughing it." Their waitress had told them that after work it was employee custom to soak in some of the hot springs along the Firehole River, the ones that were *not* superheated to 204 degrees Fahrenheit, she had laughed, because those would boil you like lobster. Even the river itself was still holding at seventy degrees because of the thermal waters entering it here and there as it made its way across the geyser basins. The Treadwells thought it would be fun, it would be the way it was when they were younger, trying things out together, nothing too risky. Adventuresome but within limits. Each other's check and balance.

They parked off the road and made their way down toward the river. There was still some orange left in the west that gave way to bruised smears of blue and purple, and then that withdrew even more swiftly than the hotter colors. It was light enough to see the clouds of steam huffing off the thermal pools and the river itself. By the time they tracked through juniper and a few stunted Douglas firs, and then nearing the river, cottonwood, low-growing willow, patches of bentgrass, and finally groves of dead lodgepole pine with their bobby socks of mineralization, the sky had devolved to a sooty gravitas, as if it had been conscripted to single-handedly prophesy the oncoming winter. Neither had thought to bring a flashlight, which of course was one of the first things that came out later. It was cold—thirty-five degrees. They could hear the voices of others not that far away, but it was a moonless night and their nudity would not be very public, if at all. He felt comfortable with her, companionable. They did not have to work at this part of their being together. This team that they had been for so long. Before the light had completely abandoned them, they had settled on a pool about the size of a station wagon whose temperature approximated their own hot tub in San Francisco. Sitting across from her, listening to her voice, the customer stories she saved from the shop to entertain him, her worries about one or the other of their sons, it seemed he had always heard her voice, all his life traveling across the darkness. Without that voice there could be no other life that he could recognize as his own life. A woman's voice, perhaps like his mother's though in truth he could not recollect how she sounded. Every now and then Molly's teeth flashed, caught by what light he could not imagine on that moonless night, and he could know when it was she smiled. She had smiled often that night. What he felt for her was real, as real as anything, and worthy.

He thought about Nichol's Ledge and shook his head, thinking, *She's still got a helluva lot of gumption.*

He would not let himself think about Charlie. What was the point?

Afterward, in the cold air, they had dressed quickly. It was so dark he grabbed her shirt instead of his, and Robert had ventured a lighthearted reference to his feminine side before passing the blouse to her. Now that she had triumphed, Molly had the wit not to leap all over that with something ill-advised, like gratitude or a teenage *whatever* acceptance of his character, or worse, another joyous trumpeting of her happiness. The canoe hadn't quite stopped its rocking. Better not stand up yet. Still, confidence was hers. Heading back, Molly led the way. She was making a hopscotch game of leaping over the dark patches of bentgrass. Robert followed about ten feet behind, not leaping but deliberately tramping across the landscape to provide sober contrast to her exuberance. Then he heard a low *plunking* sort of splash, as of something entering water cleanly and deeply, like a good diver. Her cry came as he reached the pool, reached her arm flung out above the rim, grabbed it and pulled her up and slid her out onto the grass.

"Oh, Molly," he said. "Molly, oh god . . . god damn it, Molly . . ."

Staggering, running, they got down to the river. He peeled off her clothes—she could not really help, her entire body scalded, her vision ruined. Some of her skin was sloughing off in gummy patches and then there was, apparently, a lamina of blood before a lower layer of epidermis began, all of it ruined. Then came a moment when they exchanged the same quick significant look, though how much she saw and how much she intuited he would never know. But it was a strange, hypernormal look, each knowing calmly and instantly that someone, in a single irretrievable step, has moved from life to death. He had been calling for help to those voices they had heard an hour earlier, and now here came some youths, off-duty park employees. The two young women got in the river with Molly and supported her there, floating on her back, naked, with the water of the Firehole River washing gently over her burned flesh. Molly stared up at the black night and very soon began to ask them to let her go. To let her float downstream, please, because it would be the best way to go, under the circumstances. But the young men, three of them, had already gone for help. Robert stood in the river beside her, talking quietly to her, never stopping, so that she would hear his voice and never not hear his voice, not for one second not hear his voice beside her. He wanted to kiss her forehead but he was afraid his lips might pull away more of her skin. The two young women had begun to sing softly to her, folk songs. To sing her life away. It was as good a way as any, he supposed at the time, to go.

But the chopper came and when they saw her, how red she was all over, instead of taking her into Jackson or even Pocatello, they transported Molly Treadwell down to Salt Lake City where they had a well-known burn center. So it was in the hospital, doped into a pain-free oblivion, not in the river gazing up at the stars, that Molly died nine hours later.

For the doctors' part there was a certain amount of regretful speculation having to do with how it might have gone for her if she had not been completely submerged. Her short height, her lower center of gravity owing to an extra bit of weight in the "gluteal region," had combined to immediately plunge her down and under. Perhaps a man, taller, leaner, might have kept his head, even his shoulders above the surface of the superheated pool, and then they could have had healthy skin from which to grow and harvest the grafts. And a life might have been saved.

It was over a year before he saw Charlie again. Not once had he thought of calling him. Not once. But he *had* thought about the fact that he would never call Charlie, not under the circumstances. It would have been a mistake, Robert knew, to blame himself for Molly's death, though as a nostalgic Catholic, he did feel some guilt about the fat in her "gluteal region" that had helped send her instantly down under the fatal waters. And he could not forget Nichol's Ledge; could not forget the truth that roamed like a stray dog out there at the edge of the firelight—that he had been disappointed, in a vague and inadmissible way, about that penultimate coin toss.

Mainly though, he didn't call Charlie because, as he put it to himself, he had made his bed and now he must lie in it.

Charlie emailed him, prompted by some intuition, intimation, or just time having swept things clean enough, the tawdry complications of love's early heat and violence. "I only want to know that you're okay," he wrote.

And the doors flew open.

ROGUE

*I*t is because she cannot hear the gulls that she wakes. After a minute or two, leaning up on an elbow to search the world beyond the window, she sees that there is water still standing in the street but that the asphalt is patterned with cleanly edged light and shadow. The gulls are down at the beaches, working the broad ribbons of seaweed and oceanic debris thrown up by the storms of the week. The boy is quiet too but it's the absent gulls that tell her she must do something about him. Maybe do him in, she thinks with a mental shrug that is at once small and operatic, as if she is bluffing herself at a hand of solitaire. The thought flicks away across her mind like a glint of dull light or a colorless bird, and so quickly and sub-perceptibly that she's not sure it was there at all. "A visitation," she whispers. Later when he's at school she will look up the word for its older meanings, but for now it's the partial mystery, the partially remembered connotation, that tell her it's right. There is something strange, something dense and dark furled up tight inside her that wasn't there before yesterday, a new phenomenon, an embryo. All embryos look the same for a long time, unrelated species not differentiating until the developmental equivalent of the eleventh hour. This is what she likes to tell the science class at Woodrow Wilson Junior High where she subs. It helps to keep us humble, she always adds.

But maybe this thing inside her is not new, maybe it has simply never been called upon. It has been sitting in the back row of her own occasional classroom and has always known the answer but never bothered to raise its hand. It has been folded in on itself, afraid of the light of day and the hard eyes of others.

There is a tingling clarity to the light outside, and the air seems to vibrate the way the trees shimmied in the long minutes following the big quake twenty years earlier. Even the eucalyptus trees marching along the north perimeter of the field across the street like a rank of shaggy behemoths home at last from the battle, even they are shining with relief. Shaken up, she murmurs to herself. She is used to keeping her feelings from herself and even now manages to recall from the night before only the crab bisque and Nathalie Gaultier's gold scarf, the elegant flourish she always manages just before exiting a room. But off to the side there is still that impression of a wrong she is worried about, a wrong that she really cannot abide.

Her feelings, such as they are, feel dull and colorless too, and are taking place on the other side of a screen or a heavy curtain where some sort of procedure is anticipated and for which she has already received the first of several anesthetic installments.

Is there a doctor in the house, she thinks, and the memory of the holiday flight from Los Angeles appears. "Is there a doctor onboard?" the stewardess had asked of the passengers. But there was no doctor onboard. The plane landed in San Francisco, and before the EMS team was allowed onboard, every single passenger with every carry-on and laptop and backpack, deplaned. Procedure, it was later explained to the press. By the time the patient was offered the attention he needed, he was dead.

Through the eucalyptus lies the field with its black furrows promising artichokes by late summer, and then the cement plant beyond, which is silent like the gulls this morning. They have shut down the facility for routine maintenance, two days for every six months of continuous operation. The tower, silo, and stack assembly climb into a sky emptied of cloud and tumult, and to which it does not contribute its own brand of trouble. While she's watching, the twinkling white lights that follow the pipes and braces up to the top blink off.

They have not yet taken down the steel Christmas tree wired to the top of the tower, though it's already mid-January, and its skeletal shape points heavenward as if assigning blame. The tree was meant to be a placating gesture toward the local environmentalists, intended to say, among other things, that the cement plant is human after all. Holiday spirit, etc. Tom's idea.

Tom has been there for at least an hour, sitting at his green metal desk, the fake wood grain paneling of the walls darkening the room despite the sliding glass door that faces the sea. She pities him the metal and the pressed grain, though these are not details that bother him. His is an office for bare-knuckled work, for stacked invoices, boots gritty with sand, clipboards bearing production schedules, purchase orders for cement blowers and silo pumps, clinker chemistry analyses, particulate emissions reports. The neighbors complain to her about the cement kiln dust, quoting parts per million; they point to the white film covering their roses, their windshields, their tomatoes; to their shingles where the salt air has melded with the cement dust and formed a hard gray-white skin that scabs off randomly, and leaves the roofs mottled and unsightly. They tap their chests and ask her, the manager's wife, to think, *just think*, what it's doing to their lungs. "I really have no say," she says, and tries not to breathe too deeply.

No, Tom likes his office because there is nothing soft about it, and nothing that tells the men who drive their sand trucks in what Tom Campbell is about beyond the business at hand. It occurs to her that with the men at the plant he is most truly himself.

She shoves the window up and listens; the silence of the plant is like a dull ache that has miraculously stopped. A bird—not a gull—twits from the passionflower vine closing in the front porch. And she can hear the soft commotion of the sea again. Without the storm things seem farther away—the coast road, the ragged line of cypress trees watching the beach from the cliff edge, the broadly blue washed canvas of the Pacific. Theirs is the last in a row of twelve houses, farthest from the branch line tracks now used only for servicing the plant. Twenty yards west of the tracks the two-lane highway leads down to Santa Cruz and between the tracks and the road she can see the muster of junior high and high school students waiting for the bus. In a few years her son will be there too, but for now he has Davenport elementary close enough to make in a four-minute dash.

The damp air has curled about her exposed neck. Shutting the window, she collects her robe from its hook on the back of the door and heads past the kitchen to the boy's room.

"Time to get up, Will."

"Yeah?" she hears. Nothing in it yet. And then, "So," and notes the first word loading up with scorn.

"How about waffles, couple pieces of bacon?"

"Whatever."

He's only nine. It seems unfair, that this sort of thing should start so early. And it is one thing for Tom to behave as he does, to own her, to manage her, but not the boy. She has not given him that most particular of gifts.

In the kitchen on the table she finds her husband's dishes left precisely where he has eaten off them. Tom is the sort of person who makes a ceremony of every meal, even when there isn't time or no one's that hungry. He's a gourmet cook, he encourages her to tell their friends, though there is plenty enough bragging in the way he talks about food, the airy adjectives, the French words, the stagy temper tantrums whenever guests pass by the kitchen and dinner isn't ready yet. This morning early, 6:30 a.m. she guesses, he's made for himself an omelet. There is evidence of his mulchings all over the counter: ham, green pepper, mushrooms, scallions (not green onions, never green onions), Monterey Jack, eggshells clogging the sink drain.

Very likely there was rye toast too, cut in triangles, and the requisite cup of Sumatran coffee dripped through dye-free filters. There has always been something effeminate about Tom's food preparations, the way his thick fingers pinch the edges of a tart or line up so snugly against the knife as it minces away at some culinary rarity, the fussy way he scuttles from counter to stove, the ever-frantic consultations with the cookbook, his forehead shining with effort. She's not so sure that he really is a gourmet cook, or if it's just a function of being able to read. Her friend Maggie is a wonderful cook, but to watch her in a kitchen, it's half guesswork and another half taste, all piled atop a few basics. Tom thinks that he is unassailably fair and reasonable. "If I cook, you clean up. And Missy"—he calls her Missy whenever he's in an educational mood—"you have the fat end of that deal. You get to eat what I cook." So far she has always agreed, except that he only goes to lengths for company or for himself. The rest of the time he settles for her middlebrow fare.

Tom is a big guy, not so tall but hefty with a short neck and a haircut just a week or two past a long crew, so that the hair stands straight up for about an inch and then flops slightly at its ends. He uses some sort of gel that gives it a stiff modern sheen. Most of the time, even in winter, he wears a short-sleeved plaid shirt—owns dozens of them—and a pair of chinos with brown, L. L. Bean loafers. If it's cool out, he might consent to a pullover sweater or a windbreaker. His clothes have always exposed his lower-middle-class upbringing, south central LA, his need to be careful and conventional. With no father and no siblings, and an alcoholic mother dangling a string of boyfriends, there was a lot for him to contradict. She was weak, he allowed; I had to take care of her, he explained. At the age of sixteen he drove her to a clinic for an abortion. Once, maybe more than once, she had even climbed into his own bed. The disclosure seems designed to lend a dark sophistication to Tom Campbell, for he never quite reveals what exactly transpired, only that he has had to deal with Big Issues, like incest. Now his childhood has acquired many of the qualities of mythology—there are stories and lessons everywhere and he savors the chance to invoke them. Mostly, he likes to be admired for the contrast that the life he has made for himself provides.

Lisa is small beside him, like a teenaged daughter. When she subs at Woodrow Wilson most of the boys are taller. She knows that she is acceptably pretty, but not so pretty that she didn't have plenty of girlfriends in school, or women friends now, like Nathalie, who are happy enough to praise her athleticism. Lisa was a gymnast growing up, a darn good one, as her father liked to say, meaning to aggrandize her talents, though the *darn* accurately conveyed her second and third place finishes. Yes, she has enough going for her to render her perfectly acceptable on all fronts. It hardly matters that Nathalie may have called her Miss Mousy late one party night, because compared to the beautiful and brilliant Nathalie, a corporate lawyer accustomed to the steely talk of men with power, every woman is probably a little mousy. Tom had laughed, to be polite, he said later, impugning his wife's manners. Now, when he wants to goad her, he sings, "I went down to Miss Mousy's door where I have often been before . . ."

It's a small town, Lisa reminds herself; how steely can the men really be?

When they make love Tom Campbell locks all the doors, and draws down the blinds, and hangs additional things, blankets, beach towels, over the windows too, and it happens all over the house. He is like a dog with a bird he is not ready to kill yet, and they are playing a very serious game in which words are not allowed. Maybe she is good at guessing what he wants, though even his face wears a closed, don't-bother-me look, or maybe the particulars don't really matter.

It is all about her submission, the degrees and details merely accessories. It can't be pornographic, what they do, because it's private, it's their own house and Will's at school and they are married, it's their right. But sometimes she can't help feeling strangely ashamed. Once they were in the front room and he had her up against the wall, her legs around his waist, and the next door neighbors knocked on the door just five feet away; knocked and kept knocking, but Tom only slowed down and gripped her thighs more tightly, and when they heard Mrs. Armanasco say, "I'm sure they're here, both cars are in the driveway," Tom flashed her a menacing smile. He is grave about sex, grave the way she imagines a sapper is when he's defusing an explosive, as if lives are at stake.

The next day at the post office when she encountered Mrs. Armanasco she said only, "Yes, we were home," her voice adopting a prim, matter-of-fact righteousness, but she wanted to say more, she really wanted to tell her off. Lives were at stake, she wanted to say. Can't you see that?

Will slouches into a chair and skids his elbow up to the dish of sliced honeydew Lisa has set beside his plate.

"Elbow," she says flatly.

He gazes up at her sideways, his eyes empty, as if he's never seen her before, or as if she's in the way of something he'd rather see. "Leg."

"Please remove your elbow from the table."

"We're not naming body parts? I thought we were naming body parts."

"Now."

"Stupid cow," he mutters under his breath, an epithet he has borrowed from his father.

Lisa lets another part of her head hear, the part that knows how to quickly tuck things away and get on with something that has to be more important, like the day. It is just a bump in the road, nothing requiring formal complaint or attention. The toaster pops and she unplugs it in order to spear the waffles with a knife, then arranges them on a plate with the bacon just as the microwave times out on the syrup. When she delivers the food she puts on a smile she has come to think of as biblical, the other-cheek smile. He's almost her weight already, solid like his father but with her silken blond hair and rice paper skin that in certain light exposes the blue network of his veins. In the flat light of the kitchen she can see what's inside him, how the blood branches and then branches again, a map of his little man-ness that seems to go on forever.

Out the window across the black field the cement plant rises in apocalyptic silence.

Behind her, Will burps conspicuously the way boys seem to like to do. The kitchen counters are a mess, Tom's leavings, Will's meal, the burned pot from the night before still soaking.

The morning is taking forever. The morning is forever. What can an afternoon bring if the morning is already all there is? All there will ever be?

She cannot stand the way he treats her and has a sudden urge to take a marker and scribble out the map of his veins, like a mistake she alone keeps repeating. Instead she says, "This afternoon, after school, let's go down to Panther Beach, see what the storm left."

He fills his mouth with a wad of waffle before mumbling his answer. "Got practice."

"But it's Tuesday. You're out early anyway."

He shrugs. By this she knows that he will tolerate, at least, the idea of an outing with his mother. Things may change by the afternoon.

But they do not change. The plant is still silent and the silence throbs, slow and deep, and she begins to think of it as the heartbeat of everyone who has already died together in the air all around her.

The gulls are still occupied with the large and small deaths cast up on the beaches, the kelp and crabs, maybe an unlucky seal pup, bits of grunion, nests of fish line—it is always the same ragged exhibit of casualty. And Will is apparently still willing to do something with her, his mother. This is very likely because of soccer practice. Will is not so good at soccer, too chunky and deliberate when lithe quick turns are in order. It's a small school that hasn't the luxury of declining volunteers for team sports. The other boys are hard on him. After practice Will is usually ready to find something or someone to mistreat, to make up for the injustices. Children have, Lisa realized only recently, a truly vast, a *cosmic* sense of equity, handing out corrections here for something that happened over there, making adjustments in the scheme of things as one might tug at the corner of a great tapestry to right a distant wrinkle, to smooth a mood gone awry. It is all very Jungian.

Two o'clock. At the curbside pickup he waits, his black nylon shorts hiked up his bottom, which has always been too big and faintly girlish. A couple of identically clad boys are off to his side, kicking up a hacky-sack with their heels and insteps. At the last moment the smaller one feints left and catches it with the top of his shoe and the other one whoops with approval. Will leans away from them, pretending (she suspects) to search for something in his backpack. His shorts are wedged. He is her son. Inside she feels not a wince of love or embarrassment but a kind of bleak gladness. Jungian justice at work. Soon, her son yanks open the passenger door and shoves his backpack across the seat so that she has to jerk up her arm, then fit it awkwardly atop the pack. Back at the house he changes into jeans and a sweatshirt, tosses down a glass of chocolate milk, and grabs a plastic bucket for whatever collectibles they find. She is surprised that he wants to do this with her and asks him twice if he's sure.

"Pretty soon I won't want to go," he says and she notices how relieved she feels for the threat shading his words. It seems to put things right. All's right with the world, her mother was always saying when things were least right. Her mother was a constant ironist, whether she knew it or not. Of course, Lisa's had been a picture-perfect childhood: a brother who watched out for her; a portly father who owned a pet store frequented by all the kids, since he allowed them to play with the puppies and kittens, or feed the fish, or corner the fancy lizards when their tanks needed cleaning. Meanwhile over at the police department her mother was paid to answer the phones, and so she often knew what was happening in town before the newspaper even. There were seldom quarrels, or seldom ones of any duration at the Wheelers'. Kansas, she thought. Seldom a discouraging word—it was a long time before Lisa understood the import of that lyric. "After what I hear day in and day out at the PD, we've got nothing to complain about," Nan Wheeler would say. Then she'd launch into an anecdote that they were all supposed to keep confidential until it "hit the papers," and the complaint belonging to Lisa or her brother, Sam, or to Mr. Wheeler who took his refuge in little live things, was lost in the shuffle of real complaints, the assaults, the rapes, the drunk driving that led to a terrible paralysis, the arson, the domestic violence. One day, Lisa remembers, there was not much to report: animal in vehicle. It was a hot day and some dog lover had called the police. Lisa had her own report to make: she was eleven and she had discovered brownish blood in her pants and she didn't know what exactly to make of it, but it scared her, and then a boy had held his nose and said she stank. "They *are* wearing fur coats," Mrs. Wheeler observed, obviously thinking herself both clever and compassionate. "Poor things." And then, to herself mostly, she added, "What I'd give for a fur coat."

Will and his mother duck under the confused tendrils of the passionflower vine choking off the front porch, and she glances back to count the number in bloom. Five. The flowers last a single day and she tries to note each arrival and departure, to make their lives matter somehow. "Along the coast things go a little crazy," the woman at Gardeners' Supply told her. "Roses never really go dormant and though the passionflower won't bloom profusely, it will offer random blooms even in winter, especially if the vine faces south and is located in a warmish place." Like their porch. In their early days Tom would pick one and float it in a dish of water for her, but by morning the long petals had closed, forming a hard green tubular coffin that made a little thud when she tossed it into the waste basket. She never asked him to stop giving them to her, preferring instead to hide their hasty deaths, as if she were somehow responsible, or as if maybe he would have learned something about himself that would have been uncomfortable for both of them.

In the car Lisa discovers why her son is willing to go to Panther Beach with her: there is rumor of a gray whale washed up. She turns south down Highway 1, the blue Honda climbing and dropping with the road until before she is quite ready for it, they are upon the broad gravel pullout where three other vehicles are already parked. They lock the car, scramble up the loose rock that supports the tracks, then over the other side and along the edge of what in summer will be a field of Brussels sprouts. We won't see them, she thinks, and is at once stricken by the thought, which seems to have erupted through a crack in the smooth smiling surface of her.

Will has run ahead and abruptly halted. "It's not here," he calls back to her. He is standing on the cliff edge, peering down at the sandy cove, his arms thrown out sideways and then flopped in a gesture of disgust and disappointment.

"No?" She is still walking toward him, carrying the bucket and a Ziploc of trail mix in case he gets hungry—he has always counted on her to magically produce snacks and juice boxes no matter where they are, and even today—*even today?*—she does not want to let him down. "Maybe a different beach?"

"Naw."

"How do you know?"

"I just know," he snaps. His delicate skin is flushed suddenly. "They just said it, that's all."

"Who?" she asks, but she supposes it's the other boys, probably the two with the hacky-sack, and regrets asking.

"They just fucking said it," he repeats. "Fucking a-holes."

She won't say anything about the swearing, not when he's down—they both know it. Anyway, let him have them, she thinks, his little adult moments. How many can there be? She skips up next to him quickly and joins him in looking down, taking his hand at the last moment. He does not withdraw it for a good while and she indulges in a dreamy blur of togetherness, wondering what, really, she has to complain about. It is a beautiful day, the sun warming their foreheads. Lisa Campbell and her son, Will—she sees their names as a headline typing itself out in her mind, or as a phone-in someone like her mother might take. A thousand feet below them the narrow, tawny-colored beach practically glows in the slanting light. The surrounding faces of the sandstone cliffs are softly glowing too. To the south, cutting off Panther Beach from another beach they can't see, are broad marine terraces lifting up from beneath the cliffs and jutting out into the water. The sea has slashed into them so that there are slender canals sloshing with backwash that explode in glorious white fans as each wave pounds in. When she gazes out past the breakers the ocean is a simple level blue and so hugely passive it is like a god gone fast asleep.

But beneath them around the terraces, black and glistening in the January light, there is a dirty opacity to the sea with all the sand churned up in it, and the motion of the water, trapped between cliffs and interrupted by ledges, is crazy and senseless. It is still a low tide—Lisa checked the paper before leaving the house—not such a long ways out that the terraces are entirely exposed, but far enough that some of the mossy seaweed cloaking the lower reaches are still above water. That is where they are dangerously slippery. She can see several small figures clambering about. One of them points back toward the cliffs, to the sea caves and tunnels visible only from the water. On the sand, just above the high waterline a strip of flotsam and jetsam follows the curve of the beach. "Well," she sighs, "there's still plenty to poke around in."

Will says, "I guess," and starts down the nearly vertical dirt path that drops like a rope to the cove.

In another January a decade earlier there had been in fact a gray whale washed up on the beach. By the time Lisa got there the whale was already serving various scavengers, including dogs from the migrant workers camps and a flock of gulls, lifting and luffing above the body, dropping in unison. She had gone to scavenge too, with eyes only. Marine biologists from the university were crawling around the monstrous body, measuring one thing or another, cutting off sections of her to see how thick the blubber was, examining stomach contents, peering into the small sad eyes that were rapidly shrinking from the light of day and death. It was a female, probably pregnant, heading south to Baja California and the protection of Scammon's Lagoon to give birth. Lisa remembers that part because she herself had been pregnant at the time. The whale took up so much space on the beach that at high tide her body created a riptide that continued to exist long after she was gone. Of course she was there a long time, too enormous to move. The weight of flesh, Lisa thought.

Will has a stick and is wiggling it into a tangle of kelp and drift-wood, hunting for unnamed treasure, but what he comes up with is a corner of red plastic that had once been part of an ice chest maybe, and, of all things, a lid to a pot. They are not good clamming beaches, Central Coast beaches, so it's hard to imagine where it came from, off some trawler, she guesses, where onboard meals must be cooked. She thinks about the night before and Tom's dinner for Nathalie Gaultier and her husband, a professor at the university. They have a son Will's age, which is how they met—through the boys and soccer matches. Tom is a big reader, and despite his job at the cement plant, despite his upbringing, he insists on his place on what he calls the A list. People with breeding. Last night he was playing them different versions of a Schubert sonata, the one in B-flat that always breaks Lisa's heart, so slow and melancholy, and then later wanting to dis-cuss the novel *White Noise*, and in between, jumping up to check on the meal. Lisa had done the shopping, cleaned the house, set the table, and gotten herself and Will showered and properly attired. Now her job was simple: to let him know when the crab bisque was about to boil but not boiling. That was all, he said. Could she do it? he asked. Just that one small task. "It's critical," he said. And then he added, "Sweetie" and gave her fanny a pat. Tom enjoys the cocktail hour, *libations* and "the hour of conviviality," as he likes to say, which is the only reason he assigned her the job of heating the bisque. Oth-erwise she must stay out of the kitchen and out of his way.

The Gaultiers were on the couch, drinking the sherry he had poured them, laughing at something he had said, urging him to play yet another version of the sonata, so that they might include it in the comparison, inciting him to heights of hostly pleasures. Tom was wearing his usual plaid, short-sleeved shirt. It was funny, the things that he managed to overlook in his upward rush to social status. The things he simply did not know. After a certain age, there was only so much you could naturally acquire; mostly, it became an effort, a night school class in a subject you had somehow missed. You had to really want it. And you had to know to want it, too.

Lisa is afraid that there is a lot she does not know to want. She doesn't know why but she thinks that maybe she has always been this way. It would be wrong to blame anyone else, her parents or whoever. We all have free will, she tells herself. We all differentiate at the eleventh hour and become exactly and precisely who we are meant to be. How to reconcile the two? It is driving her crazy, trying to figure it out.

There are other people wandering about the cove, a young couple, a middle-aged woman with a big white lab, and a small group composed of two Hispanic women and three children. And it is this, her studied attention paid to the occupants of Panther Beach, her confidence that, one by one, they will leave as the tide comes in, that lets her in on the secret she has been keeping from herself.

Tom's happiness is palpable. He likes the Gaultiers, their elegance and ease. He is even drinking sherry though he usually has a beer before dinner, or on fancier occasions, a vodka tonic. It is so nice, to see him this way, in his chosen element, in charge. They are talking about the boys and she hears him say with a solemn tone, "They have a profound friendship," and Nathalie looks a little surprised but agrees, because it is the thing to say. Then the music is changed to Bartok, followed by jazz, and Tom and Jack Gaultier are pointing out similarities in phrasing, Tom standing over them with the sherry bottle in one hand, gesturing so grandly with it that she's afraid some of it might slosh out. But no, he is in splendid form tonight. He is a bon vivant, a raconteur, a king in his castle. And as his and his alone, Lisa might almost feel positively regal. But she doesn't.

Will is tramping along the wet edge of the storm debris, his footprints clean and surprisingly deep, and the stick, no longer occupied with a treasure hunt, is leaving perfect periods, dark and also deep, beside each of Will's right footprints. *I am here, period, I am here, period*, it seems to say. After a while they sit down on the dry sand and share the trail mix. She begins to tell him about Kansas. She'd like someone to know about Kansas, even if it is for just a short while. What it was like. She used to tell Tom some of the things, but one day he put a finger to his temple and said, "Melba toast and bread pudding, Joey next door copping cheap feels in Daddy's Winnebago, and, let's see, the day the cat ran away. We're not in Kansas anymore, Lisa. Case you hadn't noticed. Let's leave it to Beaver, okay?" After that she didn't bother mentioning her life before him. He was right—it wasn't all that interesting. Even the accident had a pathetic and mundane quality, the three of them in their beds, as if sleeping, the gas leak inevitable, the police said, considering the age of the wall heaters, Lisa seventeen and at a slumber party with friends two blocks away. She was alive, after all; nothing to complain about. Still, she'd like to mention Kansas and her family, the way things were. The mentioning would be part of a ceremony she needed this day, the Offertory or the Memento, the last blessing.

Will says, "Kansas," and lets his eyes drift skyward. He's heard his father on the subject and that is enough for him.

She tousles his yellow hair and drops her head to stare at the sand between her knees. The sand is light browns and grays and cool wherever it touches her skin. "Well," she says to the sand, "I guess Kansas is sort of a cliché."

"Yeah," he agrees with emphasis.

"Don't you mean, yeah duh? Isn't that what you'd rather say, if you'd thought of it? Or maybe, yeah, duh, stupid cow? Say what you want to say, anything, go ahead, I can take it, Will, I'm made for taking it, actually. That's what I know how to do, take it and take it and take it. What does your father say? I'm a catcher. Right. Lisa's a catcher, Lisa's a catcher . . ." Her voice is so quiet, a breathless whisper, like someone racing through the rosary, that for an instant she wonders if she has merely thought these things, except that the boy is frowning at her.

"What's wrong?" he says.

"Nothing." She buries her hands in the cool sand and then lets them emerge slowly, buries them again and again lifts them so that it is as if they are sprouting and unfurling. Each time she plants them and they grow out of the wet sand they seem less like her own hands and more like someone else's.

Will says, "You okay?" and she answers, "Sure" without turning her head, still watching the two strange hands growing out of the sand.

The crab bisque is the first in a five-course dinner. She has been so taken in by Tom's ebullience, by the wordplay and by Nathalie's presence—such a presence—the sound of the boys making a fort in the front hall, which had been allowed only because it is the Gaultier's boy—that she has forgotten about the soup. It is boiling madly. It is in fact burning. She pours it off into another pot and tries to scrub away the evidence, but the pot must be soaked, it is so badly burned. Once the bisque cools she announces, "First course," and everyone takes a seat. What has happened is immediately evident.

"This is burned," Tom says. His voice is flat. "Burned and cold."

"The conversation was so fascinating." She makes a face and tries to shrug, but it is so out of character, so antithetical to the burst of apologies and pleadings she would have offered under normal circumstances, that the shrug is stagy and unconvincing. It is then that she realizes that the conversation was not what was fascinating, it was how phony her husband was acting around Nathalie.

"Burned and cold."

"Tom."

"Amazing." He gazes briefly at Nathalie and gives his head a single soft shake.

Humility has never been a problem for Lisa. She was always grateful simply to be alive. And then to have met Tom. The way they met. She had been driving down the Coast Highway and a sand truck going at least eighty had passed her on a curve, nearly shoving her off the road. She was so angry that she followed it into the cement plant and marched into the office. It seemed the first time that she had ever really complained about anything. Tom Campbell was just the assistant manager then, new and full of untried powers, and he had put his arm on her shoulder and told her that he'd get to the bottom of it. The sand truck driver was made to apologize. After that she belonged to Tom Campbell. Others were outsiders. No one, she believed, could really understand the bond between them.

"Amazing," Tom repeats and, for effect, he tries the soup again, as if it simply can't be so; such things do not happen to a Tom Campbell meal or to Tom Campbell guests.

"It's fine," Jack Gaultier says. "Plenty of food coming, eh Tom?" he adds in a good-natured, all's well voice.

No, Lisa has arrived at a level of humility that she realizes no one can understand. When she buys cards for friends, instead of writing in them she inscribes her sentiments on Post-its, so that they can be removed, the card still pristine, untouched by her thoughts or feelings. They think that she is cheap, that she wants the card to be reusable, but really, that is quite beside the point.

"Tom," she groans under her breath, staring at the tablecloth.

"It might occur to you to apologize," Tom is saying as he rises and lifts the bowls, one by one pouring the contents of each back into the tureen.

Her ears have begun to ring. She tries to stand, to help him, her husband, to get him into the kitchen if only for a moment, so that they can be who they are together, away from others. But Tom waves her off. "Please," he says with a firm solicitude, "please, no more of your . . . help." He glances at the Gaultiers.

"It was an accident."

"There are no accidents," he announces quietly. It is one of his favorite Est-ian remarks.

"The conversation . . ." she offers, finally looking around the table. At the corner of Nathalie's lovely, wine-red mouth, an incipient smile waits for a sign. Jack pretends to talk with his son. And Will watches his father with an eerie enthrallment.

Tom gives his head a sad shake and carries the bowls and tureen back into the kitchen. Across the table Nathalie offers a weak smile, thoroughly enigmatic—it's not clear whether she thinks Lisa has in fact done this intentionally but Nathalie forgives her, or whether Nathalie is sympathizing with Lisa over Tom's injustice. An endless purgatory of silence enshrouds them before Tom returns at last with the main course, tournedos of beef, herb-encrusted potatoes, and a vegetable medley that involves an onion confit, one of Tom's signature dishes.

"You need to apologize, Lisa, before we can properly enjoy this meal. To our friends. Our *guests*. What kind of example can you hope to set for Will if you don't? For young Gaultier here?" He nods a manly salutation to the Gaultiers' son.

Will widens his eyes and gazes directly at his mother. "*Mom.*" His voice is sharp with authority and impatience. Her son. "Say you're sorry!" Or maybe it's just that he's hungry.

Will is always hungry, she thinks now with a smile, watching him inhale the last of the trail mix. "Come on," she says, jumping to her feet, "let's check out the ledges."

It is Will who leads the way to the rocks, scrambling up, leaping from one ledge to another, getting farther and farther away from the sand. Lisa gauges how much is left of the narrow sand bridge that can take them back to the main beach: about fifteen feet she guesses. It is 3:25. The high tide is at 4:41. So she must keep him exploring the terraces for half an hour, maybe less. That should do it, she thinks, and again notes how far away her feelings have gone, so far that she really can't see what they are. After all, what was ever served by getting emotional? *Nothing served in tears*, her mother used to say.

"I am sorry," she says softly, looking only at Will. "Yes, I'm sorry. Quite sorry." She laughs, glancing around the table. "You can't imagine how sorry I am."

Jack Gaultier mumbles something vaguely kind and dismissive, and she's grateful for this man, a relative stranger, a stranger in Tom Campbell's strange land. The kindness of strangers.

Lisa gives another laugh. "Soup. Of all things."

Tom sighs. "Why don't we change the subject? Something more interesting, surely. Nathalie, tell us what you can about the Strickland case."

The others have left and the beach and ledges are now deserted. Will is on his knees trying to leverage a green crab from its hole. Eventually he succeeds, holding the creature in a finger pinch, its legs and claws wriggling, before he drops it in the bucket. She is not surprised but still mildly saddened by the fact that none of the others, the woman with the dog, the couple, maybe even one of the kids, has alerted them to the incoming tide. Everyone minding his own business, every man for himself. The sand bridge that joins the beach to the ledges is now deep underwater. Nonexistent. The marine terraces are burrowing into the wild surf. The water is suddenly very loud, very big. And the sky, still clear but not so blue with the sun so close to setting, seems to have zoomed out and away from Panther Beach, and is not watching down on them any longer. With each wave the great fans of saltwater are taller, twenty feet at least, and some of them explode across the ledges where they had dried during the day. There is a mad greed to the way the waves reclaim the ledges. She wonders if she and her son will be left with a narrow margin at the base of the cliff or if surfaces will completely disappear, only a rock or two, maybe none at all—she has never stayed this late. It is not possible to stay this late at Panther Beach, everyone knows that. Locals. Only tourists must be plucked from rocks. The Davenport Rescue Team manages twenty-five, thirty cliff rescues each year—they're famous for it. For a while Tom was one of the volunteers, but now he is not in shape for that sort of thing—too much fine dining.

"Mom." Will's face is serious. He has just been half drenched by a wave, knocked to his knees, but not pulled from the rocks. "Mom," he says again, struggling up.

The big tumult of the sea churns and seethes behind him. "I know," she calls to him. She likes how marvelously calm her voice sounds. How finally perfect she feels.

He runs over to her, his boy's arms out, the bucket banging against his side. "Mom!"

"Little man," she says, hugging him, "little man."

Then she turns him gently so that he can gaze north toward the sandy bite of land, of safety, that is so clearly impossible to reach. And she is aware that this is the moment, the one act, in which she finds a meager recompense. The cove is glowing in the western light, a warm honey tan, and a thousand feet above is the place where she and Will stood together, and behind that spot, inland maybe an eighth of a mile, is the cement plant and the stacks rising in miraculous silence and somewhere in that silence is Tom Campbell with his clipboard, enduring the routine maintenance until they can start the whole operation up again.

Will jerks his head around to her. "Whatta we do?" He has to shout because another wave crashes up over the ledge, one long wing of it sweeping across their feet, ankle deep. Instinctively they move several steps inland, though there is not much elevation change. Another wave, and another, and then two more not quite as high. It is a winter sun and she is cold and shivering and there is no point in complaining. Anyway, she thinks with an inward smile, this is my complaint.

"What are we gonna do?" Will asks her again. His fingers are clenched in the loose damp fabric of her sleeve.

"We aren't going to do anything, little man. We're just going to take it."

The boy begins to cry.

"Now," she says gently.

He buries his face between her breasts.

"Nothing served," she murmurs, "nothing served, not in tears."

Soon their backs are pressed against the rough, sandstone cliff, the water rising to their knees, hissing and bubbling as it withdraws only to surge in again, a little higher but not each time. Every dozen waves or so. She can see their tennis shoes under the water, so clean and alien down there. With the deepening water the outwash is stronger and in spite of everything, Lisa instinctively grabs at exposed stones and roots in the cliff face to keep from being sucked out. The boy decides to talk—about school, about a reptile book he's reading, about his soccer shorts and how bad they get when it's hot, a free-associating scramble that is the only way he can think of using up his last moments.

It isn't until they hear the voices far above them, and Lisa says "Oh," and stares wistfully out at the ocean, down at their tennis shoes wobbling beneath the water, and a minute later says, "Well," that her son understands she has planned this day. All of it. An expression of horror, clear and wondrous and admiring, opens his whole face as he gazes up at her. His mouth has gone slack and he looks suddenly quite innocent.

The bullhorn voice is telling them not to worry. Above them, on the cliff edge, they are setting up the Z-rig pulley and the picket system of ropes, one for the Stokes basket, another for the tender who will keep the loaded basket from banging into the cliff, and a third safety line that will connect to both the basket and the rescuer. She remembers watching Tom and the others during training. The goal was to be over the side in under a minute, because it only took one wave to sweep someone off a rock or ledge, and then rescue was more often than not hopeless.

Will slips on the ledge and she drags him by the arm up out of the water. Then it is her turn to go down, and Will's to do his best, helping his mother up. In spite of the temperature, the saltwater bears a softness not altogether unwelcome. She licks it from her lips and smiles.

The figure of a man knotted up in ropes descends toward them, kicking away from the dun-colored cliff face, swinging back, then kicking away, until he is beside them. Then down comes the Stokes basket. There is never any question that Will must be loaded first and lifted out of danger. The young man—she recognizes him from the local diner, a waiter—cinches the straps across Will's torso, then the two across his legs.

The waves are very loud now, booming around them and at them, and when the water comes it reaches to her thighs and her whole body is shaking. She is having a hard time staying upright, but the worst of the wave action, its real violence, is wasted on the seaward edges of the marine terraces. So it seems that she will be able to hold out until the basket is lowered again.

Before they begin the ascent Lisa looks directly into Will's eyes and places her hand on his chest. "You must never speak to me that way again."

"No," he says gravely. When the basket is ten feet or so above her, with the man tending it away from the cliff, she hears Will call out, "Mom!" and it is just as marvelous as she can imagine.

What a day, she thinks. What a day.

She watches the Stokes basket rise, her son's yellow hair through the wire mesh and the sandstone warm and yellow, and the distant pink face or gesturing arm of one of the men who had come to rescue them. Someone must have seen them, or seen the blue Honda parked at the Panther Beach pullout. Someone must have decided to notice and then to help. She plans to thank them.

The waves are swinging into her with a serious weight now, like bags of sand. She has pressed the length of her body into a kind of crease in the cliff face so that the waves come at her from an angle, not entirely sideways but not dead-on either, and it seems to offer more stability but not much more. A long tail of kelp swirls in about her feet and slithers out with the next outwash. Every time the sea rushes into the cave south of her it goes off like a geyser. She has stopped shaking but not because the sun, dropping down the sky, is giving much warmth, but probably, she supposes, because her lean body is genuinely hypothermic and past shaking.

She estimates that the basket is about two-thirds of the way up the cliff.

Rogue waves are not as uncommon as people think, if they even know about them, especially during storm season. Mostly, people don't see them, or know to see them. They arrive onshore after the storm, when it's all over and the sun is out and the sea recovering. There is a surge, a deep rising, out there a ways amid the processions of ordinary waves moving in long neat lines toward shore, and then, if you are facing the water, you see it climbing like a blue wall so high that you can't see anything behind it, three, four times higher than the wave train. You can see the waves leading it in, and they break evenly where all the others have been breaking, and then you see the trough as deep as a burial trench, but the rogue rises and rises and roars past that place where the waves were breaking and past the foam line and still it has not broken.

Lisa sees it when it is four waves out. It is so monstrous that, from her vantage point, it has blocked out the sun. Immediately, she checks that the basket is safe, over the edge; the man tending it as well. Sees them—or imagines them, she's not sure which and it doesn't really matter—standing there, arms hanging loose, watching. It will reach her in less than a minute. There is no time for her. After that she looks at the waves. They are not so pretty here, chopped up by the ledges and driven between circling cliffs, not like the smooth green pleats that fold neatly to the sand on the longer beaches to the south that are in her mind now, all the pretty waves on the long sunny beaches.

She thinks about Tom. Probably she would have had to leave him. And Will, the map of his manhood, his fingers clenching her sleeve, that little voice calling down to her from the basket. Yellow hair. She thinks about it all, even Kansas, there is time even for Kansas.

IN THE NOT-TOO-DIFFERENT FUTURE

Shannon hadn't seen Uncle Bliss for three years, and now that she was the beggar in the equation, it actually sounded like a long time. Not very promising. They used to get together several times a year at the halfway point between San Jose and Big Sur—Moss Landing—for a pot of cioppino at Mauro's right on the water. After that they'd wander over to Yesterday's Books and he'd give the old woman who owned the place a new list of first editions he wanted her to find for him, the books trickling in over the next six months or so, and the price, minutely penciled on the inside cover, never more than three or four dollars. The store occupied part of an old cannery built of galvanized steel and glass panes wobbled from the long western light, but she had managed to communicate a certain Old World dignity to the place, with her cardigan sweaters and her white hair incandescent in the dusky sobriety of walls made of books, and the leather and mold smell of a Scottish sanctum lost in the moors somewhere. Parked out front in the gravel wasteland where the trucks used to pull up was a yellow school bus, moribund and crippled off over one of the rear blocks, where she kept the paperbacks, ten cents each. The wayward bus, she called it.

Not once did Bliss Stewart and Shannon Costa encounter anyone else in the store or the bus. It was always as if they had arrived for an appointment and that when they departed, when they were just out of sight, in fact, the next appointment would appear. It reminded Shannon of how it had been when she was in therapy with

Steinmetz, after her mother had died; the hyperpunctuality, frantic not to encounter some sad and desperate person in the waiting room, those who actually made use of the box of tissues conspicuously placed on the little teak table beside the chair pretending to be an Eames. The fifty-minute hour was better than discreet; it brooked no witnesses. One heart came and another heart left, and each one managed to hide in the nanosecond Neverland between appointments.

The old woman at Yesterday's Books—Mrs. Godsland, was her name, a ruddy-faced Scotswoman who hardly ever spoke—disappeared one day. That was what Mauro had told them, the backs of his hands flecked with silvery fish scales. "I say she marched into the sea," he said. He paused to run the lithe contours of the fillet blade up the belly of the small halibut whose tapered face he held cradled against his palm. "She was from the Hebrides, an Islander. Those people always let the sea do their dirty work. We Genovese," he tapped his chest with two bloody fingers, "we do our own deeds."

But they weren't having lunch in Moss Landing at Mauro's, because Shannon was the beggar in the equation and this time had offered to make the drive all the way down to Big Sur. Anyway, Mauro's was still thriving but the bookstore was gone. The bookstore, not the cioppino, had always been the draw for Bliss.

"I can get anything you want online," she told him. "AbeBooks, Alibris, eBay, first editions, whatever. And in no time, a week at most."

There was a pause at the other end while he waited for a delivery truck to roar uphill past the pay phone outside Nepenthé. She pictured him squeezed sideways into the booth, half of him in and the rest of him understandably relieved to be out. "Time don't mean nothing to a hog," he drawled. The punch line to an old joke, a joke she had always gotten wrong in the telling. *Pigs don't care about time,* was how she had remembered it, and that had been funnier to Bliss than the joke itself. She liked the way he laughed; it was like water, big, clean, and uncomplicated. Still, it was irritating to be reminded of his relationship to time, his denial that life was whizzing by him at warp speed and he was lugged down in Big Sur counting petals on daisies, the same ones he'd be pushing up soon enough. And she wondered if he was aware of the *hog* connotations. It was always hard to know just how much Bliss Stewart was aware of.

"Time means something to me," she had said. "I'll find you at the Inn, 5:00."

***

Coast Highway 1 from Carmel down to Big Sur is almost exactly twenty-six miles, which is what makes it the most beautiful marathon course in the United States. The two-lane road clings to the sides of green hills that fall into a sea torn up with coves and rocks and cuts and black, hulking sea-stacks, the winding pavement always moving with the hills, swinging in and out, and in only a few places arrogant or determined enough to slice one in half and expose the sandstone. Over time the rain and wind have carved organ pipes and raised fins and spindled the buff-colored stone into delicate columns that suggest ancient ruins. But mostly the road conforms to the precipitous topography and to the ocean waiting to swallow it up, like the maw of some creature so vast that its eyeballs bob below the horizon. Once or twice a decade the winter storms are strong enough and wet enough, coming in like train cars one after another, that they load up the soil and generate mudslides that take out long sections of the coast road. But the efforts to restore the highway are usually slow—adverse economics, according to the local politicos. The Big Sur community has a year-round population of about a thousand, not enough voters to warrant a speedy response to disaster. Helicopters are usually the easiest method of evacuating community members. One year, tractoring out the new road had taken three months. Shannon had clipped the newspaper photo shot from a copter hovering offshore, showing a phalanx of matchbox-sized bucket-loaders lined up athwart a ridiculously massive dirt grade, incising a horizontal line, really just a scratch, in what was after all a thoroughly logical and very vertical rush of land down to a roiling sea. Things broke down at their edges, continents crumbled; wherever one thing encountered another that was alien, that was oppositional, damage could be expected.

To Shannon the scenery along the Big Sur coastline was so impossibly perfect that it seemed to be posing for its own picture. And the thing was, it was telling the truth about itself—no filters, no gaudy setting sun, no fancy angles. Why hold a marathon here? Beauty was beside the point, a distraction from the business at hand. She had to wonder just how many total seconds had been lost by runners admiring the view. How many ticks off of perfection?

At the Rio Road light, the last one for the next two hundred miles, she checked her own face in the rearview mirror, regarding with sober acceptance the shingled hair, brown and blunt, the eyes that were too big, like her mother's, and that seemed to betray a stupid tendency toward hopefulness, except that Shannon had long ago thrown in with determination, not hope; the durable double chin, present even in bouts of what she called disordered eating. Final and incontrovertible proof of the power of genes, that chin. No, there was nothing perfect in her face; no distraction to anyone. She had had to work for everything she had—I'm perfect at being perfect, she liked to quip—but not everything she *would* have, if this junket proved out. A smile appeared and just as abruptly disappeared; it was pleasing to her, how discrete her expressions could be. They were like scheduled events. One did not morph sloppily into another but returned directly to a position of stasis, the skin of her face pale as an oyster mushroom, and taut, admirably flat. Shannon did not *have* expressions or even *wear* expressions; she *delivered* them.

Uncle Bliss was not really her uncle, which made her mother's arrangement with him, her eccentric last wishes, all the more galling. It wasn't even clear whether or not they had ever been lovers after her father had bugged out. If they had been lovers it would have meant something, though she wasn't quite sure what. Maybe only that he knew something about Margaret Costa, secrets that only he and Margaret shared. Secrets, how a woman moved under her lover's hand, for instance, were powerful. Bliss was frustratingly circumspect, but in ways that were so out of focus, so difficult to read, the ink vanishing in its own wake, that she was hardly sure that he had in fact denied her access to information. Somehow, she just ended up knowing a lot less than she wanted to know.

Or maybe if they had been lovers, Shannon could have pretended more into the relationship; he might have been a father figure, whatever that meant. There would have been someone to imagine, someone who, under the right circumstances, might have really cared. He could have been the person she thought of when she found herself in an exotic place—*look at me, here I am in Tokyo, or Lolo, Montana, the Hebrides at Mrs. Godsland's.*

The Beemer took the curves with a pleasing tensity; no spillage at the outermost trajectory, no waste or hint of lethargy in the acceleration out of the turn and into the straight sections. A gift from management—now *that* said something. One thing it definitely said was that the clock had run out on her servitude. The time had come for her to have her own company. In effect, the Beemer had added the last argument to her own source code. Of course, they had had an Elvis year and the money was just gushing in. One of the guys in the next cubicle over had admitted that, after indulging every material whim, including that very morning a $2,600 single-cup espresso machine, he was "feeling a little queasy, you know, like, morally."

At the very least Bliss and Maggie Costa had been good friends, that much was clear. She'd even left him the cabin just up the road from Nepenthé Restaurant. It was still off-grid, but hell, what was electricity and plumbing to a retro-hippie with a Buddha complex? The money was all on Shannon's mother's side—refined sugar. Her father, James Farley, had been a sometime lecturer at a junior college up peninsula. Music appreciation. One day he'd packed his clothes and driven to Florida where, as far as Shannon knew, he was still appreciating music for the multitude. She had been ten. He never said good-bye. It was two years before they learned where he'd gone, and only because a girlfriend ratted him out. Her mother told her that he had "sand in his shoes," but Shannon figured that he had finally come to terms with the Costa family fortune, that for all intents and purposes, especially his, it was locked up in a transgenerational Rubik's cube of Trusts—bypass, dynasty, pour-over Trusts, revocable and irrevocable, living and testamentary, hopelessly arcane and sequent. The stuff of pot dreams to an attorney. Margaret's family were all gone at the time, but they had been foresighted in designing all the Trusts. Maybe they had guessed that Jimmy Farley was a flight risk, and not just because Margaret was a plain woman who hadn't aged well. The funny thing was, the money was still locked up in Trusts, but it was Bliss, not Shannon, who had been named the successor Trustee; Bliss who held the key. What a monumental joke. The big wheels of commerce run off track by Big Sur's own Big Lebowski.

Big Bliss Stewart, as he was known, arrived on the Big Sur scene in the early eighties, all six-foot-two, 320 pounds of him, looking for work, which there was a lot of at that time, owing to the state-wide boom in everything from wine to windmills. For a while he worked as a bartender at the Inn, the understated, upscale one on the east side of the highway, and as such he was unparalleled. He had come from West Virginia and had that mellifluous gentleman's palaver that soothed the spirit, and there was nothing empty or idly distracting about his palaver either. Quotable phrases cropped up everywhere. At the end of the bar most nights of the week, a former journalist from Boston stacked his arms on the gleaming copper, and it was he who used to refer to Bliss as "the last philosopher." The journalist, Mr. Nicely, still wore the rumpled serge to prove what he had been, and still enjoyed stringing together a few *mots juste*. He had probably come about as close as anyone to pegging Big Bliss.

It wasn't long before Bliss was promoted to manager, and he was good at that too. The salesmen filed in and out, and he sampled Emmentaler and Oregon Pinot Gris, and inspected the marbling of the meat, the polish of the silver; he fingered the thread count of the sheets and the weight of the menu paper, a wisp of merriment always just there behind the two blue portholes of his eyes, as if he were an imposter, the whole thing just a lark. Bliss always seemed to be a great ship moving silently over the far horizon, bearing news you had somehow missed getting, everyone onboard having a mighty fine time. The Inn was owned by a San Francisco–based corporation populated by the relentlessly youthful typical of that time in the Bay Area. He called them *my masters*, pointing skyward, which was a collective joke. His younger bosses, wanting mainly to be cool, laughed loudest. It was a time when people spoke in neo-mythological terms, a barbarous idiolect produced by the conflation of the high-tech industry swelling to the proportions of a Baby Huey on hormones, and several iconic sci-fi films of the day, like *Star Wars*. You couldn't turn a corner without encountering masters, evil empires, wizards, forms of idolatry arising from a binary system. Shannon was not unaware of the brisk harvest of stereotypes and unholy neologisms Silicon Valley had produced, but it *was* her world and she made a point of dissing it only with members of the tribe.

To sweeten the deal she had accepted Uncle Bliss's invitation to spend the night in the former Costa family cabin. The family, old Palo Alto, had five second homes, all of which had been sold off over time except for Maggie's Big Sur hideout, now Bliss Stewart's permanent residence. Maggie met Bliss at Nepenthe in the eighties one night late during the monthly celebration of birthdays. They were both Februarians, and they had both been comped the house specialty, white Russians. Bliss never talked about Maggie or what had happened. What was there to say?

***

It was a Tuesday afternoon, not a high traffic day for the coast road, but the long Easter weekend had left residuals out and about, including the occasional motor home waddling off the highway to appreciate one of the posted viewpoints, to let the mandatory yappy-little-dog take a whiz, or to shed a trailing car or two. There was one easing onto the blacktop from the pullout south of the Bixby Creek Bridge where Shannon was parking in order to take a look herself. She swung around the motor home, reading some of the stickers pasted to its billboard-sized back end: "We're spending our children's inheritance," then the breast cancer logo, a crossed pink ribbon, and a small admonition that read, "Don't postpone joy." There were others, but those three together, plus the out-of-state tags—Idaho—said what there was to say about them: a couple in their seventies probably, she a breast cancer survivor, the two of them waking up one morning and deciding that a lifetime putting off seeing America had almost reached the point of no return, or more accurately, no departure. Time to hit the road.

Such a fate would not happen to her, not to Shannon Costa; she would not be hobbled by the present while the Future bolted down the trail with reins trailing. She absolutely would not!

Shannon double-clicked the remote on the Beemer, took a dozen steps, went back to check that it was in fact locked—a tic that had somehow developed—then strolled over to the guardrail. The bridge was a single arch, poignant and graceful in its simplicity, the spokes fanning up to support the narrow roadbed, and on either end the sharp plunge six hundred feet down to the creek. West of the bridge the creek emptied into water the color of sapphire fringed with a line of white surf too bright to gaze at directly, all inaccessible. You could reach it by sea, because most of the continental debris littering the shallows lay north and south of the cove, but if you roped your way down the slopes you'd have a thicket of poison oak to deal with. She'd have given anything to stand in that cold water and gaze up at everyone yearning to be down where she was, unreachable.

She drove the marathon distance in forty minutes, the same forty minutes that might have saved her mother. The stupidity of the whole thing is what kept getting to her, even now, five years later. Maggie Costa had been strong in a quiet, stubborn way. Pain in the lower right abdomen? Appendix? She had said that she would run up to the hospital in Monterey the next morning—that was what she told Bliss who was working late that night at the Inn. There had never been a phone at the cabin, and of course no cell service. He stopped by at 9:45 a.m. and found her. It was all so stupidly preventable. What sort of person today could manage to die of appendicitis? Especially someone as educated and wealthy as Margaret Costa. You practically had to be trying, or not trying not to.

Two months later Shannon began experiencing "weird shit" was how she put it to her girlfriend. "Sometimes I can't find my way back out to my skin," Shannon had said, the words as friable as chalk. She was sitting at the foot of the bed, her back to Izzy. "It's getting easier to stay down there."

Izzy sat up and touched the flat of her hand to Shannon's back. "Where?"

"Where my voice is, the spark of me. It's very small, it's tiny. And the place is gray and muffled, not a room but a place or a pocket at the center of my body, and I don't know, my skin is like, miles up there. Really thick. There's a lot of mass, you know. You know what I mean? *Mass.*"

Izzy's hand didn't go away, but it stiffened as Shannon tried to tell her—quickly, before she couldn't—about climbing back up, about when it was just too hard to get there, to be there, and the air was fast and cold, the way it always is at edges. But the gray place was small and soft, her voice, too, very small, hardly worth the effort, actually not . . . not worth it. Actually easier to let it all just press down on the little voice that seemed to be a light too until it was gone. And really, it was just *a-mazing* how far up, how far out her skin was, like the edge of a whole planet, way out there, miles away.

Izzy did some research and found Dr. Steinmetz.

"Disturbances in body image," Dr. Steinmetz murmured, lifting his chin and speaking over his folded hands, speaking only because she had pressed him. He wouldn't have produced such a coldly clinical label without her insistence. The names for things could be comforting, because they contained the damage, packaged it up, even while they seemed to make it more serious, too, more solidly one thing and not at all another. Not debatable. Black or white.

"Will I get over it?"

"We will get you through this," he had said.

"Okay."

He studied her with kindness. Or with a kindness that she was willing to believe.

"Did I say something? Did I say okay? Could you hear me say it?"

"You said okay. You are not so far inside that I cannot hear you."

"Okay."

He looked at her and the looking made her close her eyes and fall slowly and heavily back down to the muted center, to the soft twilight and the soft walls. She could feel her breathing go slow and slack and an easy gentle pressing-down sensation develop on the top of her head.

"Shannon. Do not go back down there," Dr. Steinmetz said. "We need to work together. Your mother isn't there. Your father isn't there. Nothing is there."

"I'm there."

"No. You are here with me in this room, and this room is safe."

"I'm a tiny little pinch of light here, a tiny, tiny spark inside a huge blimpy thing, this body."

"I want you to occupy all of your body, to flow out to your skin, like a great happy wave."

Dr. Steinmetz was a small man with patchy gray hair and hands that moved in adult gestures of wan acceptance, *such is life*. Words like happy did not sound credible in his mouth. But Shannon understood that he was appealing to her age, or to the standard optimism twenty-three years on the planet assumed.

In the car, in her tailored J. Crew outfits, 40 percent discounted to staff, Izzy was always waiting. After half a dozen visits to Dr. Steinmetz, Shannon realized anew that Izzy's lips were pretty in a tidy, plump, compacted way, and clearly not afraid of the edge that they occupied. She kissed them and Izzy said, "Don't worry." It took a lot of courage to be sweet. Izzy was always sweet. In a terrible world, Izzy never failed to be sweet.

It was for Izzy that Shannon wanted to provide. To *shine*. To always be there and never to leave. They had been roommates at Berkeley and what had begun as a straight/bi-curious experiment had become the real thing. Or something like real. Izzy said love, shrugging off the obvious, but Shannon remained uncomfortable with the concept; after all, love had a pretty crappy track record, especially the American version. Shannon didn't want to trap what she was feeling inside the word, just in case what she was feeling needed more room. Being with Izzy wasn't exactly effortless but it was easier somehow, less foreign than being with other people; she was not an edge but a continuation, or at most, a gentle transition.

After graduation, Izzy's summer job at J. Crew became basically her job, while Shannon desk-surfed Silicon Valley, working her way up through various tech companies. Now she was really ready to have her own gig, a software company specializing in applications, branded apps for networking sites, mobile applications, game apps, whatever. She knew enough people eager to make the jump over to her start-up, and if Bliss Stewart would release the funding from one of the Costa Family Trusts, they'd be golden.

Izzy, blond and scrubbed, with her beautiful derriere and brave lips and her hand steady on Shannon's back, wished her luck as she settled into the Beemer earlier that afternoon. No, Shannon simply could not lose Izzy. She must shine for Izzy.

***

The road straightened before Point Sur, the steep hills sighing into long gradual sweeps of pastureland that flowed east to west and disappeared into white beaches and broken lines of surf. The green pastures were dotted with black Angus cattle as unmoving as statuary, the picture restful and reassuring, as though all was as it had always been, as though her mother were beside her and they had just made a shopping run up to Carmel and the Crossroads, and were coming home to the camp cabin, bustling with purchases, soup ingredients and strawberries and *pain au chocolat* for breakfast. Then the road burrowed back into the redwood forests, the land rising sharply again, past the River Inn, Ripplewood, Fernwood, Pfeiffer State Park, and finally Shannon found the discreet turn into the Cooper Inn and followed the right fork up to the restaurant. His old white GMC pickup was in its usual spot, at the far end closest to the walkway. She saw that the rear tires were bald. At first she circled past Bliss's truck and stopped at the distant end of the lot, to spare the new Beemer random nicks, but remembering, she rolled back up to the truck and parked beside it. He liked to walk her to her car, a hump for a man his size. The gallantry—if that was what it should be called—was respectful, not contrived or showy. You could see that. You could see that it was important to him and that it came from something at the center.

The first thing she noticed was that Bliss was not at the manager's desk, visible through the door off the entry vestibule. He was behind the bar. And the second thing she saw was that—incredibly—Mr. Nicely was sitting at the far end of it in his usual location, the last stool adjacent to the slot where the waitresses ordered up. There was a couple, tourists, judging by the fanny packs and sunburns, at the other end enraptured with each other, dangling tentacles of calamari into each other's mouths. In the distant lounge area, at a low table, three young men had managed to surround a covey of long-necked beer bottles.

"Well, hello darlin'," Bliss said as she came up.

She leaned over the bar and kissed him on the cheek. "Hey."

"You are making my eyeballs feel good."

She smiled in spite of what she knew about her looks. "You're still a crappy liar." But the fact that he was a crappy liar also suddenly, unexpectedly, wadded in her throat.

Bliss pulled back and straightened to his full height, and it was then she could see that he had lost weight, not what would be called a good deal of weight, but a definitely noticeable cut in poundage, the extra that had always qualified him for jolly rotundity. "I never tell a lie," he said.

She veiled her eyes patiently, then nodded toward the end of the bar. "That's scary," she said *sotto voce*.

"What?"

"He's still here."

"So am I, darlin'. And in the not-too-different future, I shall be here yet." There was a funny lisp to his words.

"You work here," she said, hopping onto a stool. "I'll have a tequila sunrise."

He mocked surprise.

"I'm into them lately. They have bite I can trust." With that she raised her eyebrows to communicate something to Uncle Bliss, something important for which she had no interest finding words. The things that were nice and easy could not be counted upon, but the hard, hurting things, why, they never changed, did they? They never stopped coming.

She watched him make her drink. His white short-sleeved shirt was wavy along its hem, not crisp as it should have been, and his hair was riding the bottom of his lobes. Bliss was always vigilant about haircuts, getting them before he really needed them and keeping his wispy blond bangs shorter than a man his size with a face that round ought to. But what concerned her—that was the feeling she seemed to be having—was that he was missing a couple of teeth, an incisor, plus one of the smaller of the molars to the south.

He set the drink elegantly before her atop an embossed cocktail pad, then braced both of his soft meaty hands on the bar and took a couple of shallow breaths. "So how are you, little sister?" The appellation had never made any sense to Shannon.

She shrugged off the question, not yet ready. "What are you doing behind the bar?"

He looked around as if he had just discovered himself there. "I fancy it," he said with a wink, leaning in and whispering, "faster access to local news."

"News."

A Cheshire grin eventually cowered her gaze. She took a sip of her drink and watched two thirty-something women glide across the parquet and out the big glass doors, obviously rich Inn guests with boyfriends or husbands off doing something rugged; weekend warriors up from LA. "Anyway, you did this to yourself."

"It was my selection, if that's what you mean."

She didn't know what to say. He sucked the toothless gap again, and she wondered if the change in his employment status had affected his health-care benefits, among them, dental insurance. "By the way, you've got a couple of bald tires," she said finally. "Maybe four."

"New shoes for the old girl. Top of my list."

He poured himself a drink, Scotch, which she'd never seen him do at work, and then he checked in on Mr. Nicely with a gentle double pat on the copper in front of him. Nicely tried to shake his head but it bobbled like one of those car toys instead. There was a tiny slick of drool out the corner of his mouth and an eye was wandering away from its mate, toward the overhead light fixture, something rustically elegant, of course, wrought iron and mica. "Yyyyou ever been to Loz-Angeleez?" he shouted down the bar at her. "I was in Loz-Angeleez. 1983. Angels, angels, angels." He trailed off into gibberish punctuated by cartoon gestures of grief, digging a fist into his eyes and burbling wet red lips.

Shannon decided not to hear and not to answer. Obviously something bad had happened to the journalist from Beantown.

"You don't like money and success?" she asked Bliss when he returned.

"Got enough."

"So you gave yourself a demotion."

"Yup."

She let out a stagy huff of incredulity, puffing out her lips. "Well, at least you are always original." The singsong in her voice bothered her; what was she so pissed about? He hadn't said no yet.

A group of regulars came in and while he sorted out their drinks and money, and they swapped corny ritualized greetings, she tried not to watch him. Every few minutes or so, he checked on Mr. Nicely, not to refresh his drink but just dropping in a few words, letting him know he hadn't been forgotten. If not for Mr. Nicely and what had happened to him, she would have brought up the Trust funds; Mr. Nicely and the couple with the calamari who were irritatingly public in their affections. Irritainment, the guys at work called it—annoying but you couldn't stop watching.

Bliss paused before her and again placed both of his hands on the rounded rim of the bar, drinking her in as he said her name, *Shannon*. She tipped her head to one side, conceding it was she, because he had said it in a pretty way, the name belonging to an earlier edition of herself, before her mother died, before the world stopped making a certain kind of sense. In the year following she had sunk into lots of NLB—nonlinear behavior—and then simply gone off-line, emotionally speaking. In the gray cubicles of Silicon Valley she had been able to live a life that was removed from life. Or at least that was the formulation Steinmetz seemed to be guiding her toward. What good were they anyway, emotions? Mainly, they slowed down the work.

750k was a lot of money but that was what she would need for the new company. She was twenty-eight and ready for the future, ready to grab it and run. Ready to keep keeping the past at bay and the present an endlessly loading screen of pop-ups and distractions.

The bar was filling and Bliss kept having to make drinks. She finished hers and slid a twenty across the copper. "Dinner guy's late tonight. Comes in at 6:00," he said, and slid the bill back toward her, making a dismissive face and sucking the gap where his lateral incisor had been.

She did want to know what had happened to his teeth and didn't want to embarrass him, but it was going to be hard to seem not to notice. "I'll meet you back at the cabin. You don't have to walk me out."

***

Pitted and calving at its margins, the one-lane driveway dropped west from the highway through a cool canopy of live oak and bay, made a gooseneck turn and came to its conclusion at the board-and-bat structure that had been Maggie Costa's refuge from the rat race of Palo Alto. Shannon grabbed her duffel from the backseat and went in. The cabin had never once been locked. The table was set for two with a faded red cotton cloth, paisley napkins—wrinkled and stained, but clean—and two new candles; there were pans on the propane stove ready for dinner, a bottle of Barolo on the plank counter, and an hors d'oeuvre dish of mixed nuts covered in cellophane. The open shelving held sundry items, from Blue Diamond matches to a porcelain ginger jar that had been her mother's, everything clean and neatly arranged. In spite of the patchwork exposure of his entire domestic needs, there was a stillness, a purity about the cabin. On the deck off the kitchen the view still caught her breath, the nearly vertical hillside pitching down to a sea that fit itself in and out, like puzzle pieces locking together. Here it seemed less like an edge, like a dangerous clash of opposites, than a consolation, one medium embracing another, land and sea in agreement. On the western edge of the deck nailed to the railing was the small metal sign she and her mother had purloined from the state beach when Shannon was eleven or twelve: *Never turn your back on the ocean.*

Shannon found his Swisher Sweets and smoked half of one, then went back in and poured herself some Scotch, two fingers, plus a cube. Afterward, she stood in the doorways of the small bedrooms, the one that had been hers with its faded blue and white sailboat quilt and the one that had been her mother's, a yellow ring quilt. Several pages from an Ansel Adams calendar were still thumbtacked to the wood walls, and so was the Matisse poster of the dancers hand-to-hand around a three-legged table. On the dresser Shannon's childhood, oblivious to time, carried on inside glossy black frames. She had been a cute kid, all cheeks and eyes, dark curls. The chin hadn't mattered then. The bedside table held a neat stack of books, hardcovers naturally, a brass lamp, and a pastel of Bliss and Maggie seated in front of the Nepenthe Phoenix. It had been done by one of the many amateur artists Big Sur harbored from the real world. The window faced the sea, hugely soft and blue, like something out of a good dream about the whole world. When the front door hinges sang their old three-note melody, in came Bliss, rocking painfully from one leg to the other. He saw her stalled in the doorway of her mother's old room and said, "Go in, go in."

"S'okay."

"*Go*," he said, motioning with his head, insisting.

So she stepped into the room for the first time since, and stretched out on top of the quilt, resting her head in the rich down pillow her mother would not do without, and looked through the window to the sea. It was a fine place to die after all. As fine as any.

Bliss fried up a plate of thinly sliced rounds of Yukon potatoes and set them aside on a blue Spode plate. When she was ready to talk she got up and propped herself inside the doorframe that separated the kitchen from the deck. The deck, the plunge down to the sea, had always been an intimate part of the life of the cabin. She listened to his rough breathing, the effort he had to make, moving, and saw that his brow was misted in sweat as he began to sauté four petite lamb chops, expensive and no doubt acquired from the Inn.

"I want to start a company."

"Grand," he said.

"Applications."

"Well, I don't know what those are," he shook his head apologetically, "but it sounds grand." His eyes he kept on the sauté pan.

"I'd like you to release funds from the Trust."

He flipped the chops, then messed up some rosemary sprigs into the browned sides of them.

"I know I'm not thirty yet; I know you don't legally have to, but I'm asking. That's all." It was hard to watch him, with her big wish hanging in the cramped space between them. She glanced away and read the sign on the deck again: *Never turn your back on the ocean.* The tide came in, waves, random big ones, and there was just the ocean too, the ocean itself, deep and cold with life and death. "750k," she added perilously, to get it all out and push it toward him across the cubicle kitchen. Now the only thing that separated Shannon from

Bliss was the wish, the desire. It was huge and ready, like something that needed to be lanced.

Bliss cracked open a mason jar of applesauce and held it under her nose. "Homemade," he said. "'M-boy."

That was when she knew that he would not release the funds.

"'M-boy," she said flatly. The plunging hillside had deepened into silhouette against a western sky bruising with the onrushing night. Somehow she had missed the sunset.

"You only have two years to go. Two years," he said, lifting his eyebrows wistfully. "Nothin'."

"Do you have any idea how long that is? In my field?"

"Have to confess I don't know much about your field t'all."

"No."

He shifted his gaze to her. "Maybe a little about life."

"Whose?"

Neither of them said a word as together they made the salad: watercress, goat cheese, piñon nuts, dried cranberries. Bliss was a graceful cook, the kind who paid attention to details, like salt-cellars and color combinations. His grace and its incongruence with the rough cabin, with his size in it, left her feeling even more apoplectic, as if an overfilled bubble inside her head was about to burst.

Finally he whistled softly. "That's a fair chunk of change, little sister."

"Forget it."

"No. I'm listening, I'm thinking."

"No you're not."

He came up to her and held his face about six inches from hers, so close that she could see the faint etchings in his lenses that circled round his blue eyes. He had poor vision and the lenses were thick and cloudy with grease, and his eyes really did look as though they were floating behind portholes. "Well, I did make promises to your mama and I aim to keep them if the gods let me."

"Things change, Bliss."

"Less than you think."

"But you know they do, they have. Right now, I could really make something, something big."

"Shannon, the Trust has rules, specific language."

"My welfare. You could do it under that clause, and you know it."

He handed the Barolo to her with a wine opener and she pressed the worm into the soft flesh of the cork, twisting quickly and decisively down, then she set the tooth and pulled up on the levered arm. It was the newer kind of cork, a composite, and the damn thing broke on her. She tossed it past him, into the corner. It had just missed his arm. On the second try she eased the remnant from the neck, wiped the rim with a napkin, and gave them each generous pours. Bliss didn't say anything about the cork on the floor, though she could feel it over there throughout dinner, pale and accusatory. He always kept the cabin so tidy.

After they had sat down, and he had raised his glass and said "Bon appetite," she cut herself a hunk of lamb, purposely too big and impolite, as if she were merely fueling up. The meat still in her mouth, she said, "So what happened to your teeth?"

For a moment or two he let her see how sad her question had made him. Then he abandoned that, and let her see the abandonment. "Oh, a year or so ago, couple of hooligans . . ."

"Hooligans? God, that's right out of the dark ages."

This time he did not smile. "The words change, Shannon, but not those things they are emblems of."

"Don't you get it, Uncle Bliss, time is running out." She slammed her fork onto the table. "People die, all the time. We're all dying! We're dying right now." Suddenly she was up, moving down the narrow hallway. There was no place she knew to go or wanted to go, except away from the table, so she simply hid in the bathroom until whatever had happened to her passed. It felt catastrophic. To make use of the time, to give herself cause, she changed her tampon, washed her hands, and checked her eyes in the mirror, hating the way they looked. She wasn't a child any longer; how was it that she couldn't seem to get that look out of her eyes?

***

The next morning the sky was gray, the color of concrete, the sea, too, like poured concrete, and between the two, insubstantial tatters of fog drifted up from the still surface of the water. She lay beneath the blue and white regatta of her sailboat quilt, not cold, not anything except lonesome, for what she couldn't say, not even to herself. Her room was on the east side of the cabin with a window that focused down the ridgeline where a three-part compost bin stood, followed by the garbage shed, and then the wild flora, the needle and oat grasses, foxtail, brome and mustard, outcroppings of sage in the sunniest barest spots, and finally the trunks of the stunted oak with their heavy, snaking limbs. Everything felt still, the only movement coming from the ground that was faintly huffing the heat it had held on to through the night. Then she saw Uncle Bliss out there. He was carrying a galvanized tub, the kind people used for keggers. It had been years since she'd been to the cabin, and she had forgotten the toilet routine: a steel tub lined with a plastic bag, the small bottle of lye, the clamped bin where he stored things until it was time to dispose of it all, usually twice a month. He would have seen her used tampons. He was making it fresh for the morning, for her.

At that moment she knew what it was she was missing: the time when all the love was there. The time when what she did didn't matter so much, so critically, because no matter what, all the love was there. Her mother was there and before that, a father from whom she had inherited her chin, some recognizable features. The solace of genes. He used to play her folk songs on the piano. He had been a nice man, limited but nice. For a while she had carried his name. And around their trinity, the whole Costa family, grandparents and grand uncles and aunts, and even faraway cousins who sent Christmas letters that didn't mean anything except that someone had taken the trouble to write out their names on an envelope. Someone had assumed they would care. What was left?

Through the single paned glass, quite clearly, she could hear Bliss talking pleasantly to himself.

Bliss was left. Bliss and the Family Trust.

***

"Why don't you and that girl of yours take a trip? Have some fun?"

"Izzy."

He stepped back and opened his hands. "Hey, I have no problem with that."

"Yeah, I know," she sighed.

"I'm for love. Only that."

"Right. Peace and love, love and peace."

"O-kay."

She delivered one of her concise smiles, on/off. "Okay."

He stood on the porch, she in the driveway, and again she saw the weight that he had lost, the sallow skin, the gaps in his mouth. He had already worked up a habit around the gaps, sucking as if there were trapped food, an obstinate seed forever there. Without looking at him, looking instead at the pea gravel between them, she said, "Just how sick are you?"

"Little sister," he said, swinging his big head side to side, "I am so sick that you are going to have to scoot on down here on a regular basis. And bring Miss Isabel, just in case there's a bride or two to give away."

Izzy. Really, Izzy didn't care about the new company. Only Shannon did. Work had become the default mode. "Uncle Bliss," was all she could think to say. And then, to save or shield herself, "You are going to think about it. Right? My company?"

"I will. If you think about easing up and having some fun. Stop running."

What Izzy wanted to do was go to Hawaii. She had never been. There were pools, she had said, with floating bars that you swam up to, and coral reefs in the lagoons, and pretty fish.

As usual, he was not giving her enough information. "How are you doing, really? I want to know."

There was no expression on his face except maybe the distant impression of something long decided upon, or laid to rest. He locked his hands behind his head. "One becomes accustomed to the civility of solitude."

***

On the drive up she decided not to think, to try not to think. She set the iPod on shuffle and let even the bad songs play through without skipping them so that she would not have to consider whether she liked or disliked them. She just didn't want to have to feel anything. Feelings called for decisions. They made you move through things that might hurt too much. With the advancing day the sky had brightened some, but it was still like concrete, heavy and impervious. Out beyond the pastures toward the naval facility at Point Sur the surf lines were almost indistinguishable from the vague movements of an ocean pausing between tides, between breaths, not quiescent but nearly so, the deep uncertainty visible as mere scribbles across the water's surface. When the road began to climb and twist and run along sheer edges, she caught up with a handful of cars trailing a motor home. Within a mile they bunched up practically bumper-to-bumper and she could see that it was the one from the day before, its back end plastered with the identifying platitudes. California vehicular code requires that drivers pull over if they are holding up five or more vehicles, but those Idaho plates meant that it was just as likely that they would do nothing for a while. Anyway, there weren't that many pullouts.

The Beemer had a standard transmission and the constant shifting up and down began to grate on her. Twenty-five miles at fifteen or twenty miles per hour. She did the math, then scanned the iPod for something slow, Ben Harper or John Mayer, maybe some Norah Jones, to help her settle down, chill out. There were four cars in front of her; opportunities to pass would probably never come. Behind her cars were accumulating. When the motor home went by a perfectly usable turnout, Shannon began to feel remotely peeved. Did these people ever look in their rearview mirror? Just one fucking peek behind? Were they oblivious or just flat-out rude? To make it worse, every time they came to a hill the beast let out a toxic cloud of diesel fumes that prompted frantic window lowering all down the line.

At the Bixby Creek Bridge, the car in front of her bailed into the viewpoint lot; that left three. Around the next bend, miraculously, another took the road down to Rocky Point; two. Her chances of passing had doubled. Mile after mile the motor home lumbered along at its stately pace, blissfully entitled, witless, seeing America at everyone's else's expense, holding up the world. Even the road straightening now and then did not inspire the driver of the motor home either to speed up or to slow so that at least a handful of cars might have been released from the creeping, twenty-six-mile-long chain gang it was creating.

Behind her, like dogs at bay, distant honking rose up in protest. If everyone honked all the way up to the wretched hulk, it might have worked. But somewhere along the chain, one car, then another wouldn't do it, and soon the honking subsided to random bellows of frustration. Presently she noticed a yellow car braiding its way up the column, passing on nearly blind curves, darting in and out. It had a scripted quality, like a line dance. On one of the straight sections, impressed by what she had become a part of, she counted the cars: thirty-two. He was almost halfway up the line. Now drivers were making room for him, easing over and urging him on, their agent of justice. Someone had to make a run for it, and this guy was willing to take the risks. Someone had to say *enough is enough*.

The motor home drove by another perfectly acceptable pull-out and Shannon's brain went dumb with anger. *Unbelievable.* She pinched the iPod into silence and lowered her window, inviting the air to cool her down. *Un-fucking-believable.* One hand gripping the wheel, the other thrashing down the gear shift, a perverse inspiration momentarily seized her: that the motor home not *ever* pull over, that some kind of mad purity of offense be achieved, a record set, that they would reach the Crossroads as one, hundreds of captives united for life, released into life.

In her rearview mirror she saw the yellow sports car, an older MG convertible, tuck in behind her. A gasp of triumph escaped her. Lifting her foot from the accelerator and grinding down to first, she waved him forward and he made the jump to the slot ahead of her. Her heart was pounding, as if it were she running for it: this guy was going to do it, he was going to make it out. He was not going to let this golden-geezer hold up his life, not one minute longer. She watched him maneuver around the last two cars until he was directly behind the motor home.

How controlling; how stubborn and controlling these people must be, how arrogant, to think that they should decide for all. By virtue of what? Being big and slow and old? Like Uncle Bliss, she thought, and immediately felt ashamed.

The MG was bouncing back and forth behind the motor home, jittering at every turn, waiting for the slimmest, death-defying chance to scurry out and pass. He would not be held hostage while some addle-headed retirees strung out on Paxil took in the scenery.

Finally he made his move, sprinting by the motor home and slipping in front of it and . . . stopping. Stopping completely. The motor home stopped, the two cars in front of Shannon stopped, she stopped, and in the rearview mirror, she watched everyone in the line simply come to a stop. The road had swung west toward the ocean and she and at least a dozen other cars had a clear view of the yellow MG and the motor home. It seemed very quiet in the world, in her head. The Beemer engine purred quietly along with the idling cars in front of and behind her. The honking had ceased altogether. A mood of expectancy sent a low charge through the scene, and even the onshore breeze had dropped and was quivering nervously among the blades of spring grass.

Ahead, the man in the yellow MG convertible climbed out of his car, not bothering with the door, and straightened into a tall figure as sharp and vertical as an exclamation mark. His pace was confident yet measured as he strode back to the motor home; he seemed to possess a plan. Apparently the driver of the motor home either already had his window open or he opened the window for the approaching driver. In any case, she saw the man from the MG reach in with his left hand and then immediately the right hand shot in, delivering (offstage) a single punch that bore the collected rage of every driver down the line. It was shocking. And silent . . . so silent. Like a strange vision in a strange and unsettling dream. And it was exactly what they all wanted to happen.

Shannon looked away, embarrassed. The words, *never turn your back on the ocean*, wandered across the empty sands of her mind. She thought about Mrs. Godsland letting the sea do her dirty work, and about Mauro, his hands bloody from the fish he was gutting, and then she looked back at the man from the yellow MG.

Just for an instant, he acknowledged the road south with its long idled procession of vehicles. The audience. It was all so silent, so formalized, like Kabuki theater. She almost expected him to cross his eyes and strike a pose. Then he climbed back in his car, started the engine, and drove away. The motor home did not follow. Slowly, eventually, one by one, every car passed it, the big, wounded monstrosity with its stickered back end and its undersized tires. When it was Shannon's turn, she couldn't help glancing sideways, but the driver and his companion had drawn back into the shadows.

She thought of Bliss and his missing teeth, standing there on the sidelines, heart and hands open, trying to be the soft place for her to fall into.

The cars along the road had stretched out and spaced themselves peacefully, each in its own moving world. Each heading homeward where someone might be waiting.

Maybe she would bring Izzy down the next time. Maybe that was what it was time to do.

TWINS

*W*hen you are a twin, the world is your sister. *Nina.*

Clair was the first out and the biggest, and so far as the doctor knew, the only one. But then came Nina and Nina did not come without a fight. There was a lot of blood, several transfusions, and it might be a certain unconscious resentment. Louise Bugato was not fond of surprises. She did not love easily, but once she did, she loved with a deep and durable promise. Her people were Bavarian, three generations in California, and they kept the transplant's loyalty to origins and its customs. Like her mother, Louise ran a tight ship. So: twins. And there was only one of everything back at the house and now a scramble of last-minute duplicate purchases had to be made and because it was September and picking season and Henry was needed in the fields, a nursemaid to help. But Henry was beside himself. Twins!

Nina . . . Nina was the prettiest, her features falling expertly into place, her demeanor calm and watchful, despite her embattled entry into the world. As the second born, born almost an hour after Clair, she was the perfected version, as if in that hour God had made quick amendments to His initial effort. Though they were fraternal twins and there were clearly two sacs, they looked so remarkably close to identical, yet not close enough, that the pediatrician began to talk about a new category of twins, near-identical twins, or half-identical, she had read about, the babies sharing 75 percent of the genetic inheritance. A tightly timed sequence of cellular events, the egg fertilized by two sperm, and then immediately, the egg dividing, not dying as it ought to have, and then two separate placentas, two babies, two lives bound forever by the thinnest of threads, infinitesimal timing.

They were warm-skinned babies with ginger tones in their dark hair, and as they grew and their hair thickened, sunlight made a game of spinning unexpected titian filaments. For a while Clair stayed the bigger of the two, but by the time they were three there was little difference in their height and weight. "Nina is catching up," their mother remarked to the pediatrician during a checkup.

"Well," said the doctor, reviewing the two charts, "it's not that. Clair has slowed down." And she showed the mother the graphs, Nina's growth rate angling up and Clair's beginning to flatten.

Mrs. Bugato smiled with cosmic satisfaction. "Twins . . . everything's got to be fair."

Nina was the prettiest but she was not the most loveable. She expected people to come to her, parents and friends, even the dogs, and whenever they did not it was as if an invisible emissary had carried instead a tiny somber weight to her shoulder so that by the time she was five, she seemed already to bear a grudge against the world. Her dark eyes acquired a look of wary calculation, and she developed a habit of asking questions to keep others from finding ways in, questions with answers that might go on a while and to which she paid only sideways attention. She seemed always to have a secret and she laughed at odd moments, and long after they had stopped being babies, for no apparent reason or gain, like a psychological non sequitur, her voice would climb and pinch into babyish inflections.

But Clair . . . Clair was *obvious*—running to her father when he came in from the cellar or the vineyards, or wrapping her arm around her mother's leg as if it were a pillar made for just that purpose, for hanging on to, or jumping in bed with her parents as soon as they awakened each morning. She was not exactly demanding, just so happy that they were there when she was there, great living comforting god-toys, happy that she belonged to them and to that mountaintop west of Napa Valley where patchwork vineyards fell from the summits in quilted folds and billows. Children seem to have no religion. Their parents are their religion and they are born zealots. Gods, sometimes monsters of God, but always godly.

Did she remember that Nina was still back in their shared bedroom, or notice that she was winning some unannounced competition? It came so easily to Clair, winning, that almost from the beginning, it felt entirely natural, like air to breathe and sleep when you were sleepy and food the instant an aimless pang of hunger quickened into something like anxiety. Would there be food? Of course there would be food. Food and comfort, victory and fellowship.

One morning she returned to their bedroom almost as soon as she had bolted from it. She felt uneasy. Suddenly it did not seem right that Nina never piled into their parents' bed each morning to jump about and hide under covers and generally demand the affection that a whole night away in sleep had rendered vaguely unreal and unreliable. Parental love. Nina was out of bed too, standing at the dresser, her back to the door. There was a knife in her hand, one of the harvest knives that were kept in a wooden box, its thin, sickle-shaped blade as shiny and lithe as a fingerling cutting through fast water. They were not supposed to play with the harvest knives, or even to enter the field house where the picking equipment and sulfur and other dangerous things were stored. Harvest knives were very small and very sharp, so that a good picker might reach up under the canopy of leaves with one hand to cup a bunch of grapes and with the other, and the slightest flick of his wrist, sever it from the vine. Any child could hold one in her hand, they were so light. But no child was supposed to.

Nina was cutting something into the top of the dresser. Clair came up behind her to inspect the carving, just a line of small o's, and then x's over them. Nina was not the artist that Clair was. She preferred to build things, like the boys down the road, with Erector Sets and Tinkertoys, not draw pictures or fashion things out of clay, and when it came to stories in books she was remarkably . . . *dumb* about why things happened the way they did. It was so surprising to Clair that she almost didn't believe it. But it hardly mattered anyway, because Nina had no interest in Clair's explanations. If it was something she didn't know, then it wasn't worth knowing.

"Nina?"

"What." There was nothing in her voice and that worried Clair. The skin under her arms began to tingle. There was no point in telling her sister that she would get into trouble.

"What are you doing?"

"Nothing. Thinking."

"What about?"

She shrugged. "Things."

Clair was trying to figure out how they would hide the o's and x's. Maybe they could put one of their mother's runners over the markings, or color them out with brown crayon. Burnt Sienna, that was the color she would choose. "Like what things?"

"None of your bee's wax."

"Why?"

Nina swung around. "Well," she said, her tone utterly different now, informative and friendly, "I have a thought and when I'm done having it I cross it out and have another. There are lots of thoughts.

Thoughts can't do anything bad. Uncle Sal told me. They're just bubbles in my head that pop."

This seemed so perfectly reasonable, or it was said in a way that implied that there was nothing *un*reasonable about it, that Clair said simply, "Oh." And then, after a pause, "Like what thoughts?"

Nina smiled brightly, and even to Clair at that young age, she saw how very pretty her sister was and felt proud, and maybe scared too. Her prettiness was a force in and of itself, apart from her, apart from the two of them together. "Like pierced ears. I was thinking about pierced ears."

Some of the girls who belonged to the Mexican pickers, girls their age and even younger, had pierced ears and in them wore the tiniest jewel studs—rubies and sapphires and emeralds. Clair had been longing for blue stars on her ears, and the girls had been after their mother to take them to the shop in town where it could be done. But Mrs. Bugato said not until they were at least eight, which was so far away that the girls knew it would never happen. She may as well have said when you're grown-up, which was also a faraway place that they would never get to go to, like the North Pole or Disneyland or Lake Berryessa.

"We have to wait," Clair said—it was a statement—running her fingertip along the crude line of x's.

"I don't see why."

"She said."

Nina gazed thoughtfully out the window. "If one of us has pierced ears she has to let the other one."

This was irrefutable logic, Clair knew. With twins everything had to be fair.

"I'll let you go first. I don't mind waiting a little," Nina added. Once again, this made sense to Clair: if Nina was going to get something out of it then there was really nothing left to question. And Nina possessed an uncanny talent for patience and timing. The whole deal suddenly acquired the weight of plausibility, and with that, broad permission. It was like going to the beach where the instant you set foot on the sand, customary rules no longer applied. You could take off your shoes and get wet and sandy, and run off, a long ways off, and throw things and dig up things, eat with your fingers and pee in the water.

Sometimes when things hurt, their mother put ice on it. And so Clair was told to fetch a tray of ice. Nina's thought was graduating into something more than a thought that she might think and then cross out. When she returned, Clair lay down with her head against the pillow, and Nina held cubes of ice to her ear lobes, one in front and one in back.

After a few minutes she said, "Now I'm going to make the hole for the post, so don't move." Clair watched her sister. There was a calm concentration about her face, an authority in the way her small pink lips tightened to the task. Nina was the meticulous one, her side of the room always tidy, her toys lined up like obedient soldiers awaiting instructions, her playtime plans premeditated and sequenced in a way that convinced Clair and their friends that she knew what she was doing and ought to be in charge, and so she was often in charge.

Clair felt something warm against her neck and it was running down, and she touched it and it was the brightest red blood, so much of it that Nina straightened, a strange look of surprise in her eyes, followed by something like fear and a smile that was . . . unsound. The smile seemed to be trying to undo what she had just done. She had the good sense to holler for her father, but it was Louise Bugato who came; then the great fuss of words, a towel pressed to Clair's ear, the flurried ride to the doctor's office down in St. Helena. The lobe was hanging by the last little bit of itself, and had to be stitched back to the rest of Clair's ear. The doctor positioned a green sheet over her face, and then folded back one corner by her ear, so that she could not see his expression or what he was doing, she could only hear the tools clinking softly in his hands and his breath coming and going in a series of sighs, breath that smelled vaguely swampy. "It's just a teaspoon of blood," he said several times, in between telling her how brave she was and what a fancy little scar she was going to have to brag about, and why—*really*—had she let her sister do this? Then in the car winding back up the mountain, her mother asking what could have *possessed* her.

After that, whenever she was nervous, Clair fingered the fine white scar as if it might offer up some truth she couldn't quite make out.

A winery with its own vineyards was a grand place for a child to grow up on. There was always something happening and plenty of people around, field workers and cellar workers, and then the monthly tastings with neighboring winemakers and their wives or husbands, the borrowing of equipment and picking crews, the barrel rackings, the bottle lines that arrived in a big white truck, the dark, high-shouldered bottles of Cabernet Sauvignon laid down and stacked in long low walls, and the moldy vinous smell of the caves dug into the hillsides. The Mayacamas Mountains were developing a style recognizably distinct from the valley wines where the soil and drainage and climate were different, loamy and deep. The soil on the western slopes was volcanic, porous with an orangey hue. It drained more readily and held fewer nutrients, so the vines had to compete. Competition was a good thing, Henry told them; the grape flavors were concentrated and the yields lower but the grapes more prized for their character and complexity. Their vineyards were above the fog line but not the frost, and their harvest always came later than the valley floor, later by two weeks, with maybe lower sugars but higher acids, and Cabs that were reticent, taking longer to age and open up, to give themselves over to the deep sensuality of their innate character.

It was the early seventies and subregional fraternities were beginning to form, terroir to terroir, microclimate to microclimate. Each growing area had its own problems and those problems were only just being sorted out and talked about. Bugato Vineyards were up on Spring Mountain, a twenty-minute drive from St. Helena. "Well, what are they doing over at Mt. Veeder? How is Mayacamas dealing with the high acids this year? The bunch rot? The hard tannins are shutting down the flavors ... how to soften them, reduce the aging time ..." Except for the wine judgings, the competition between the growing districts and the wineries was mostly collegial. In those days, putting Napa Valley on the international map was the primary objective, and whatever sibling rivalries there might have been were easily driven beneath this purpose. They were mostly small wineries often founded by people who had had earlier incarnations as lawyers, doctors, entrepreneurs. Henry Bugato had been a banker in San Francisco when he and his brother, Sal, a restaurant owner in the city, decided to buy fifty acres in the Mayacamas Mountains and plant grapes. The Bugatos were originally from southern Italy, and Henry's father, Mauro, never let them forget the wines of his homeland, Lacryma Christi from the slopes of Mt. Vesuvius, and the dark drama of Primitivo, the same but not quite the same as the Zinfandels of California.

Yes, a world of vineyards and wineries was a fine place to grow up in, where farmers were artists and artists rode tractors and the Paris newspapers complained about the California growers who never had to chaptalize and where you could drink the wines in half the time it took the wines of Bordeaux to mature; where the wines were big and ripe and dramatic, saying everything that the grape might say on its best day, in a perfect year. The French said, "La beauté du Diable"— the beauty of the Devil.

"What does that mean?" Clair asked her father.

"It means that something is too good to be true."

By the time they were six, the twins could use a corkscrew like master sommeliers.

They were always referred to as *the twins*—a singular entity that demanded a unified response. Everything had to be equal, everything had to be shared, and if something was not equal or not properly shared, it must be publicly officially evened out so that whoever was on the short end of the current negotiation would know that swift measures were being taken that would put things right. Their fancy clothes were the same, but different colors; their candlewick bedspreads identical; their doll cradles pink and white. For Christmas Clair was given Malibu Barbie while Nina received Busy Barbie; their wagons were respectively blue and red, as were their battery-powered toy VWs that terrorized the dogs. Stuffed animals might be different, but they had to be approximately the same size, and neither could have more than the other sister. Louise believed in chores, in being a "good citizen of the house," no matter their age—so the twins were assigned daily jobs that were theoretically equivalent in duration and effort.

One morning Clair was to dust the living room furniture and Nina told to water the potted plants on the patio. But Nina always seemed to take longer than anticipated, or she dillydallied, and then Clair might be told to help her, or even assigned a second chore to give Nina a chance to catch up. Clair could see her sister through the window aiming the hose into the air, or up at the wild doves that liked to nest in the wisteria vine trained along the eaves. Every now and then she might let the water find a potted lemon or the box of red geraniums under the big picture window, but when she caught Clair watching through the window, she shot the water at the glass and laughed at Clair's startled face.

Clair ran outside. "Why'd you do that?"

"You were watching me."

"So?"

"I don't like you watching. It's not nice." Nina's eyes never wavered; she said this as if everyone ought to know, and Clair immediately felt bad.

"Well I only want you to hurry up so we can go find Daddy and sit on the tractor."

"I don't like ugly people watching me."

"But we're the same."

Nina's lips thinned into something like a smile. The sun was behind her but Clair could see the stripe of white that was her teeth. "Not quite." Not quite was what everyone always said about them, *not quite* identical, a phrase that seemed to contain miles of difference that Nina regularly paced out and measured and enforced.

Clair glanced back at the window where the hose had sprayed. The force of the water had kicked up potting soil from the geranium box, so the glass was not only wet but spattered with bits of dirt and bark. "She's gonna be mad."

Nina stuck the hose in the next pot and casually said, "If you clean it, I'll do the watering. Then we can find Daddy."

So Clair cleaned the window with rags from under the kitchen sink, and soon enough the two girls made their way down the hill into the lower vineyard where their father was working. On the way, Nina took her sister's hand and Clair gave two skips, one for each of them. She was happy. Their baby brother had arrived that year, and his presence, along with their mother's preoccupation with him, had cinched the lines between the girls. Nina did not often take her hand. They were always together, but not quite. Some of their friends had made-up sisters or brothers who thought or did things, often things that might have gotten them into trouble, bad impulses or naughty behavior, like taking change from the coat pockets in the hall closet to buy candy from the Oakville grocery, so it was a great advantage, Clair decided, not having to imagine a sister who looked so much like you and who could be and act so contrarily. She already had one who was real. From the beginning Clair's job was plain: to be the good girl.

It was May, and the flowering vines were giving way to fruit set so that at the end of each slender shoot clusters of tight green buttons, the size of the smallest rounds of lead shot, had formed. The mustard weed made a yellow haze down the center of the rows, and in some of the wetter depressions were lingering patches of lime yellow oxalis. The wild marigolds took the margins; poppies and lupines grew here and there as reminders that it was still spring, and they were still king and queen of California wildflowers. Henry Bugato was bending over, inspecting a vine, his head half concealed beneath the canopy of grape leaves. Clair never noticed his skin, except when someone remarked upon it, a friend or an overheard adult, but that day beneath his straw hat, it was noticeably describing of her father. The amorphous areas of light and dark pigmentation that, to her, were like land and sea on maps, or good and bad, never seemed to bother him. She liked to trace her finger along the edges of one to the next, good to bad, land to sea, and he in turn tolerated her explorations. She was like a blind child learning the landscape of his face. They had even begun to name the light continents and the dark seas, to dream of journeys little girls might make one day. In spite of the pigmentation, he was a beautiful man with a quiet smile, never so big that you couldn't trust it, and never so restrained that you wondered about his true feelings; and his soft eyes, even if he had wanted, could not hide the simple native intelligence he brought to everything.

Clair ducked under the canopy and forced her father to regard her. "Hi," she chirped, and he let his fingers wander blindly to the tip of her nose, as though it were a pink grape.

"Almost ripe enough," he said, musing. "I just might have to sample this one, see how sweet it is."

She clapped her hand over her nose and peered up at him. The sunlight was coming through the brim of his straw hat in tiny diamonds, so that his pigmented face was twinkling with stars.

Straightening, he hoisted her up and swung her onto the tractor seat where Nina had already staked a claim. "Scootch," he told her.

Nina didn't budge. Instead, she asked him about the fruit set, the twins having already acquired all the lingo of making wine, and that led him away from the issue of sharing the tractor seat to harvest speculations, at least for a minute or two. But eventually he told her, "When you're big enough to take up the whole thing, you can have it. For now, share it with your sister."

"No," she said, looking determinedly ahead and gripping the steering wheel, as if she were driving it down the row. "No, no, no."

He smiled gently. "Nina for no. That's a word you use too well and too often, little one."

Clair did not want to get her sister into trouble. With their father they would never get into much trouble, not like with their mother, but as a rule she did not want their parents to take sides. Everything had to be fair, even when one of them was wrong. She squirmed out of his arms and wandered down the row, picking up dirt clods and tossing them at the trunks of the vines. She had wanted to sit in the tractor seat, she had been looking forward to it all morning, but it seemed more important to Nina, and anyway, there were other things she could do and maybe like just as well.

Released from his Solomonic duties, Henry followed the course he had already begun, stopping to check the occasional vine, cupping the green clusters, palming up the canopy of leaves to ensure that there was enough protection from the sun. By the time they reached the bottom of the row where the oak trees began, Clair had begun gathering wildflowers for the vase on the kitchen windowsill. She was enchanted by plants, plants of any kind, and she had a remarkable facility for remembering leaf configurations and the particular places where each green thing liked to grow, what it seemed to need from the little disk of world surrounding it.

Suddenly behind them Nina pushed the button that sent the wailing call of the tractor across the vineyard. Henry had had a horn installed that year, because of a nasty accident last season on one of the steeper slopes. The tractor had rolled, crushing a worker's leg, and he had lain there the better part of a morning, waiting for help.

Henry stopped, dropped both arms, slowly turned and pointed to the ground. Nina climbed down and tramped back up to the house. Clair watched her sister yank one of the clusters of baby grapes from a vine and toss it where her father would be sure to see it. Before that could happen, Clair would have to collect the cluster and throw it away.

Why didn't Nina care about making them mad? Why did nothing nice matter to her? She didn't even like being hugged; she was always watching from some corner, or acting like things didn't interest her. She was always up to some secret something.

Henry Bugato was a tall man, beautifully educated in Jesuit schools, then Carnegie Mellon, and possessed of a mannered, old-world bearing that he had deliberately adopted from his father, Mauro, to honor him. He never raised his voice, and it was well known among the workers that the angrier he was, the quieter he became, so that a whisper from Henry Bugato was as thunderous as a sonic boom. He had a mellifluous voice, the voice of a tenor who happened at the moment not to be singing but who kept the phrasing and syncopation of song. There was nothing nicer to Clair than late afternoons finding him in the barrel room with Eric, his assistant winemaker who lived in a cottage on the property with his wife, tasting from each barrel, and keeping up a running commentary on the developing wine while the assistant made notes in the cellar book. She could hear her father's voice long before she had sorted out where exactly he was, winding her way between the stacked barrels and puncheons, his voice a trail to treasure. For a child the barrel room was not a safe place to be, because what if there was an earthquake and one of the barrels came loose and rolled off and crushed her? So when she did find him, the first thing he did was to lift her up to safety, and then would come the gentle reprimand, "Clair, you'll end up flat as a flat worm," or "How will I find you when the barrels come tumbling down?"

But later that afternoon she did not go to find her father in the cellar room. Instead, their mother took them shopping for spring clothes. There were other winemakers coming to the house for a meeting, and Louise wanted to give them enough time without the Bugato offspring underfoot. Clair was in the dressing room, trying on birthday dresses, and it was Nina, not her mother, occupied with the fussing baby, who brought Clair things to try on—pastel dresses with lace and puffy underskirts. She was being so very nice to Clair, so attentive and motherly, calling her Clairsie and cocking her head like an eager and trusting puppy.

"But don't you want to try some on?" Clair asked when the last batch arrived.

"I'll pick what you pick," Nina said. So she was in a good mood; she wanted Clair to get something they might otherwise fight about.

"But a different color," Clair said, clutching the yellow one to her chest.

"I like the blue anyway."

"Okey-dokey."

"Hunky-dory."

"Peachy-keen."

"Holy-moly."

They laughed themselves into hiccups until the store clerk herded them out of the dressing room and back to their mother, who had finally managed to placate the baby. Nina stuck her fingers under his chin and tickled him so hard that he began to scream again while Clair pretended that it hadn't really happened. His name was Tony. So far as she could tell, he wasn't much fun yet, except that he did make goofy sounds with his lips and was crawling all over the place, like a piglet, and now and then she liked to imitate Tony, which got her mother's attention. For a while, she might even play along, pretending that Clair was still a baby too. Nina was especially scornful of this game, and usually had to leave the room whenever it began.

So the near-identical dresses were purchased, one yellow, one blue, and they went home. The meeting was just breaking up. Henry was loading the dishwasher with the wineglasses they had used to taste Cabs from the last vintage, and a dozen or so vintners were clogging the front hall, their faces rosy with alcohol and camaraderie. When they had finally left, the last one a little wonky on his feet and being towed off by another, the girls tried on their new birthday dresses for their father.

"Princess one, princess two," he declared and off they went while dinner was cooked.

Everyone was tired after dinner; everyone wanted the day to end. But it was a day that would never ever end. Not for Louise, not for Nina and Clair—it might have grayed and tattered and found some cubbyhole to fit itself into, wadded up in a drawer in the back closet of the mind where clothes you would no longer wear found refuge, former selves and unpleasant memories, things you ought never to have done or seen or tried. And not for Henry; not especially for Henry who didn't seem to have a drawer or a closet in the back room where no one ever went any more. For Henry, everything was eternally present, demanding the same accounting day after day, with the same results year after year.

The baby would now eat spaghetti, along with the rice and pureed fruits and vegetables Louise regularly prepared from scratch. Sitting in his highchair, he squeezed it up into his rubbery mouth, swallowing a tiny portion in a way that seemed purely accidental, then out it would come into his plastic pelican bib where Louise, practical about such things, would spoon it back up for a second ascent. The girls watched with fascination his happy barbarism, red sauce smeared across his face and one noodle clinging like a tracing of a future big smile from the corner of his mouth clear round to his ear.

"Anthony, old chap," Henry said, "you've disgraced yourself." Henry liked to address his new son in highbrow borrowings that seemed especially to please his wife as though she were solely responsible for introducing aristocracy into the House of Bugato.

Tony answered with something like a high-pitched extended *Ha*, and then broke into his version of song, his fist crammed into the corner of his mouth and a babbling repetitive eruption, *labba-labba-labba*. Nina egged him on and Clair collapsed in laughter, and then their mother said, "Enough," because she was exhausted, she said, and didn't "you girls" have anything better to do than to get the baby all charged up at the end of the day. A bath would calm him down. A warm bath always calmed him down.

"Go and fill the tub." Or had she said, "Go and fill his tub" or "the baby tub?" No one could remember. "I'll be along in a minute." Everyone remembered that. She was busy swabbing off the worst of the spaghetti and lifting Tony down into his walker chair, the one that he could maneuver by himself around the house, his fat little toes and feet slapping the hardwood and sending him wheeling about. Henry cleared the table and began emptying wineglasses out of the now-dry dishwasher so that he could refill it with the dinner plates. He held one of the glasses up to the light where it winked in flawless clarity back at him, and satisfied, hung it from the stemware rack. He had been meaning to set up a different water heating system for the house and winery, one that didn't have to be set so high, and that hadn't happened yet. In the meantime, the tanks had to be sterilized, the cement floors hosed down, the glasses washed free of residue. But he hadn't gotten around to it yet; he had been meaning to, he said later, but he hadn't gotten around to it. There was always so much to do at a winery.

Clair flounced down to her parents' bedroom where there was a full-length mirror, wanting to see all of herself in the new dress before having to take it off for bed. She could hear the water running in the hall bathroom and more distantly, her parents talking in the kitchen.

It took a long time for night to come to California, for the late afternoon yellows and pinks to withdraw from the sky, emitting what she imagined was a soft fizzling sound, and so even though it was late, the big window that took up the south wall of the bedroom was not black yet but the deepest peacock blue. So that was behind her, peacock blue. In the mirror her yellow dress was especially pretty, with the blue behind her. She remembers that, yellow and blue. And then going into her parents' bathroom to rummage through the caddy that held her mother's makeup, finding the lipstick, the orangey one, the one her mother wore to fancy dinner parties. Clair remembers running it back and forth across her lips, and before she left, studying a tampon from the box on the back of the toilet and thinking that it was some kind of fat straw and liking the crinkly sound of the paper, like wrapping paper, but also knowing somehow the way children do, that she should not ask her mother about it, that it was still too big a mystery, maybe a bad and dirty mystery, else why would live only in her mother's bathroom?

She could hear Tony's walker pinballing down the hall. The walls were scuffed with dashes and darts wherever he had run into them just above the baseboards, and Louise was already planning to repaint, once he was walking on his own. She liked to keep up with things, minor repairs and the like. Not a day went by that she wasn't deadheading flowers, or polishing a piece of silver she had inherited from her grandparents, or changing the hem on a skirt to keep up with fashion. Once a year she sorted through everyone's clothes, culling and bagging them for the Goodwill truck that parked down at the edge of town every weekend. Sometimes an item of clothing would go missing from Henry's side of the closet, last week a pair of brown cords she was famously tired of seeing him in, and he pretended to be angry and she pretended that she didn't know what had happened to them—the dryer ate things, like socks. "It does," Clair assured her father because she too had been missing one of her favorites, the sock with the ladybugs, though that had eventually turned up in Nina's drawer.

Behind Clair on her parents' bed was a pink duvet cover. Not candy pink, but cameo pink, faded and old-looking. So there was that color too—pink.

From the kitchen, the sound of a glass breaking. Her breath caught; someone would be in trouble. But no, her mother was laughing. Maybe they were kissing. Things were always happening when people kissed, glasses broke and stuff went unnoticed. The pantry door squeaked (he was going to fix that too), broken glass swept and rattled into the metal dustpan, voices, softer now, murmuring. The bath water still running. Tony singing his *labba-labba-labba* song, then one of his sudden *Ha*'s shot down the hall, and back to the *labba-labbas*. The walker charging another wall, plastic on sheetrock, *thwump*.

Now it really was getting dark and she decided to put on more lipstick and show herself off to Nina, but this time the lipstick broke. She had pressed too hard. Opening the window, she tossed the orange bullet out into the night. The crickets and tree frogs were so loud that she stood for a moment or two, just listening. They were ringing or singing or screaming at each other all at once, and it did not sound alive but like machinery gone haywire and sending up an alarm. The air smelled of wet dirt with something sweet but not nice-sweet on top, dying flowers, but it was too early for them to die so she didn't know what it was, she only knew that it was not a good smell, not a spring smell. Not far from the house stood four young redwood trees that her father had planted, the color disappeared from them now. They were just black cutouts with a gray lacy fringe along each bough, the four of them pointing straight up and keeping their line as they nailed themselves into the sky. Up in the sky, the stars were fizzy and bright. Something big flapped down from one of the tall Douglas firs that stood beyond the redwoods and she closed the window. An owl maybe.

And then there was a different screaming, singing, ringing, screaming, a crazy mad sound, the sound of air shattered and space wobbled and time stopped, especially in her head, and her ears hurting as she's running out of the wobbly room and down the hall where the steam is coming from, and then in the bathroom, through the steam, Nina, her hand or her hands on the faucet going one way, going the other way, and Tony's walker taking up the middle of the cramped room but Clair does get past it, does see what's in the tub, it's just the color red, that's all, the most amazing red bubble puddles, small ones and big ones with streaks swirling curling feathering off. Her father is behind her now slamming into the walker, into her, and she feels the water splashing, hot water, and it seems he has Tony in his arms, but it's not Tony, it's something lumpy and red with peels of pink coming off. Behind him now her mother with her arms empty and strange and shaking down to fingertips, and her eyes as black as the trees that were already nailing themselves into the night.

Yellow, blue, orange, pink, black . . . *red*. Red was the memory of that night, the color that took over all the other colors.

Before they fled with Tony, Louise glanced with a look of horror and confusion at Clair, at the lipstick gashed across her mouth. "I don't understand." That was all she said. *I don't understand.*

They only had to eat one of Eric's wife's meals, instant oatmeal, not the cooked kind their mother made in a pot on the stove, that took so long and held its shape even with milk cratered around it. Susan was her name. She was pregnant. Susan wouldn't look at either one of them, but the next day it was only Nina she wouldn't look at. By late morning they heard tires crunching through the pea gravel, two car doors, then the front door opening, voices in the entryway, Susan saying, "Oh god!" and not long after there was the sound of the front door opening and quietly closing again. The girls were sitting on the floor of their bedroom playing a board game, Chutes & Ladders. Nina looked up. "Hi," she said. Someone passed, no one answered.

Soon their mother called them to the kitchen and set two plates with grilled cheese sandwiches before them, two glasses of milk, fruit salad in a big bowl. Much too much fruit salad for two girls, enough fruit salad for all the children of the world. How long had she stood there, peeling and slicing and chopping up fruit, her hands trembling, her hair uncombed, a runaway look in her eyes? After she had put the food down she straightened and paused and smoothed down her apron, the way a waitress does after she's delivered the order to the table and asks *Do you have everything you need?* They didn't see her for three days. She had done her duty and was released now to flee into the shelter of madness.

All that first day Henry kept them with him wherever he went, into the vineyards, the winery office, the caves where he inspected ullages on the older vintages, one bottle at a time, but he didn't seem to be paying much attention because the ones with low fills went right back where they had been in the rack with the others that were not flawed. Two sheriff's cars came up the drive and not long after they left, the cleaning lady's Honda showed up though she had already been to the house that week. Finally Henry walked them up through the vineyards and around the courtyard to the kitchen door, stooping to brush his fingers across the oregano and thyme growing between the cobbles and stopping again at the door as if an invisible beast had knocked the wind out of him for a minute, and he stood there, staggered, his right hand gripping the frame, unwilling to reach for the doorknob. At the stove he heated up a can of alphabet soup, keeping his back to the twins until it was time to serve the bowls, the crackers, the glasses of milk for them and wine for himself, no food. It was nothing like dinners their mother prepared and so in that respect, more fun, like camping, or like the times when the babysitter cooked and then let them eat more than the allowable number of cookies.

In his quietest, gentlest voice he said, "It's time for you girls to say now what happened."

"Where's Tony?" Nina asked.

Clair said, "The water was red."

Henry winced. "Before that."

Nina had just spooned up some soup and was blowing across it. "It was too hot." And then after slurping the soup into her mouth, "Mama said to fill the tub."

"Too hot," Henry said to himself.

Nina nodded.

"But you were helping your mama."

Clair fiddled with her spoon. Nina stared across the table at her father. Finally she nodded.

"She was trying to help," Clair said with a rush of encouragement as if this was the way out of all of it, out of the dark spell that had taken over their family, the spell of silence, of strange people coming and going, of nothing being paid the old kind of attention.

Her father was looking at her with sudden alertness. The pale parts of his skin were pinking and the dark patches were the color of grapes. "Where were you?"

"In your room . . . mostly. I wanted to see my dress in the big mirror."

He dropped his head. "Lipstick . . ." he said to the floor.

"It broke. I'm sorry. Will you tell Mama I'm sorry?"

"She doesn't care about lipstick. Who gives a . . . a tinker's damn about lipstick, Clair? Why would anyone care about lipstick?"

"But I'm sorry."

Now he turned to Nina. "Nina, what about the little tub, Tony's tub? Why did you let the water fill the whole tub? How did you lift Tony into the tub? How did you do that all by yourself? Clair didn't help you?"

"I don't need Clair's help. I don't need anybody's help."

His twin hands had been folded in a calm affectionate bundle on the table, but now he pulled them apart and lay them very carefully, as if they were breakable or hurt or in need of a time-out, palms down and fingers splinted straight out, each one separately on top of each thigh. Nina was intent on spelling out her name with the alphabet noodles, assembling the letters beside her bowl, then swimming her spoon through the soup for the next letter. It was only the A she needed now. "Is that why you didn't wait for your mother?" he asked, trying to corner her eyes. She was still fishing for the A in the yellowy depths of the soup.

"Sure."

"Sure?"

"Yeah, sure."

"But is that why?"

"Is what why?"

Something flashed across his face, a shadow, and Clair thought of the owl from the night before, the shadow of its great wings against the shadow of the night.

Henry whispered, "How did you get his clothes off?"

Nina glanced up brightly. She had captured the A now; it was floating all by itself in the hollow of the spoon. "Oh, they came right off. The diaper too."

Clair was watching her sister, her eyes so sparkly, so pretty, so proud. She had the purest features, like a doll's. Nina placed the A at the end of her name and, using the edge of the spoon, neatened up the letters.

"It wasn't poopy," she added, as if, had it been, she might have waited for her mother. And nothing bad would have happened.

Slowly Henry rolled his head back and forth, his eyes closed and the eyeballs bulging behind the lids. He took a sip of wine and set the glass carefully back down, then he decided to take another longer drink, then he just ran his thumb back and forth along the bottom edge of the glass, faster and faster. Over the counter the clock was ticking and outside Clair could hear the crickets and the frogs setting up their alarm, and down the hall, the loud and forbidding silence of her parents' bedroom door shut all day was booming up from the depths, from the dark earth underneath their house clear up to the base of her throat and filling it with a hard hollow shape as big as a walnut.

"Is Tony okay?" she said. All day she had been afraid to ask and Nina had seemed strangely uninterested. But everything had happened so fast that hardly anything seemed to have happened, or could possibly have happened enough to be real and bother any of them, so why *should* Nina wonder?

"Tony?" His lips moved in a strange unbidden way. "Tony is gone. Anthony Mauro Bugato," he said, reeling out the words as if he were introducing a character in what was now a storybook, a little prince, a perfect boy. His voice was very soft, very beautiful, a trilling, a little song of sounds, but Clair heard too something like astonishment. "My boy is gone."

For a long while no one said anything. Henry poured himself more wine and the girls ate their soup and the clock kept ticking slow unwilling ticks and out the window it sounded like a jungle with the tree frogs and crickets and the piercing cry of a single screech owl and then Boomer, one of the winery dogs, giving voice. The indoor silence grew bigger.

Full of twitches and worries, her lower lip quivering, Nina's face was not looking like her face. "Daddy?" she said.

"What?" He did not lift his eyes from the table, but then, as if finally he had to, as if there was another father in the room even bigger and older than he himself telling him to, he drew his head up and regarded her with spent indifference. "What is it you want to say? Nina." Adding her name did something, broke something—the silence, the spell, the ticking clock.

"Nothing."

"Nothing?"

"Nothing. I . . . I spelled my name," she said as if in afterthought.

Henry rose from the table, gathering their dishes, and when his back was turned, Nina used her spoon to smash the letters she had taken such pains to align, and her face had gone back to the way it usually was, pure and untouched.

THE BOAT ON THE LAKE

*A*ll day they watched the boat on the lake. There were no waves, no breeze to make them. The day possessed an ambiguous calm owing, they decided, to the midsummer heat. Yet the boat, distant and masterless, fared ever south and east, moving on the deep unseen currents that recognized no master, no source, no justification but that of existing somehow below the surface. A glacier had cut the lake from granite, and so whatever force of configuration there was down below had been there a long, long time.

From Bill's room, which afforded the best view of the lake, the boys monitored the boat with binoculars, leaving and returning to the window as other distractions failed and they were thrown back upon the One distraction. Was there a body in it? A cache of treasure? A picnic, Miriam, their mother, guessed, the boat having somehow escaped its former occupants as they waded ashore onto some tree-dense thrust of land. The picnic was the least attractive of the theories. And anyway, it was morning when they had spotted it, too early for a picnic.

Miriam came and went too, mostly for Bill, but also to assess the boat's progress down-lake because, by late afternoon, it had acquired the status of a lost and mysterious living thing.

"You boys there, get out now," Bill said.

"But why, Father?" It was Bryce, the older of the two, the first to ask why, the one who could stand the greater uncertainty all questions inevitably awakened.

"Butternut bread, that's why."

The younger one, his eyes flashing, twisted to look over his shoulder toward the bed. "That's not a real reason."

"It's the only one I need. Now get out."

Just then their mother appeared in the doorway. "Boys," she said, all the tenderness of the ages in her voice.

"But Mama . . ."

And so they left.

She went to her husband bearing efficiency in her hands now, folding back the linens and dressing his bedsores as she did every day at that same hour. It was why he had sent his sons away. He let out the occasional moan, or he used his name for her in warning—*Mimi*. One sore had developed within a patch of the shingles where even the movement of air across the rash ignited the nerve endings. When she had finished, he tossed up his chin in challenge. "Why do they call you Mama and me Father? Have I been all that remote?" He was still breathing hard from the pain of her cleaning him.

"Yes," she said without elaboration.

They had known the answer, each of them. The question was not seeking an answer, only the intimacy found in reciting aloud what they both knew. They had reached that stage in their marriage and in the third year of his disease where the things that were said were often said in ritual, though lately she did not always supply the customary response to his prompt. The old sentences were making her sad. And he had been too sick to do anything that might have made new ones. His face had lost its color, was as hueless as tallow, or as the dusk of an already clouded day. She could not say exactly when the dusk had descended but she knew it would be dark soon. Pain, she thought, not unaware of the ongoing generosity in the thought that let him off the hook, for now there were thoughts that kept watch over other thoughts, until it seemed there were no longer any thoughts at liberty in her mind. They had been careful years, these three. Filled with care.

Piero arrived only minutes before the boat did. *Piero*, she said to herself, keeping sight of him as he came down the path through the ferns, light on his feet and fast, a duffel slung over one shoulder. Something was crowding up her throat—maybe gratitude, for she had asked and he had come, or maybe only the ache lying just beneath every act of kindness—and she had to look away. We can be good, she thought, we humans.

They had been waiting on the beach, Miriam with the boys, when here he came in white shorts, elegantly boyish. There was some sort of random stitching and gathering along the outside seams that reminded her of parachutes, nothing straightforward about them except the color. Designer shorts from Milano. Piero was forty-two, almost accidentally rich, and au courant, but only because, in his international world, such a state of affairs was unavoidable.

By then Miriam had been carried away by the boys and their imaginings, and she would not let them wade out to meet the boat, just in case there *was* a body. All things loose on the lake ended up in the sandy shoals of the southeast cove, unless captured along the way by someone else. Bolton's Beach as it was known by the locals. It was the Bolton cottage that they had rented these last three summers, to cheer Bill up, to get him out of the city heat. To cheer them all up.

Instantly, Piero was charged with intercepting the boat, the water lapping up over the waistband of his shorts and his soft Italian eyes widening with horror to goad his two nephews onshore, upping and downing on the soles of their feet and straining to see over the gunnels, their cheeks pinked in the late-afternoon humidity that had gathered in on them, heavy and expectant, like a mood, like an aimless and sullen throng. But the corpse for which they had half yearned throughout that long hot day was not there. A painter trailed alluringly in the water, and Piero took hold of it and towed the boat in to shore, the narrow hull rising and dipping as if on rough water, resisting capture, until the sand grasped it with a *shush* of earthly reassurance, now that the day's journey had at last come to an end.

It was some kind of dory, fifteen, sixteen feet long with a modified transom that could support a small outboard. Once, in more recent times, it had meant to be green, but the paint was peeling down to an older white here and there, and then beneath the white along the gunnels and ribs and the aft edges of the thwarts where a rower's legs must have rubbed was the final gray of the wood itself. Why did all things end in gray, she thought. Piero reached in and retrieved a stiffened pair of leather gloves whose size did not betray the owner's gender, not so big, not so small. There was also a peavey, the long wooden pole with a metal hook and spike at its end that loggers used to maneuver timber. She'd seen Emory with one down at the landing where trucks sometimes loaded pulpwood that loggers had driven in from their wood lots. The anchor was attached to a coil of braided yellow nylon, the cheapest of line; two oars still rested in the open hands of their locks, each blade stowed along a side; and there was a plastic cider jug reused for drinking water. It was a poor village, except in summer; everything was reused for something else, and then something else again. About the boat there was no odor of fish, no evidence of fishing whatsoever. Sometimes metal brackets were screwed to the gunnels in order that a lone fisherman might prop several rods—in a lake as long and deep as this one, where the lakers stayed down in the colder water during the summer months and the rainbows fed from surface to bottom, trolling was popular—but there were no brackets. Around the stern there was not a single oil or gasoline stain, and no splintering where an outboard might have chewed away at the transom. In all, something strange and virginal enveloped the boat, as if, though it had been clearly used, it had not been used in any of the usual ways. This in itself sent Miriam's heart toward it. She wondered if something had happened to it, something unforgivable.

"It hasn't a name," Miriam remarked, running a hand along the narrow prow, trailing her fingers across the starboard planks where a name might have been painted.

"Buck!" William shouted. He was practically incapable of not shouting, a childhood mannerism that grated on his father. "Let's call it Buck for the way it bucks in the water."

"Not ours to name," Bill said. He had made his way on his walker to the open window, and for Miriam, his cool toneless voice had the effect somehow of tripping up the moment. The moment when the boat had come to them freely, of its own accord.

Piero raised his hand in greeting. "Billy," he called up cheerfully. "*Come stai?*"

The sick man nodded once and turned away. "*Abbastanza bene.*" After that he did not bother with lies of courtesy.

Bryce was telling his brother, "It's a girl. All boats are girls."

The next morning Piero fixed notices to the village market board, the town clerk's wall, and the post office door. But until someone claimed it, the boat belonged to the Cappellettis, and the boys seized it wholeheartedly. It was theirs now and could belong to no other.

In honor of the boat and Piero's arrival, they planned a picnic. Miriam called Emory and, knowing that he would show up almost immediately, she had everything waiting on the porch, even Bill's thermos of gin martini. Emory and Miriam were exactly the same age, forty-seven, and having little else in common she made an effort to mention old popular songs that they would both know, to rouse conversation during the long drives to and from the airport, or whenever he came to help her with heavier chores; or, in the previous two years when there was still some hope, Emory would come to help get Bill in the car for trips to the hospital and doctor's appointments; for the tests, most of them inconclusive, for the plasmapheresis that had done nothing but gobble up four hours each visit in the jumbo vinyl seats populating such rooms for such endgame antics, as Bill sourly referred to them.

Emory was a broth of a fellow, impossibly shy, his hands always stealing into his pockets, his head slinging sideways whenever it was time to name a fee for his various services, his thick curly hair long to his shoulder not for any reason other than that he hadn't had time to get it cut. As one of only two village handymen, he was always busy, *right out straight*, but never too busy to help Miriam Cappelletti. What was she doing with him, he heard himself pondering more than once. Locals did not think, they pondered on things.

Piero came up behind her as she watched the pickup roll across the gravel, Emory climbing down from the truck with an awkward air of apology, as if he might be intruding. He was always embarrassed around the summer folk; they knew so little about so much.

"That's a shaggy fellow," Piero remarked quietly. "Right out of *Braveheart*."

She gave a little laugh. "Yes. He reminds me of those Highland cows past the village. Quiet and strong."

"And primitive."

"Emory's a prince."

"A prince to you is a prince indeed," he said, now leery of the man.

Piero had been away too long. He could have come up on that last trip to New York, but Bill was such a *figlio di puttana*, such a bloody bastard, and Piero was sick of being cowed. Cowed, he thought—*perfect*. Why was it that he had had to pay the price all these years for Babbo's affections? His stubbed toe, as the Americans said.

Emory mounted the porch steps, in passing indicating his hello—it was never quite clear how—and then headed up the old narrow stairwell to the second floor and Bill's room. Once Bill had been a solid man, never heavy but certainly ample, with an assertive chest that suited his work as a criminal attorney, and then later as first assistant to the General Council, State of Massachusetts. But now Emory carried him without trouble to the waiting boat where, in the bow, a king's throne had been fashioned from the cushion of a chaise longue, with throw pillows for side support and rolled beach towels for padding here and there, and finally, after he had been placed on the throne, a blanket despite the relentless heat and humidity. "Christ, Emory, Jesus H. Christ," Bill had said as they were descending the stairs. There were more invectives, guttural and yet accepting, against which Miriam had learned to cauterize her heart. Bill had always been a difficult man, more difficult with increasing status and age, but in commerce with what he jokingly regarded as minions, he played the munificent, cantankerous squire.

Piero squeezed her shoulder and she brought her hand up to acknowledge her brother-in-law before following Emory out with the picnic things. The sand was soft and grainy and tea-warm where waves had lapped in and soaked down, and then brought up to temperature in the summer's heat. William poured his little body over the gunnels, then Piero with Bryce, twelve years strong, shoved the dory out into the cove. Moments later as the boat rocked with their suddenly acquired weight, Bill squeezed his eyes against the pain, but once they were rowing smoothly and evenly out toward the main body of the lake, he seemed to relax.

Miriam sat facing her husband in the bow. Piero was behind her, facing the stern where the two boys were busy jointing and rigging their rods.

"Como," Bill grunted to his younger brother.

Piero smiled broadly. "And Babbo bellowing from shore."

"That's what he did. He bellowed," Bill said. "Fine man that he was. Incurable swordsman," he winked tiredly, accusingly, "but Pops was a fine old Dago. Fine old swordsman."

Rights of primogeniture were in full force between the Cappelletti half brothers, Bill's mother, the American girl from Beacon Hill, and Piero's, the first love from back home, but the second married. Thus the argument had been rendered equally unwinnable and unloseable.

"What was it," Piero asked, "that he was always bellowing about?" He kept rowing, tilting forward and back with each pull, the water plashing softly as the blades caught and cut down, his rate so measured and slow and the air so heavy with moisture that the bugs kept up with them until a breeze off the point sent them away.

"He was sure I was trying to drown you out there."

"Weren't you?"

Bill closed his eyes, remembering those July days on Lake Como in Italy when the boys got to be together, when the two mothers annually recognized the importance of family and set aside geography and lost battles and lost husbands. "Of course. What the hell did I need with a little shit like you in my life?" Bill was struggling against one of the pillow props and Miriam reached to make the adjustment he needed. He was looking into her eyes when he drew a labored breath and said, "Little shits, that's what I'm left with. That's what I'm leaving."

Side by side on the stern thwart, the boys dropped their lines. Like Piero, they had their backs to Bill.

"Did you use a *piombo*?" Piero asked.

The younger boy did not turn around. "A what?"

"A weight. A bit of lead to take it down."

Then William's quick terrier eyes were on him, so alert, so charming, so indifferent. "I've fished before," he said.

His uncle only smiled.

William made a great show of spinning the reel and letting out line, sending his lure deep, tugging against the water's pull as if he might have a great fish on the end. But Bryce simply trailed the neon-colored lure along the water, watching it spin and waggle, knowing that nothing could be caught trolling at the uneven pace their new boat must submit to, because of his father's illness. So many things had to submit to so many other things, because of his father's illness. He did not bother to tell his brother, three years younger and still sure of himself, that trolling required the monotony of a motor.

Past the point, they tacked north into the breeze and headed up the lake, staying close to shore so that they could tour the other cottages and their docks, the canoes and kayaks and sunfish lying like giant beached fish. Miriam, the only member of the party who could see where they were going, said "raft" whenever they approached one, and then Piero would give the left oar a long deep pull and send them farther out, away from the anchored floats. Some of them were empty, some supporting a congress of gulls, but others were swarming with kids diving and clambering back up, or draped with teenaged sunbathers engaged in the logistics of lust. Only the older people relaxing in Adirondack chairs onshore raised a hand as they glided past. The Cappellettis did not really know any of their summer neighbors. The disease had isolated them, and they had had no boat to get around the lake in. It was a quiet family lake, waterskiing and the like not permitted, and to reduce pollution, no two-stroke engines. One of Bill's colleagues had suggested it during that last conversation when phrases like "no longer appropriate" and "this time with family" had dubbed in for the usual, neutrally empty, legal commerce. His time had become *this* time, with all the specificity of an end in sight.

At last they came to the brook that spilled out of the woods. There was a rocky swath of beach along one shore and a shelf of shallow sand and mud lake bed to the south where the brook had delivered enough silt to form a small lopsided delta. This was the largest of the lake's four inlets. Piero eased the dory up the brook a dozen yards or so, grounding her with a gentleness that even his brother could not fault. *Dolcemente*, Piero was thinking, *dolcemente* . . .

William was reeling in, the tip of the rod bobbing as if something were indeed on his line. "I've got something," he shouted. "I've got a fish. It's a fish!"

His father snorted. "You've got a load of milfoil."

"There isn't any milfoil in this lake," Bryce said informatively. Bryce was the thoughtful one, prone to convictions and rituals only he and his mother could appreciate. They were alike, just as William and his namesake were.

"Let's see then," Bill said.

But Bryce insisted. "There are people at the boat launch, they take turns checking out boats. The bottoms and the propellers. You can't put your boat in if there's anything on them. I watched them one day. They were very careful."

"We're all careful," Bill said. "What good does it do?"

"They do check the boats," Miriam offered.

Bill was studying his brother as he lifted out the canvas bags that Miriam had packed with lunch. "Something always manages to sneak in."

It wasn't a load of milfoil, but it was a knot of reeds that, in their similarity of appearance, seemed to portend milfoil, and then would come zebra mussels, and slowly the lake would die. It was the way of things, to let fear hew out a path into fear's reality. In short order you found yourself standing in the country of fear itself.

Sitting onshore, the boys consumed their sandwiches. Miriam and Piero took the thwart facing Bill. It would have been too difficult getting him off his throne to the beach. Bill was taking regular doses of OxyContin, synthetic morphine. When he asked for a second martini, Piero rummaged through the small ice chest for the thermos and no one said anything.

Finally Bill asked, "Can you smell it?"

Miriam stared at him.

"They say dogs can smell it coming."

Piero shifted his weight. He had a habit of touching his fingers to his thumbs whenever he was especially pensive, or a little nervous, occasionally rolling one or the other and signing a private O of wonder. "Billy . . ."

"Two martinis and no one peeps. Amazing." He gazed off across the water. A sudden breeze had sharpened the ripples to thin blue blades chopping shoreward. "*I like a martini*," he said, "*two at the most; three I'm under the table; four I'm under the host.*"

"It's a picnic," Miriam sighed. "No rules today. That's all."

"Dorothy Parker. Funny broad." He held out his plastic cup. His hand was shaking so badly that Miriam had to grasp it as Piero refilled.

"Let's talk about Como," Piero suggested.

"Let's not." Bill brought his other hand up to steady the cup as he carried it to his lips, pursed and quivering, until the rim reached him, then his eyelids dropped as the chilled liquid found its way in. His hair was greasy, his skin glazed in the heat, but when he opened his eyes a cool assessing formality had settled about them. "You two make a nice couple."

"Don't," she said. "Please."

He asked for another egg-salad sandwich. Several weeks earlier he had announced that he would stop eating, starving to death being preferable to letting the damned thing run him down. At least he would have retained some control, some say in the matter. But now the disease was taking him faster than starvation could erode what was left of his body, so there was no point to be made. It was the first time in his adult life that he was not master of his world. Except for those earliest months with Mimi.

They had met at a party, a fund-raiser. He had been the one not trying to talk to her and that proved, apparently, enchanting—or at least a point of curiosity. Any girl who liked him for his worst traits was a good bet with a long payout.

"Let's play hooky," she said, taking his arm. And off they went not to a fine restaurant but to an all-night deli for liverwurst sandwiches and then an hour south to Buzzards Bay because what she wanted to do was to feel the wind come off the sea without the world pressing in around it, mixing things up, confounding all that was clean and purposeful and straight. They were funny words to say on a first date. She had always been a funny girl, too serious for her own good, but yes, funny in a way that now and then made his chest hurt.

The boys were thigh-deep in the water, having discovered three feet below the surface a school of perch nosing into the brook water as it entered the lake. Carefully, so as not to disturb the dory, Miriam climbed out and joined them. The brown strokes of life shuddered and tightened and held into the current. They were so pretty in their random order, each one shaped like a small extended hand and all the hands keeping together, all of them somehow unanimous. In a moment of joy, she scooped up a flume of water and splashed her sons. A fight ensured. The silt was deep and soft, the three of them chasing and staggering in the shallows, Piero laughing in that single-hearted way of his and even Bill looking over from his makeshift throne with imperial indulgence. Miriam had always been athletic, and the two brothers, briefly united by the happy spectacle, watched her sleek calves glistening as they disappeared in and out of the water, the tie of her halter top flapping at the nape of her neck, like the wings of a white bird just learning to fly, and her big smile seeming to gulp all of it in, her sons, her husband, her brother-in-law, the perch, the blue water, the air soft with moisture, the sun above beaming down on Miriam's world. William was just about to catch her when she said quietly, "Oh," and fell sideways. They could see her foot, her two hands around the ankle, the rest of her sinking in the shoals, her head coming up, and in the pale arch of her foot the blood fast and pinking as the water drained with it, and then in the long instant she kept it from the water, the flow a bright ribbon of red.

Piero and Bryce had hold of her under the arms and were dragging her to shore. She kept the foot up, out of the water, and used the good one to help them. William never moved. He had dropped his arms and was simply standing in the water up to his knees, scowling with worry because his mother was hurt and now who would take care of him, then scowling because the game was over and he felt cheated, which was safer and easier than worrying about his mother.

"What was it?" Piero said, trying to see the wound through the blood, using his thumb to wipe it away.

"I don't know. It was so sharp I hardly felt it. It was very sharp," she added, feeling a little afraid now because she had not really experienced any pain, only the knowledge of damage. "Like a knife. I could feel it go a long ways in."

Bill said, "Here," and tossed one of the towels that she had made into padding for him. There was something in his voice, anger or disappointment, that he made no effort to conceal. He needed her whole, but not so that she could take care of him. Any hired nurse could do that. No, he had never really believed in the world until he met Mimi. He did not believe in it yet, and at the rate he was going, probably never would. But with Mimi around, there was always some doubt. Sometimes when she entered a room and smiled that smile of hers, that big open smile she let loose like a friendly dog, it almost seemed that all was right with the world, that he had been mercifully wrong and it was okay to care. It was safe. And there would be no foolishness or shame in it.

Piero wrapped her foot tightly and with Bryce again, helped her limp to the dory.

There was that winter when Bill and Mimi had been cross-country skiing in Vermont. The night before had brought a hard blow from the north, ice and snow. They had come upon a birch bowed to within five feet of the snowy land, and Miriam had set about trying to rescue it, using her ski pole to knock off the mantle of wet snow clinging to the north side of the tree, and then pausing to watch it inch upward, measuring her height against it as it slowly lifted its ivory arm back into the air. But beneath the snow there was still a coating of ice, and Mimi had gone the next morning with a chisel to break it off. "It'll take a while to stand up," she informed Bill back at the cabin. Her confidence was so disarming that he hadn't known what to say, and so had simply watched her as she removed her knitted cap and shook out her long blond hair. In the bright morning light it was almost the same color as the birch. At the end of their week while she was packing up their things, Bill had skied over to the meadow where the birch had almost lain down. He had meant to report to her that it was standing once again. And that was just what he told her.

A doctor from the next village gave her a tetanus shot, stitched and bandaged the wound, and they went home, each one differently shaken.

Piero's cell phone rang often, and some of the calls he took outside to the porch, the ones from women. In the way he held his back, in the compressed explanations of his left hand gesturing close to his stomach, she could tell.

"Why have you never married?" she asked him one night.

"Why have you never divorced?" he replied.

Miriam stood up then and went into the little kitchen to turn on the heat under the corn chowder she had earlier prepared. It was the season of corn, after the strawberries, in the midst of tomatoes, but before the apples, and you could not stop eating corn, it was so sweet, so available. In a few minutes Piero joined her. "*Mi dispiace*," he said, his hands empty at his sides, palms out. "I have never known what I wanted from you. I'm sorry."

Untouched by ambition, Piero Cappelletti's life had been cluttered nevertheless with success. This was not to say that he did not work hard, only that he cared very little about outcomes. It was a strangely charged position, not caring. The business came to him. The women came to him. He let himself acquire the particulars of his lovers, so that at least in the details they were not iterations. It was never a good idea to bring to the bed games and techniques from other lovers; the landscape could only and always be new. But they were always iterations on the subterranean level. He was considered a good lover—thoughtful, firm, with an early potency that flattered, and a stamina that satisfied even the most nervous, the *slow-burns* as he had come to think of them. Toward his women he felt grateful, enthusiastic, apologetic. In that order. He knew himself to be a victim of his early success, of his affection for womankind. His mother had waited a decade to reclaim the man that was hers. And during that decade, while Babbo was off sporting about in America, a future older brother had appeared. Bill.

"You didn't answer my question," Miriam said. Her angular back was to him as she stirred the soup, and her blond hair, tied in a single band, divided the valley between her shoulder blades like sheaved wheat. "Why haven't you ever married? Why are there so many of them?"

"Because of the not knowing."

Then, for reasons she could not let herself name, she discovered that she was trying not to cry.

Bill died a week later. He had lain in bed three days, concentrating into himself, the beams of his eyes fogging over, his breath scuffing in the back of his throat. At first he would reach out only for her, and then, when he let go of his awareness of who it was sitting beside him, he would take the arm, or pat the hand, of anyone. He did not seem to be seeking comfort, only to offer it, uncharacteristically—or perhaps characteristic of the man she must have hoped was cloistered all along.

In the boat that had come to them, the Cappelletti family took his ashes out onto the lake early Sunday morning, so early that the water was still as smooth as polished marble. Just beneath the surface were thin veins of movement that would later acquire direction and grow into conflicting currents, and then even later, as the wind gathered, the little confusions would surrender and the abiding currents would take over.

They took turns rowing the dory. It was Bryce's idea, so that they would each have a hand in keeping his father company that day, or in doing something for him, a last service. It was a day he wanted to remember with his body. In his back Bryce could feel the oars pulling and the water resisting, the rough wood of the thwart scraping the place behind his knees; he could smell his mother's perfume, which she had stopped wearing two years earlier, but which she had put on that morning for her husband. There were sounds, too, like William sighing—when it wasn't his turn to row he devolved into a kind of miserable impatience. There was the sudden whir of a raft of mergansers taking off thirty yards away; then, as they neared the center of the lake, his mother's voice reading a poem, Wallace Stevens's "Sunday Morning" the words *she hears upon that water without sound . . .* and Piero saying her name when she got to the end of it, *downward to darkness, on extended wings*, and broke down. Then William reciting one of his father's pet limericks, the one about Tim and the woods and Timbuktu, his mother smiling weakly, forgiving the naughtiness of it. Now she was looking to him, to Bryce.

His throat compressed around something that felt like a stone. For two days he had been thinking about what to say, a hundred things, a thousand words, a lot of questions he would never have answers to now, at least not the ones his father might have given. They were not always welcome, or even nice, the things that he said, but eventually they had some use, like those funny old tools in the shed behind the Bolton cottage, the ones whose original purposes Bryce could not figure out, but then one day a perfect new use would appear. And he would know how to be thankful for his father. It seemed important to him now, to be thankful for his father.

They were all waiting for him.

It was going to be hot and humid again. The sun had somehow already climbed above the hills east of the village and was forming a diffuse yellow smudge over the place they had come from. Out on the lake, around them, a white haze furred the water's surface. Here and there, from the underwater sanctum of the lake, a fish tapped its ceiling and sent out delicate disappearing rings. It was pretty on the water in the early morning; prettiness seemed to make it easier. "We should always say good-bye in the morning," he said at last; and then, "Good-bye, Father," in the dear gravitas of youth.

His mother tipped her head and regarded him with a big sad love. "We should always be together," she said, touching her fingers to his cheek, "whenever there are good-byes to say."

Finally, his mother took the oars and began to row so that Piero could spill the ashes into the water. He sang an old Italian folk song for his brother, one that their Babbo used to sing for them summer nights on Lake Como, *Mamma mia, dammi cento lire che in America voglio andar* . . . He had a nice voice, a talking way of singing.

After helping Miriam settle Bill's affairs, Piero returned to Milan. It took two weeks for him to leave, although she urged him to go back to his work sooner, to the consortium of high-end wineries that depended upon him to negotiate for them with American distributorships. To belong to the Cappelletti House was considered *moltissimo bene*. It took him two weeks because, without Miriam's knowledge, he had contacted Mrs. Bolton and offered her enough money for the place, twice what it was worth, not only to preemptively settle any question of a negotiation, but to confirm for old Mrs. Bolton that summer folk were as profligate and foolish as their reputations promised. He had money enough, more than enough. And then there was the boat, after all, that needed a home now. For no one had come forward to claim it. Like his sister-in-law, it had been abandoned for one reason or another.

In Milano, away from her, he missed her unexpectedly and in a way that made his head vibrate inside so that it was sometimes hard to think clearly. A woman he knew came with him to his villa outside the city one night and he had her quickly and without appreciation. "*Fottuto*," she said, dressing in a rush, taking his car keys. *Worthless fuck.* Still, the next day, she telephoned him. She drove out with his car. Her hair was a sheenless yellow from multiple dye jobs, the roots deliberately left dark as was the fashion now among chic Italian women. It reminded him, enraged him, defeated him.

"I love you," the woman insisted. "*Ti amo!* Why do you treat me this way?"

"Stop pretending," he said. "I can't stand these lies. These lies!"

"Piero . . ."

"Your hair . . . it disgusts me."

He had never been a cruel man, and now he found that he could be cruel. That he was heartless and shallow and indiscriminate. Like his father.

It was almost a year later that he remembered that night, and then only because when he first saw Miriam at the lake, one hand held high and still in the summer air, a greeting that was her practice and that brought to mind statuary, he saw that she had cut off her long yellow hair. A day passed before either of them mentioned it. She had had beautiful hair and the loss was something they knew to feel timid about in each other's presence, a new scar whose source was worrisome.

"I wish that I had had just a little more time," she said.

"More time?"

"More time getting over what happened. Bill's death." She rolled her eyes helplessly, smiled, and added, "Bill's life." Then she rose from the porch chair to fetch the wine he had brought, a wonderful old Barolo from Pio Cesare.

"But more time before what?" Piero asked when, for the second time, he heard the screen door behind him.

She leaned to pour the wine, her white linen blouse untucked and loose about her torso so that he could not see her fine shape. "Before I had to cut my hair."

Several minutes passed. From the sunsetting west, a canoe slid out of a dream and disappeared into the green secrecy of the cove where they could hear a kingfisher working from the low overhanging branches of a cedar hedge.

He did not bother to tell her that her hair was still pretty. That it felt like a quiet declarative, straight and cropped about her small ears; that it still possessed the movement of clean heavy hair; that it would always signal health and candor. Or that, long or short,

Bill had been unworthy. They knew each other too well for trivial homage; it would have undone itself in the saying. He did not bother to tell her that, even without her hair, she was a woman. And a woman he wished he did not want.

"You have had time now. You should meet someone. Have you begun to see other men?" he asked.

"Other?"

She watched him blush and quickly compose himself. "I have had no interest," she replied.

They sat in silence long enough for the canoe to pass back across their frame of vision. Piero waved and one of the three canoeists waved back. The water carried not their words but the quiet companionable tones of a summer day's end. Then it was just the cove and the kingfisher and the silhouette of a single loon dipping its head underneath the water's surface, searching. When it dove at last and there was empty water before them, she said, "I like you," as if she had been waiting for that, for the empty water and the world stopping. She had not known it was coming but it had come. Her voice lacked any inflection; it was as grave and as profound as granite. Many times over the years she had told him that she loved him, or she had signed her notes and letters with the word *love*. They were family; it was customary. This was different.

A month after Bill's death, Miriam had returned to Boston with the boys. It seemed strange to her that he had died in summer. People died after summer, or after holidays, but never in the middle of loveliness. It was a weirdly accurate comment about Bill, his aptitude for contrariness. Her job as administrator for a small, private preschool awaited, the children swarming her knees, the teachers, all women but one, afraid of her loss, relieved for her, too formal. The last three years especially had formed a kind of prison, and one did not quite know how to speak to the newly released in the wake of the newly deceased. To be happily sad, or sadly happy. Anticipating all of it had heightened her awareness of time and resources. Her resources had diminished. She was forty-seven. Probably along the way she had sold herself, but not often, and not much of herself. People who sold themselves inevitably wanted to buy themselves back. And that was harder to do as those resources diminished. She had had one affair, or two if she had to count that night in Austin. The silliness of technicalities intruded—no penetration, no penalty. It was the teenaged way.

But she was not a teenager.

The heart compensates, she thought, as one foot compensates for its damaged mate; after a while, it too would need help, need caring. She had given herself to the boys, to her work, to the children at the school, and they had given back in measure. But behind that, her heart was struggling. It had lived without enough sustenance, or had lived in a kind of mourning for something that had died too soon and too young. And then the heart began to decompensate. And she and Bill had been reduced to trafficking in plot and script—*How are you/Thank you, not well*—with terms of endearment coming thick and fast, *honey, sweetie, Mimi, darling*, like roadside rescuers who tell their dying victims repeatedly, "you're okay, you're okay, you're gonna be fine," the sirens screaming into the night.

What she had wanted to do—after Bill's death—was to lie with Piero. It would have been an act of creation meant to challenge the destruction of a life. That was what the books on grief stressed in their comforting and facile expositions, the same way, the same careful unraveling, she employed when explaining things to her preschoolers. It was quite common (said the books) to desire sex following a death, and not to feel guilty, not to worry. It was perfectly normal.

Now it was a year later and nothing had changed. Except that it wasn't sex she yearned for—necessarily. It was an extent of seriousness; it was a sudden recognition, an onrush of joy.

Bryce strolled across the grassy clearing adjacent to the beach that was now theirs—theirs because of Piero—and then out toward the dock. She closed her eyes and listened to his tennis shoes softly drumming a tattoo out the wooden planks to the end where the boat was tied off. Each evening Bryce had taken it upon himself to check the bow and stern lines secured to the cleats. Now, because Piero was here, she could not watch her little man as he went about doing what he could to take care of things for his mother. Now, because Piero was here beside her, she wanted not a man, but this man.

"What kind of woman is it that you like?" she asked him. "Exactly."

He did not know how to answer. Or he was afraid to say. Or afraid for her, of him. With Miriam, in her presence, he was forced into an intense significance. Everything seemed to count. "I am afraid," he began, not looking at her, swirling the wine out of habit, studying its color in the dimming light, "that I am maybe like Babbo. That no woman ends it."

The water had gone brassy in the sunset and she could not take her eyes from it. "Yearning," she murmured simply.

"Something."

How did two gentle people ever come together? Some degree of aggression was required, some increment of taking had to *just* exceed the underlying percentage that was caring. Taking, caring. To take or not to take? To love without love's body. To care—to care hugely— and have not the privilege of caring's expression. To accept another's caring, to surrender to that, but to no more. The taking balanced the ledger. Without it, she could hardly stand it. And so to be in debt without funds to repay. To have no tools that might repair the distance that separated all humans.

He would always come. And he would always leave. Suddenly angry, she stood. "What do I have to do?"

In the dusk her blond hair was a shock of illumination. "Nothing. Be yourself."

So.

So, she would have to guess.

What he wanted to say was *I think I knew from the moment I met you that I would love you for the rest of my life. I have had many women, none of them you, and all of them together not even close to the youness of you. "Nothing, be yourself."* That was his only answer. He would not take her.

Emory came the next morning to go over the specifications for the new boathouse. The boat had had to lie outside all winter in the snow, and there was a little less paint now, a little more exposed wood. She wanted to keep it safe, she wanted it to last. Miriam had grown up poor with itinerant parents and a perpetually sulky and quarrelsome sister, the four of them living at times in residential motels or trailers at the low wet edges of rural properties in the Midwest, once even in an auto body shop that had been converted to a rental and that smelled not that faintly of petrol, while her father took one temporary job after another. It had been a childhood that had not led her to want more, or a lot, but to want a few reliable things that she might care very well for. It did not take too great a wind to scatter the family once the girls achieved maturity. One could be quite unhappy, one could be living a shadow life, and never have a chance to know it. It was like that deep wound in her foot last summer . . . she had been aware of the damage but she had not felt the pain of it.

This boat had come to them and this boat would thus be cherished.

The Cappellettis made suggestions while Emory took notes, Miriam wanting dark green paint, Piero, racks for the fishing rods and gear, for skis if they were to come up in winter, and the boys requested bunks so that they might camp out right at water's edge. And then

Miriam went off with Emory to choose windows, a side door, latches and the like, while Piero stayed to conduct business online. Some of his wineries were getting nervous about the length and increasing frequency of his American vacations.

They drove to the next town, to a place that recycled building materials. The teenager at the counter nodded toward the yard, and Emory with Miriam in tow prowled the abandoned windows and doors, the stacks of posts and timbers, the trapezoidal brick formations, the wooden boxes containing hardware, selecting and purchasing for later pickup. The yard was hot and exposed, and at some point Emory removed his shirt. He had a stalwart physique, his skin tanned from summer work, his belly unashamed. How could she not admire his comfort or the absence of expectation?

In the truck on the way back Emory said, "Ever seen Stone Pond?"

She had not.

And so he took her to Stone Pond.

On a narrow path through the maple woods she followed him, aware of the movement of her summer skirt, aware of her bare arms and of the sheen of sweat that coated them, aware of the color of his flesh against the green blur of foliage and fern, aware of time and resources, aware of the old essentiality of their predicament and the nowness of it, this man, this woman on a sultry day alone in the woods, aware that it was Piero for whom she longed.

The pond, she saw—no, she could hear in its stillness—was eutrophic. The surrounding land was eating it up, the inlet choked off, the outlet damned by beavers, plants slowly smothering it. One day soon it would be a bog, and then a meadow, then soft woods giving way to hard woods. The stone of Stone Pond rose vaguely ominously at its south shore, a glacial erratic. Slipping off her flip-flops, she stood in the water to cool her feet. As a native New Englander, Emory rarely removed his boots, and he did not break form even that day. The water was so flat and motionless that a dark concavity was revealed, a portent of forces pulling down and in. At the end of August she would return to Boston, faithful now to faithfulness itself, the heart's concavity. Bill was gone; Bill had been gone almost from the beginning, his malice causeless and aimless. And Piero . . . Piero was accustomed to many. Anyway, what she had to offer he very likely could not appreciate. He needed women who could be casual or gay or reckless, who would not care too much or think so seriously . . . in any case, no woman like her. She felt terribly alone suddenly, terribly cheated and out of place in the world.

She was still staring at the water when Emory said from behind her, "I think about you."

"Emory."

"I don't want to say, but it's a lot. Let's just say, I think about you."

She glanced over her shoulder. His hands were fiddling with a long brown stalk of some kind, perhaps the stem from a cinnamon fern. Without the usual tools—chain saw, peavey, crowbar, hammer—he looked even more awkward and undressed than he was. She heard herself sigh, then she bent to pick up her flip-flops, hooking their straps with two fingers, and climbed up the grassy bank. His hands seemed to hold her entire rib cage, and for an instant she felt like a child in need, being lifted up.

Well, if Piero wanted her like that, or women like that, she could do it. If that was what it took to have a place in this world.

Piero and the boys were down on the dock baiting crayfish traps with chunks of raw meat. She took her time in the cottage, putting away beach towels, wet tennis shoes, the croquet mallets; then she set a pot of water to boil for the pasta, tore into strips fresh basil from the farm stand down the road, chopped tomatoes and sautéed sweet sausage. Finally she changed into chinos and the linen blouse, and wandered down to the dock with a plate of sliced pecorino. The boys had ridden their bikes to the village for marshmallows, chocolate, and graham crackers, planning to make s'mores later at the town beach with friends.

"You were a long time gone," Piero remarked. He patted the warm dock boards for her to sit beside him, cross-legged. "Did something happen?"

There was a pause during which she considered lying. "Yes, something happened. What you wanted to happen. What you advised."

It did not take him many moments to understand what she was saying; the earlier conversation had never stopped looping his mind. "Oh," was the abbreviated sound that came from his throat without warning, not as a word but as a small sudden breach in his soul.

Miriam kept her hands flattened palms down on the dock, they were shaking so badly, not daring to reach for the glass of Orvieto that had been waiting for her.

He stood now and padded barefoot out to the end of the dock, swinging the crayfish traps down into the water and tying them off to the cleats. She watched his gestural precision with the ropes, his beautiful hands, the elegance of his body's shape as it dropped and folded and perched in a single swift motion against the ambered light of sunset. "Well, good. That's good," he said again and this time there was a kind of resolve. "I want you to be happy."

She said the word, "Happy."

Only then did he venture to look at her, his eyes cleansed of something. "Nothing would have changed."

"No, probably not."

"So it's good."

"Sure, it's good. It's good and casual and just what you wanted." And she added, "You can sleep with me now."

"Miriam."

"It won't mean anything and that's what you want."

He left her on the dock and went up to his room and lay in his clothes atop the covers, ready to leave if that was what needed to happen. It occurred to him that he had ruined her and he hadn't even touched her.

She told the boys that their uncle was not feeling well, setting aside a portion in case Piero changed his mind and came down to dinner. She wanted him to come down. She had hurt him and couldn't bear it, the way that she had hurt him, because none of it was how it should have been, all the years to have landed in this place, this time. But he did not come down.

Once again Emory showed up in the morning, this time with the load from the lumberyard. Piero watched them together, alert for signs of intimacy. His cell phone buzzed and he took the call, not bothering to go outside to the porch, not leaving his post at the kitchen window. Miriam was making a wide box with her arms to indicate the place next to the shed where she wanted Emory to stack the lumber, Emory nodding, releasing one hand from his pants pocket to fish the invoice from his shirt pocket. She didn't read it; Miriam was trusting that way. She was animated. It was one of the things about her, a kind of breathless interest, like a girl who has rushed into a room of somber adults, bearing some discovery, great for its small particularity, a bit of moss with a cocoon living inside it, or a story about an old man who took his first plane ride at age ninety-eight, what he thought about it, what he said. The preschoolers could not help feeling at home with her.

They were not standing close to each other; nevertheless, they kept their backs to the house.

Presently, with another nod, Emory went to work, pulling the two-by-sixes from the truck bed and sliding them across the stringers he had already laid out. She said one more thing, maybe *see you,* or *thanks*, or *let's talk later*, or perhaps even, *thank you for yesterday*, then she walked up to the house. There was something sad and resolute about the way she came, her gaze dropped in thought, her arms swinging a little as if to help her along.

Quickly he moved away from the window. His appetite had not yet returned, but when she entered the kitchen he selected one of the muffins she had baked that morning and began to devour it. What right had he to punish her?

It was a beautiful day. Single clouds floated in place, and though it was still humid, the sting of heat had dulled. Temperatures were dropping. There were a number of domestic chores that needed doing, and they went about them in silence, Miriam and Piero together, washing up dishes, stacking a small wood pile that had fallen over because the boys had not made good corners, re-gluing the leg on a wobbly side table, weeding the flower boxes around the porch. The way that they did things together made sense. The way that they moved in the same room or in a small space spoke without speaking—of anticipation and comfort and knowledge, but mostly of a kind of caring that seemed to say they were each there to make the day less difficult for the other.

Finally someone spoke, maybe about the weather, or one of the boys. Did it matter? A new order was trying to establish itself between them, and the path felt rough and precarious, and they had to take each other by the hand and work their way across the strange terrain, and talk in short, safe sentences with no objective in mind but human contact.

Midafternoon brought William and Bryce in from their summer day wanderings. Piero had promised to take his nephews trolling out on the main body of the lake. The two-horsepower trolling motor—electric, as Miriam had insisted, so that it would be quiet and not contaminate the water—had arrived several days earlier. The weather was supposed to turn, so the outing would have to happen sooner.

From the porch she watched the boat that held her family glide quietly out of the cove toward the open water. When they had been in the cove, inside the circle of trees, the water was green and flat like jade, and the boat made a clean V, but at its mouth was a line past which the breeze from the northwest chafed the surface and the light on it was so bright out there that it had gone black somehow. She thought how good it was for her boys to have Piero, to have a man to do things with. They needed him, and what they needed, at least, he could give.

They ran their lines out around the point where the bottom of the lake dropped off. Almost immediately Bryce had something. Piero spun the boat to keep from crossing the taut line, Bryce horsing the rod and William netting up the trout for his brother when he'd brought it in along the starboard side—a big handsome laker, maybe two pounds. This one they would keep for eating, and maybe another too, if that happened. After that they would use barbless hooks.

"Why can't we keep them all?" William asked, already anticipating some deficiency.

"How much can you eat?" Piero said.

"A lot."

"You don't like trout."

"Well I do," Bryce said, taking his brother's side.

So that revealed their mood. They were sore at him for taking so long at the house with their mother. Or they were sore because he was not their father. Or because it was time, for the older one maybe, to rebel, as boys are bound to do. "There's no room in the freezer," Piero reminded them. The cottage had an old refrigerator with a tiny freezer compartment that swiftly closed in with swelling walls of frost. "Your father would use the barbless hooks."

Bryce said, "He's dead," and Piero could hear an uncharacteristic anger in his voice.

"We are all Cappellettis, and we are all here in one way or another," Piero said.

William simply turned away. The two brothers let out their lines again as their uncle steered the boat, following the curvature of the shore but staying above the deepest coldest water. Bryce hooked the second one too, and by now his younger brother, jealous and increasingly uncertain of his skills, begged to land it. When he was older he would know not to ask that of another man, but this time Bryce handed over his rod. At last a rainbow flopped into the dory, smaller but prettier than the laker. Bryce ran his fingertips along the bands of color, the fish trembling at his touch, then he covered the plastic tub, and they re-rigged with the barbless hooks.

Piero could not say exactly when it was that he realized she had lied.

Bryce was explaining to his brother how to remove the hook without injuring the fish so badly that it could not go on to survive, how to hold it without damaging the gills, turning the hook along its curve, away from the flesh. His father had taught him.

Piero could not say what it was that unexpectedly entered his mind, or why, but he could see Miriam with Emory, tossing out her arms broadly, her natural enthusiasm fully present. And he knew she had lied.

An hour and a half passed and nothing more was biting. They decided to head to the north shore and try working the submerged ledges. The sky had been filling in with broad sheets of cloud cover and the air had changed, the wind huffing now and then on the water but steady high up in the branches of trees along the shore. After the days of unimpeded sun, the light, now entirely crepuscular, was a relief. There seemed no clear intent about the change, just a confused, almost peripheral shift away from what had been toward something that had yet to be imagined. From the north shore steep hills mounted and the fishing was cooler, shadier. The boys had fallen into silence and that too was a relief. The engine made a low hum. Here and there he could see down to the sedate olive-brown ledges stepping off into the lake. He was happy.

It was only moments after the engine stopped that William's lure sank and caught up. "Crap," he shouted. "Double crap."

"Take it easy," Piero said, "*calma.*"

In the end, the line had to be cut. And what he had forgotten, what the boys didn't know, was that the charge on the electric engine lasted not much more than two hours. They would have to row back.

Again, as on the day last summer when they had scattered Bill's ashes, they took turns rowing. It was not long before the wind developed muscle and the water assumed an iron gravity with white bursts advancing the collapse of wave after wave, and then each of the young brothers took one oar and together almost equaled Piero. The new air from the northwest was shoving into the warm air still laden with moisture, and a kind of angry free-for-all had fomented mid-lake. Leaden clouds boiled down on them and they began to hear distant thunder. Bryce counted aloud the seconds between the sound and the lightning flashing and dropping from the sky in sudden ropes of fluorescence. Nine seconds, nine miles.

"This is cool," Bryce exclaimed as the first wave washed over the gunnels.

William said, "Totally."

Piero stared at the two of them, these boys who were brothers, who were her sons.

They were horsing around with the oars, adding their own deliberate splashes to the waves that were now regularly violating the dory. It had started to rain.

"Row," he told them. "There's no time to fool around." But they paid no attention.

"*Non abbiamo tempo!*" he repeated.

Still they continued to carry on, jostling each other, tangling their arms and mugging for an imaginary camera.

"God damn it, boys, I said row . . . here, give me the oars."

Then, as if they had earlier consulted each other, as if it were central to some age-old scheme of things, the brothers simply stopped. William pulled in his oar, draped his arms over it, and gazed without expression at his uncle; Bryce tucked the oar grip under his knees so that the shaft and blade angled sharply up over the water. Idle in the chop, the boat was canting and tilting crazily. At least when they were moving, making progress toward the cove, there was enough momentum to shave off the crests and flatten the troughs a little, but stationary they were at the mercy of the lake itself, which in turn was subject to the storm barreling in on them with all the menace of time and indifference.

"What are you doing?" Piero demanded, angry now.

Again, as if by agreement, the two did not answer.

Piero started forward, moving on his knees. "Give me the oars."

"No," one of them said.

"This is very dangerous. The lightning . . ."

William snorted nervously and glanced at his brother. Their little game of challenge had suddenly taken a turn, had become serious. Bryce stared across the turbulent water, his mouth finding a moody defiance.

Against whom now could they test their young male mettle, their father dead, their mother a mother, and alone?

Piero grabbed William's shoulder and his oar popped free, but Bryce was stronger, bigger, and he pressed his weight into the oar tucked under his knees, clasping the thwart with both hands and somehow winning the battle. His brother had fallen backward into the bow and was looking rattled and confused. The rain came in heavy lashes. A cross-wave knocked him against the tub that held the fish they had caught, and he let out a whimper.

Again the two struggled, Piero and Bryce. The older boy began to cry. He was not used to the actuality of a man or of a man's concerns, and it scared him. His uncle, out of breath and holding on to opposite gunnels as the boat lifted and fell, dropped his voice, "Do you want to drown? Don't you understand, she needs you? Both of you."

In spite of the cold rain, the boy's cheeks were hot with the bloom of anger.

The last lightning flash had been close enough to infuse the air with a momentary grayish-pink hue. Then there came the boom and he could feel it inside his chest.

"She needs us! You understand?"

Bryce jerked his head sideways, hiding his face as he released the oar. Piero nodded aft, meaning for him to move there, then he took the oars and began rowing, deep hard pulls that made the boat jump. "Get down," he told them. "Lie down."

So Miriam could not see the boys until the boat cleared the point and was cutting across the cove. In the hour that she had been out there on the dock, waiting, the cove had become a cauldron of heavy waves and wind, branches with bobbing twigs and shaking leaves, sections of rafts that had been torn off, a blue beach ball, the pale white board of a windsurfer. The waves were breaking over the dock, the dock vibrating with the force. She would not sit down, though it would have been safer. When the boat came in Bryce threw the line to her and, without a word, the boys scrambled up and made for the house.

"My god," she said to Piero.

"I'll tell you later."

The storm was passing to their north now, and in its passing the clouds let go a drubbing rain whose weight they could feel and hear. Not impatiently, they turned to walk up and before they reached the end of the dock, Piero said, "You lied."

She looked at him for a long moment, the two of them stalled in the heavy ubiquity of the rain. Then she took his hand. "*Si*, I lied."

Muted drums of thunder, as quickly distant as they had earlier borne down upon them, led the storm away. He was tired from rowing but he felt a kind of strength too, a kind of promise. Nothing more; nothing less either. In this world it seemed enough for now.